THE SUN WILL RISE TOMORROW

THE SUN WILL RISE TOMORROW

William Shymkiw

Suite 300 - 990 Fort St
Victoria, BC, V8V 3K2
Canada

www.friesenpress.com

First Edition — 2020

With contributions and assistance from Rita MacPherson

ISBN
978-1-5255-7215-9 (Hardcover)
978-1-5255-7216-6 (Paperback)
978-1-5255-7217-3 (eBook)

1. FICTION, SHORT STORIES (SINGLE AUTHOR)

Distributed to the trade by The Ingram Book Company

CONTENTS

CREATOR and CONTRIBUTOR

AUTHOR
William Shymkiw BA, Bed.

William (Bill) Shymkiw is the author of this book. Bill is a retired Senior and lives in Olds, Alberta. In his earlier life he was a farmer, gardener, and teacher. After his vision failed, he pursued former and new interests. All his life Bill has been an avid gardener. Today with Rita's help the garden is a creation of beauty. Then he took up landscape painting. The book cover picture is one of his paintings. At age ninety he took up writing and this book is one of the results. It is his hope the reader will find it interesting.

ASSISTANT
Rita Rose MacPherson

Rita is Bill's caregiver. She is also the assistant in the publication of this book. Rita was born and raised in Nova Scotia in a family of nineteen children. Today she is a proud Albertan and she also lives in Olds, Alberta. In her earlier life she raised a family, Church involvement and advanced in customer service. Seven years ago she came to work with Bill. In producing this book she provided encouragement and prepared all the parts for publication. Like Bill, she hopes you will find the stories enjoyable.

1.
JOHNNY'S BICYCLE

"ASHES TO ASHES AND DUST TO DUST," THUS SPOKE LYDIA Dahl as she sprinkled prairie soil on the casket, that held the earthly remains of Mary McLeod. Lydia Dahl was the celebrant from the United Church. Before the few left, she announced that there would be lunch in the United Church basement. An elderly man took the arm of a boy and said, "I your Grandfather and you come stay with me."

The pair walked towards a battered old truck when a young lady came running.

"Mr. Starchuk Mr. Starchuk! Stop! I'm Helen Hayes and Mary asked me to help you with her possessions. Johnny will show you their home and I'll get in my car and follow you."

When they arrived Johnny took his Grandfather down some steps to a basement suite. Everything was so neat, clean, and homey. Helen took a big cardboard box and said, "Johnny, put all your things in the box."

Mr. Starchuk looked around, "Johnny take the bedding."

Helen gave Mr. Starchuk a black case. "There are important papers in this case."

Later Mr. Starchuk and Johnny would learn that the case held certificates, a will, a white Bible, and photos. A few were of a soldier in uniform.

On the thirty mile ride from Watson to Margo, neither spoke. Each was absorbed in his own apprehensive thoughts. Mr. Starchuk never had a boy nor did he expect ever to have one. Johnny had lived all his life with his Mom and there was never a man. Who was this Grandfather?

When they reached their destination Mr. Starchuk turned off the highway. They drove down Main Street, across the tracks, and into a yard.

"Dis my place and dis be your home."

Johnny looked around and saw a small house, sheds, some machinery, fences, trees, and animals.

Everything looked old but well kept and orderly. When he got out of the truck, a black and white collie ran to him and sniffed his pant legs. Then he licked Mr. Starchuk's hand as if to say the boy is OK.

In the house Grandpa said, "Dis be your room. Long time dis be my Mary's room. When you finish come eat."

Mr. Starchuk prepared some potatoes, meat, and cheese, but Johnny would never remember what he ate. He was so worried and excited. After Mr. Starchuk washed the dishes he said, "We go out I show you."

In the yard he told Johnny the names of the animals. The collie was Sookee. The billy goat was Baran. The two girl goats were Donya and Sonya. The three kids had no names yet. In the goat shed on a shelf was Kotzar, the tom. The mother cat was Mila and the two kittens had no names. The chickens, geese, and pigs had no names, but Johnny could give them names if he wanted.

Before he went to bed Johnny took a little book and wrote: "*June 25 1978 Mom died. Helen said it was pancreatic cancer. I am going to be with my Grandfather, Mr. Starchuk. He is old, but OK. I like my first friend here. She is Sookee, the girl dog. Mom, I know you are in heaven and your body has a nice place to sleep. I love you, Mom.*"

Next morning on Saturday there was a breakfast of porridge, milk, bread, and jam. Grandpa washed the dishes, then said, "You come I show you."

First Sookee was fed porridge, a little bread and a little meat on a bone. Then all the other animals got fed and watered. The goats went into the pasture. Then Grandpa did something different. He took a pail with some grain and a stick and beat on the pail and called, "Coo Coo." Eight pigeons flew from the loft and landed at his feet.

They came back to the house. Grandpa did his Saturday work. He washed clothes and baked bread.

He showed Johnny how to wash the linoleum floors and which plants in the garden should be watered. In the evening Johnny was to take a bath in the tin tub. Then he was to take the water from the tub and water some plants in the orchard. That evening Johnny was tired and fell asleep as soon as he laid down.

On Sunday Johnny fed Sookee and the chickens. Then he went and changed into nicer clothes. He went to Grandpa and said, "Grandpa on Sundays Mom and I went to Church and Sunday School."

Grandpa looked at Johnny in his nice clothes. He said, "Johnny someday you go, but now work to do."

Johnny changed his clothes again. He and Sookee just walked where the goats had their pasture.

He did not mention Church again. He learned that Grandpa had a pattern of things he did on Sunday.

He would finish anything that had to be done. He checked the animals, garden, orchard, and fences.

He shaved his whiskers and would read a paper the one with funny letters. Sometimes an old friend would come. Grandpa would take a bottle from the cupboard and poured some drinks. They talked, laughed, and argued in a strange language.

In 1947 Mr. Starchuk came from a DP camp in Austria. He re-united with a friend in Margo, Saskatchewan. With his friend's help he got a job with the CNR Section gang. Two years later he married Ann Shumay. A year later a girl was born and they named her Mary. At first they lived in the CNR bunk- house. Later they bought ten acres at the edge of Margo. With each year they worked and added to the farm. Mary was a likeable girl. She had excellent grades in school and at home she was an eager helper for both Mom and Dad. In her teens she worked on Saturdays in the grocery store. Many an evening Mike and Ann dreamed and hoped. They saved money so Mary could be a nurse or a teacher.

In 1967 Mary graduated with honors from high school. Mike and Ann awaited their daughter's decision- would it be Nursing School or Teachers College? Then a bombshell was dropped!

"Mom and Dad, I know you wanted me to go further, but I decided to get married and I hope you will approve."

Mike in a loud voice, "who dis man you marry?"

Mary softly replied, "He is Tom McLeod. He is a soldier who lives with his mother in Watson."

"A soldier! Why?"

With tears in her eyes Ann said, "Mary we saved for you, maybe wait. Think this through."

"Mom I have. I promised Tom I would marry him as soon as I graduated."

"Promise! Promise! I tink you crazy like he."

Ann burst into tears and left the room. Mike pounded the table and swore ********

Mary took her already packed suitcase and walked to the grocery store. She phoned Tom and waited. Tom and his friend came and they drove to Watson. Tom and Mary found a Justice of the Peace who married them. Their honeymoon was in his mother's house.

A week later Tom got a call to report to Camp Borden. It was a sad day, but Tom promised to ask for a PMQ. Then he would send for Mary. In a letter Tom wrote there would be a PMQ available, but for now his Unit was being sent to Yugoslavia for a six month stint in peace keeping duties.

On July 16, two soldiers came to the house with news that Tom had been killed. Mary was devastated!

Mary got a job in Johnson's Lucky Dollar Grocery Store. Living with her mother in law was trying.

Mrs. McLeod seemed to always have dirty dishes, cigarette butts all over, and sometimes she was drunk.

Mrs. Johnson from the store, invited Mary to join them for a service in the United Church. People in town knew about Mrs. McLeod. An elderly Mrs. Anderson met Mary and said, "I have a comfortable basement suite. All you will have to pay is utilities and a share of the taxes."

Mary moved in, and eight months later on March 23 gave birth to a son. She named him Johnny.

Mrs. Anderson babysat and later cared for Johnny while Mary worked. Mary's life centred around Johnny.

She was both Mom and Dad to the boy who was a perfect child. Mrs. Anderson and Mary doted over him.

When Johnny was born Mary had sent a card to her parents, but there was never any response.

After Mary left that day in June 1967, the Starchuk home seemed to descend into an atmosphere of gloom. They hardly ever spoke and covered their disappointment with endless work.

In 1974 Ann died. Two years later, CNR phased out the need for section work. Mike was given a small pension.

On the second Sunday of July 1978 Grandpa said, "We go show you school."

They crossed the tracks and then walked down Main Street. Johnny read the signs on the buildings: Margo Hotel, Korol's

Grocery, Harry's Shoe Repair, Chan's Cafe, Sally's Salon, Pete's Pool Room, Jones & Jones Lawyers, and then Larson's Hardware. Johnny stopped and starred. There in the window was a bicycle. What a bicycle, red and silver! Grandpa was ahead and he called, "Come."

At the end of the street they stopped.

Grandpa pointed, "Dat School and Dat School."

On the way back Johnny stopped to admire the bike. Although he saw the card that read $185 he wished that the bike could be his. He had to run to catch up to Grandpa.

That evening as Grandpa was reading his paper and Johnny was doodling, he could not help it. He said timidly, "Grandpa do you think I could have a bike?"

Grandpa lowered his paper and asked, "How much money you got?"

Johnny in a small voice said, "I have nine dollars and twenty cents."

Grandpa replied, "Not enough- no money no bike."

Johnny kept silent and went on doodling.

Once again Grandpa lowered his paper and said, "Mr. Weber at the drugstore is looking for a paper boy."

So Johnny became the official carrier. He delivered the Leader Post to twenty one homes. He had three extra in case someone might buy or sign up. When all the figures were calculated he had about twelve dollars at the end of the month from the paper route.

That evening when he counted his earnings it was still twelve.

"Grandpa it's no use, I'll never make enough."

Grandpa kept secretly eyeing Johnny. He said, "You know we have some extra eggs, some honey, and cheese. Maybe some might buy. That money be yours."

So Johnny became a sales boy. Whenever he had a chance he would ask a woman or man in the house, would they like some eggs, honey, or cheese.

That month his income jumped to sixteen. Maybe by next summer there would be enough thought Johnny.

On the first Monday in September Johnny was excited and anxious. Grandpa had bought notebooks, a pen, one pencil, and a box of crayons. He also put a brown paper bag with a lunch for Johnny.

At the school that morning the halls were a mass of boys and girls talking about which class and teacher they would have.

A teacher noticed Johnny and said, "You are new here, let's go and see the Principal."

It was decided he would go to grade five, but if he excelled they might move him to grade six. His teacher would be Miss Wright.

When he got home he took his sandwich of homemade bread and meat and began eating. He was hungry.

Grandpa asked, "Why you not eat lunch at school?"

"Grandpa the others have a different lunch. Mom made lunch with white bread, peanut butter, some fruit, and yogurt."

Grandpa asked, "What dis ting yogurt?"

Johnny replied, "Yogurt is like a pudding."

Grandpa said, "No problem, I take goat milk and honey. Dat be yogurt!"

Johnny burst out. "No No Grandpa! You have to buy it in the store."

The next morning Johnny never knew how, but in his lunch bag was a peanut butter sandwich on white bread, a banana, but no yogurt. He liked school. The lessons were easy and it was fun to play football at recess and at noon. He liked his teacher, Miss Wright. When she walked past his desk she smelled like peppermint. He also liked coming home. He always stopped to look at the bike. When he got home there was Sookee always happy and the other animal friends were glad to see him.

Not everything at school was fine. There were two boys Jack and Brian, who said hurtful words at recess and noon. They would say, "Is your Grandpa a dumb Uke or a crazy Pollack?" At other times they would say, "Hey McLeod, you stink like goat shit." His fists would clench, but he still remembered his promise to his Mom. "Johnny you are not to fight." Why did she make such strict rules?

On those bad days he remembered a wrestling match on TV. He would close the door and practice punches. He would be like Mad Dog Vachon and beat the crap out of those bullies.

There was one boy Stevie Boyko, who became a best friend. Stevie's Dad had a small garage at the corner of Main Street. Some Sundays Stevie would come to the farm. By this time Grandpa had said this was their farm. Stevie said he had no use for the girls in class. Johnny said he didn't mind them and Peggy looked nice.

Stevie said, "Johnny we need to make a pact. We should promise that we would never ever marry any girl." Johnny wasn't that eager to promise, but Stevie knew what was best. However he said, "If there is a girl like Mom, I would break the pact."

For Halloween, He and Stevie had plans. Grandpa said Johnny could go trick or treat. They decided to be pirates. They found a red cloth for headbands and some charcoal from the stove to paint their faces. Stevie said they should plan for some nasty things. Johnny said no, many of the homes are my paper customers. So Stevie agreed, it would just be treats and no tricks.

One Sunday Stevie's dad took the boys fishing at a lake north of Margo. It was fun. They caught the limit and Johnny took home three jacks. Grandpa helped to scale and prepare. That evening he and Grandpa ate fried jack. It was so good! He wondered if his Mom had ever gone fishing.

On the first of November- Johnny was shocked. The bicycle in the window was gone! Instead there were hockey sticks, skates, and skis. Johnny went inside and asked, "Mr. Larson did you sell the bike?"

Mr. Larson smiled, "We put it in the back. When spring comes it will be in the window again. If we sell it, we will order another." As he walked home he felt a relief.

Other events saddened him. People came to help Grandpa butcher chickens, geese, and pigs.

Some meat was put in the smoker and some put in the freezer. Most was sold. The yard seemed so empty and sad. Even Sookee was not her vigorous self.

Johnny asked Grandpa, "Why do we have to do this? Why can't they keep on living?"

Grandpa replied, "There is a Plan. There is a time to sow and a time to reap."

Johnny had heard this before, but still he thought it was so unfair. Johnny wondered if Mom's death part was of the Plan?

With the snow and the cold Johnny had other problems. His skates were too small. Grandpa bought a used pair that was a larger size. Whenever he had time he went to the rink to skate. He wished his skating was better. They might choose him to be on the Margo Marlins team. He was sure Mom would be proud when she saw him in the red jersey with McLeod on the back!

In mid December there were Christmas decorations and lights all over town. He asked Grandpa if they would have a tree?

Grandpa said, "No but you could hang up stockings."

Johnny knew the Santa story, but it was still fun to hang his stockings. When he woke on Christmas morning there was an orange, some nuts, and a chocolate bar in his stocking. Beside the stockings was a brand new hockey stick.

In the afternoon Stevie came and they had fun playing road hockey. Grandpa's friend came over and they all had a Christmas dinner of ham, potatoes, carrots, and some canned pears. Johnny thought about the Christmases he had with

Mom and Mrs. Anderson. He wondered if they did Christmas things in heaven?

With the new year came more snow and cold. Grandpa tried to make the animals comfortable.

Johnny made a warmer bed for Sookee in the porch. Johnny had his school and paper route and a few other duties on the farm. Sometimes Stevie came over or Johnny went to Stevie's place.

In April the skating was over. There were new surprises. There were new chicks and goslings. Mila had four new kittens. Donya and Sonya had two kids each. Maybe Grandpa was right. There was a plan.

Someday he was going to ask Grandpa why the plan was not working for Sookee. Why couldn't she have pups?

At the end of May Johnny counted his money. He counted twice. He had $180.20. One more month and he would have enough.

A week later Grandpa said, "Johnny, why you not go and get bike?"

Johnny replied, "Grandpa, I don't have enough."

Grandpa said, "Maybe you not count good?"

Johnny went to his room and got the can with the money. He spread the money on the table and counted. He was puzzled. There was $185.20.

Grandpa said, "I tell you-you not count good. If you ready tomorrow we get the bike."

The next day they went and bought the bike with the money Johnny had earned. He couldn't ride, so he guided it. For the next two weeks whenever he had time he practised and got better and better.

Grandpa allowed Johnny to keep the bike in his bedroom.

Each night before bed he spoke to a photo of his mother. "*Mom, I have a bike. You should just see it!*"

On the last Sunday in June, Johnny woke up and in the kitchen was Grandpa in his better clothes.

"Johnny, today we go to Watson and see where your mother sleep."

Johnny asked, "Can I take the bike?"

"Sure."

Johnny put the bike in the truck box. At the cemetery he took the bike and guided it to the grave. At the head was a plaque that read, *Mary McLeod 1950-1978.*

Johnny started to tear up but he fought back. He remembered what Mrs. Anderson said, "Big boys don't cry." He tried to hold back the tears, but it was no use. Tears came and came. "*Mama why did you have to go?*

Mama I have a bicycle. Can you see it?" Johnny noticed that Grandpa was also wiping tears from his face.

On the way to the truck they looked back and saw dandelions with heads bent over the grave. Did Nature use the lowly dandelion to sanctify this special place?

While still going to the truck, tears and thoughts had lifted the burden of grief. There was a feeling of elation. Grandpa said, " I tink your Mama is happy. She wants us to be happy."

He said, "We stop at Mrs. Anderson's house."

Johnny was happy to see her. Mrs. Anderson said, "Johnny you have grown bigger!" Johnny told Mrs. Anderson about all the exciting things on the farm and at school. He showed her his bicycle.

After the visit Grandpa said, "We stop at Highway Diner."

They had hamburger, chips, and a sundae with a cherry on top. Grandpa had coffee and Johnny had a cherry soda. On the way home they talked about the sights along the highway. At home the animals acted warily. They sensed something happened to Grandpa and Johnny.

That evening before bed Johnny wanted to thank someone-God or Jesus. He knelt beside the bed and recited the Lord's

Prayer and then added, "*Jesus, thank you for looking after Mom. I know she is happy with you. In case she doesn't already know, tell her my school grades are all A's. Grandpa and I are making our farm better. I have a good friend called Stevie. It sure would be good if you could change the plan so that Sookee could have babies. But make sure you tell Mom I have a beautiful bike.*"

Johnny laid down and closed his eyes. Something strange happened. The room was filled with the scent of lilacs. Yet they had stopped blooming a month ago. Then came the dream. Out of a cloud came Mom. She was so beautiful in her white dress. She was smiling.

"Johnny I love you and I am proud of you. I like your bicycle!"

He fell into a deep sleep.

In the morning the sun was high and Grandpa was at the table waiting for him.

"Grandpa, I had a dream and I saw Mom! She was happy and she liked my bike!

"I know," said Grandpa. A big smile broke on Grandpa's weathered face.

"YES JOHNNY, THAT IS THE MOST BEAUTIFUL BIKE IN THE WORLD."

2.
RELUCTANT BRIDE

IN THE AREA NORTH EAST OF EDMONTON, JULY 26 IS A date that almost everyone observes. For Catholics it is the Feast of St. Ann. It is the time of year when it is a slow time for farmers. The haying is almost done and harvesting will be in full swing in three to four weeks. For the folks in town and villages it is summer holidays. Business is slow so there is time to go to the beaches.

This July 26 for the Gaston Dumont family it promised to be an exciting day. They all piled into the panel van. It read Peter's Plumbing and Heating. When they parked in the parking lot of St. Judes R.C. Church other parishioners wondered what was the problem with the Church's plumbing?

After the Church mass they drove home, had a quick sandwich, and changed into casual clothes- shorts, loose shirts, and sandals. Today they were off to Muriel Lake. When they arrived at the Lake there were many other people already there. Everyone was moving to their particular group. The men congregated beside Samson's truck. They talked about haying, cattle, combines, swathers, and of course politics. The mature ladies were in their own age group talking of young single men and ladies, plans for fall suppers, and new recipes. The younger women with toddlers were on the beach watching their little ones splashing in the shallow water. The young men were watching the water sking, the cars, and motor boats. Really they were watching all the young women. The young women had their earphones on and pretended that music was their only interest. Of course, like the men they had their sunglasses on and were sizing up the guys.

Ann Marie and her sister Bonita were casually strolling and observing everything. The two young women stopped when they came abreast of two young men sitting on lawn chairs, drinking beer, and tending a barbecue.

"Would you like to join us for a beer?"

"No, we don't drink."

"How about a Coke or Pepsi?"

"Sure."

One of the men got two folding chairs for the young women. The other went to a cold chest and picked two cans of Pepsi from the ice.

"We are having steaks but it will be no problem to put two more on the barbecue."

Ann Marie said, "I don't know, maybe we should be going?"

"There's no hurry and if steaks don't suit you, we have some smokies and wieners."

"OK, smokies will be fine."

The younger guy put four smokies on the grill.

"My name is Gabriel Peladeau and this is my younger brother Joseph. What are your names?"

"My name is Ann Marie Dumont and this is my younger sister Bonita."

"Do you go to school or have you graduated?"

"Why are you asking all these questions? Are you police detectives?"

"No, we are farmers and we live about twenty miles from here."

There were no more questions. They talked about: music, bands, sports, and coming events.

Ann Marie rose and said, "We have to go and we thank you for the smokies and the drinks."

Gabriel spoke, "I would like to meet you again. May I have your phone number?"

"OK." 556-65XX

A few days later a phone call came to the Dumont home.

"Hello this is Gabriel Peladeau and may I speak to Ann Marie?"

"Hello this is Ann Marie."

"Ann Marie, there is a Sports Day in St. Paul on Sunday afternoon. Would you like to go?"

"Can my sister Bonita come?"

"Oh sure, she can come."

When Gabriel drove into the Dumont yard that Sunday it was a surprise. There were three derelict cars. One had been converted to a truck. The only functional vehicle was the panel van with the Peter's Plumbing and Heating sign on its side. There were two tractors. One was lacking a rear wheel. The other was split and scattered wrenches were about. Someone was in the process of repairing it. Behind the fence were two cows, their calves, one horse, and some pigs. In the main yard was everything else. When he stopped his car, turkeys flew up on the car roof, geese nibbled on the car trim, and three dogs each marked the tires. The chickens, guinea hens, and cats were looking for a chance to get into his vehicle. Gabriel thought, what have I got myself into? But then Ann Marie was a prize worth pursuing.

The next time he phoned her he asked, "Would you like to go to a dance at Elk Point?"

"Can Bonita come?"

"I don't think it would be appropriate."

At the dance all the men were attracted to this intriguing young lady. Ann Marie was very discreet. She declined many requests and reserved every second dance for Gabriel, her escort.

When he took her home she would give him a passionate kiss and then slip out of his arms. Gabriel wondered how does she do this masterful escape!

The next time Gabriel phoned, "Ann Marie, would you like to go with me to the Agricultural Exhibition in Edmonton?" At the grounds Gabriel went straight for the cattle pens. He looked at each animal with an experienced eye. He took some pictures. Then it was off to the Machinery Row. Each machine he examined carefully. He questioned the attendant. Then off to the display home. It had everything.

"Ann Marie how would you like this home?"

"I think I would wish for nothing more."

Next they went to various booths: Insurance companies that could predict your life span, Financial planners who could teach you how to make a million, the kitchen gadget salesman that promised that with the gadgets you could make a healthy meal in four minutes. Then there was the cosmetic booth. There were lotions that could transform any common Jane to a glamourous queen. Ann Marie was interested, but she wasn't convinced she needed all that magic. Of course they had lunch and drinks. It was a long day and Ann Marie was tired. Gabriel offered to get a motel room, but Ann Marie said her parents would be waiting for her. Once again they parted with that elusive kiss.

Later on he phoned, "Would like to meet my parents?"

She said, "I would be delighted."

When they arrived at the Peladeau place it was impressive. At the gate was a large sign that read:

A. Peladeau and Sons Farms-Ranches-Construction The yard looked like it was out of a picture book: manicured lawns, landscaping with flowers and shrubs, and buildings so new. She counted ten grain bins. Even the fence posts were painted. The machinery was so new- shining red, green, and yellow. There was a yellow caterpillar with a huge blade in front.

Gabriel introduced her to his parents. Theresa Peladeau embraced Ann Marie. She was so friendly. Aristid Peladeau was more reserved, but he too responded to Ann Marie with genuine delight. Theresa had prepared a colourful and delicious lunch on the patio. A golden retriever came and settled herself at Ann Marie's feet. Was this heaven?

Driving back to the Dumont home Gabriel asked Ann Marie, "Would you consider marrying me?"

"Oh course I would, but you must ask my father. Come for Sunday dinner and there will be an opportunity to ask."

Gabriel did arrive for Sunday dinner. Those darn turkeys! The family was seated at a long table. Gaston Dumont pronounced, "Today we have a special guest may God bless him. We will start with a prayer. Petit Jean it is your honour today."

Everyone rose and crossed themselves. Petit Jean spoke softly, "In the name of the Father, Son and Holy Ghost. Our Father in heaven we thank you for this food, for Mama and the girls who prepared it, and we thank God for bringing Gabriel Pela .... to our home. Amen." Everyone sat down. In front of each was a bowl, spoon, and a fork. Mama Maria Dumont carried a pot and a ladle. Into each bowl she put a full ladle of pea soup. Ann Marie followed and gave each a bannock biscuit. After everyone was finished, Bonita placed a huge bowl of poutine in the centre of the table.

Papa Gaston said, "Each will take as much as they want and we will start with our guest."

Petit Jean spoke out, "It is not fair, when the bowl comes to me there will be nothing left."

Papa Gaston responded, "Now now Jean, remember we have a guest so we should not complain."

"I'm sorry Papa." After everyone was finished, they rose and said- "Father, Son and Holy Ghost, Amen."

Ann Marie, Bonita and Madeline went to wash dishes. Mama Maria sat down. She seemed so tired.

The others went outside except Gabriel and Gaston.

"Monsieur Dumont, "I came today to ask for the hand of Ann Marie in marriage."

Gaston was tapping his finger on the table but he was gazing at the ceiling. He said, "It costs so much to raise a child and when they are grown up and able to do some work, they are off to someone's home to work for them. Now I would never stand in the way of a daughter if she wanted to marry, but now my thoughts are out there. He pointed outdoors and said, "The hay should be cut, I had two horses but one died. So, what can I say?"

"Monsieur Dumont, our family has horses we no longer use."

Gaston replied, "May heaven and God bless you my son!"

There was no definite answer to Gabriel's request.

Two days later a horse trailor brought a horse to the Dumont farm and Ann Marie assured Gabriel that her father would consent. "Let us talk to Father Damien."

After Sunday Mass when everyone left, Gabriel approached Father Damien. "Father can we talk to you?" Father Jean Damien suspected what the couple wanted to talk about.

"Let's just go in the Sacristy and have this talk."

"Father Damien, Ann Marie and I want to get married."

"Congratulations, God smiles kindly when a man and woman decide to join as one in holy matrimony."

"When can you marry us?"

"My dear hopefuls, the Catholic Church does not rush into such a life long commitment. We do not do marriages during Advent or Lent. First we must do some preliminary work for the Government. I have to check if you are of age. Next, I have to make inquiries if you are already married or if you are facing any criminal charges. If all that is concluded satisfactorily, then you must take a prenuptial course. This will be with me three Saturdays and three hours each time. Make an appointment and bring your certificates. We will meet in the Rectory where I have an office. Go with God and we will see you soon."

They drove to the Dumont home, urgency was on their minds.

"Father Damien wants to see our birth certificates."

"Ann Marie get that black box behind the radio. Mama go through those certificates and find the one for Ann Marie."

Mama Maria went through all the certificates, once, then twice. "It's not here, but where could it be? This is not going to be good."

Gabriel said, "We cannot wait."

Gaston said, "We will search and search, and if we cannot find it we will ask the Government for a copy. There will be a problem. It will be a month before we can sell the calf for some money."

Gabriel took out his wallet and pulled out a fifty dollar bill. "Just get a copy!"

"We will do it right away. God bless you my son."

Three days later Ann Marie phoned Gabriel, "We found the certificate! It was in the glove compartment of one of those broken down cars."

Gabriel phoned Father Damien for an appointment.

At the Rectory Father Damien welcomed them. He took out a Government form. He filled in the spaces- Gabriel Peladeau, single, age 28, no encumbrances. Ann Marie Dumont, single, age? He could not make out the tampered space. He took an eraser and a magnifying glass. She was fourteen. Father Damien said, "Oh no, we can't proceed."

Gabriel and Ann Marie hung their heads and had that forlorn look. Gabriel spoke, "Father is there no hope at this time?"

Father Damien saw the hopelessness in their eyes. He said, "There is one possibility. If Ann Marie gets a consent letter from her parents we can proceed. I will be away for a week. If you get the consent letter and bring it to me, we can take the next step. God be with you my children."

They drove back to the Dumont home.

"Father Damien says I have to get a consent letter and then everything will be fine."

Gaston said, "Maria get a paper and pen. I don't know what we are going to do? You can see by Mama Maria that God will give us another child. The girls will be in school and who is going to do all the housework and all the fall canning? Someone will have to look after Petit Jean, he's only four. I am already two weeks behind in my work. It is time to swath, but my Case tractor is all apart and I need a clutch."

Gabriel said, "How much is the clutch?"

"It will cost $200."

Gabriel took out his wallet and peeled off ten twenty dollar bills.

Gaston said, "May God bless you a thousand times my son. Maria start writing. Say I, Gaston Sebastien Dumont and I Maria Celestine Dumont, do give permission for our daughter Ann Marie to marry Gabriel Aristid Peladeau esq. So Help Me God."

Maria said, "What is the esq for?"

Gaston replied, "It's what all official letters say."

Then Maria said, "What's may God help us for? I don't think you need to put that in the letter."

Gaston folded the letter and said, "We need an official seal. Maria if we put a blob of corn syrup and you and I press our thumbs on it, that will look real official."

Gabriel took the certificate and the consent letter. He was in a daze. He didn't even notice the turkeys on the car roof. Slowly he drove away.

Two days later Ann Marie got a letter. It was from the Mensa Association. She remembered that about six months ago she had been called to the Principal's office. The Guidance Counsellor and the Math teacher were there. The Principal James Harder said, "Ann Marie you have a rare gift. You have already skipped grades four, seven,and nine. We think the Mensa Association would be interested in you. Here is an application form."

"Mr. Harder, I just want to get married and have a dozen kids."

"We recommend that you talk to your parents and then decide."

Ann Marie talked to her Mom. "Mom do you think I should apply?"

"Ann Marie, to have children is one of God's gifts. Take the scholarship and there will still be time for a dozen children."

Ann Marie phoned Gabriel, "I have some news I want to discuss with you. If you have time come and we will talk."

The next day Gabriel came. Ann Marie said, "I am offered a scholarship for $2500 and a possibility for a further $2500. I could finish a four year degree in two. Two years from now I will have my degree and we will get married. I will be all yours!"

Gabriel looked at the ground and then looked at her. "Ann Marie, I think you are stringing me along and your father keeps raising the bar. I've had enough!" He took the certificate and the letter, tore them in half and tossed them at Ann Marie's feet. "I've had enough, you may think I'm stupid but I have come to my senses. You and your family can go straight to hell!" Gabriel walked briskly to the car. He didn't even bother to chase the turkeys off the roof. He gunned that motor and spun the tires. Turkeys and chickens flew in all directions. The geese and the dogs scattered for safety. There was dust and smoke as he ripped out of the Dumont yard. After all the dust and smoke cleared, Ann Marie just stood there. She didn't cry. She didn't scream. She just stood and watched. In Ann Marie's world practicality and logic dominate. Misplaced passion and futile action were not for her. She may have lost a battle, but there was still a war to win. She turned and walked to her loving and "crazy family". She remembered a wise saying, "When One Door Closes, Another Will Open."

3. WHO AM I? — A LOVE STORY

SARAH FRANK STARED OUT OF THE TRAIN COACH window at the passing darkness. Once in a while a white railway sign flashed by. She was on her way to Winnipeg. The train would make a brief stop in Kansack and then the next stop would be Dauphin.

She was a bit nervous about this trip. She was not concerned about Aunt Naomi. Her real worry was about Ben and his parents, the Goldsteins. Ben had promised her, but would his parents approve the marriage?

Abe Frank had come to Canora in 1930. He opened a general store in a rented wooden building.

He immediately attracted customers. Ukrainian and Russian farmers and towns people came to his store because he could speak their language. A few years later he bought the corner lot on Main and Railway. He built a larger store of brick. A big sign in front read "Frank's Department Store".

In 1960 Abe's son, Isaac inherited the business. For a few years business was good but as the next generation replaced the older, the new one spoke primarily English and patronized the other stores. In 1980 he placed a sign in the window "Business For Sale".

As the train passed Kansack, Sarah closed her eyes and remembered that week last summer.

Aunt Naomi had written that the Goldsteins, a very respectable family had a son who would like to meet Sarah and her family. Would they agree to a visit? Mirium Frank wrote a reply that the Goldstein's son Ben would be welcomed.

It was Sunday evening July 7th when Ben Goldstein drove up in a late model Mustang. Ben was quite handsome. He was six feet tall, with slightly curled black hair. His smile was infectious. Sarah was shy, but attracted to this stranger. He said he was going to the motel, but he would be back next morning.

The next morning Monday Ben, was at the Frank home. He asked, "Would it be alright if Sarah showed him the town?" Isaac replied, "I think it would be alright." Mirium joined in and said, "Ben, I want you for supper at about six."

As they drove slowly, Sarah pointed out the various businesses. They stopped to admire the two churches- Orthodox and Catholic. They stopped at the mall and had a Coke. At the last stop they parked in front of Canora's signature statue, the Ukrainian Lady holding a loaf of braided bread. They talked and asked questions. Ben had completed two years of Law. After he received his degree and passed the Bar, he would join his father in the firm, "Goldstein and Harmon."

Sarah said she would complete grade twelve and then maybe she would go to Saskatoon or Winnipeg to pursue a Commerce degree.

Time passed so quickly. They had so much to talk about. Ben looked at his watch and it was fifteen to six. They quickly drove to the Frank home. Then they washed and came to the dinner table.

Isaac and Mirium were waiting. Isaac put a prayer shawl over his shoulders and said a brief prayer in Yiddish. Mirium had prepared latkes and lamb stew. They drank a small glass of

Manishewitz wine. After supper Sarah and her mother washed the dishes and they joined the men in the living room.

There was more talk and Ben was a good listener and a good talker. Time passed so quickly and at ten Ben said it was time to return to the motel, but he would be back next morning. Ben thanked Mrs. Frank for the delicious supper.

Ben was there on Tuesday morning. Sarah suggested they go to Good Spirit Lake. Mirium saw that her daughter Sarah was captivated by this handsome stranger. She called Sarah to the bedroom.

She said, "Be careful with this charming man, he may charm you but do not let him cross the line."

At the lake they swam and walked on the sandy beach. They talked, joked, and laughed. Ben did not suggest any improper act. They had a milkshake at the resort cafe. Towards evening they drove back. Ben said he would return the next morning.

On Wednesday Sarah suggested they go to the Crystal Lake Resort. At the resort they rented some golf clubs and golfed. Both had golfed before, but neither was very good. They never bothered keeping score. It was not important. They seemed to be enthralled with each other. They went to the beach, waded and swam. After enough water, they spread a blanket on the sand and basked in the warm sun.

Ben took Sarah in his arms. "Sarah, I love you."

"Ben I love you too."

Both were aroused, but then Sarah edged back out of his arms. "Ben I am not ready and I want my husband to be the only one."

Ben also drew back. He muttered some inaudible words of his disappointment. Yet instinctively he realized the gem that Sarah was. This girl had smarts and high moral standards. He would be a fool not to claim her for his wife.

Sarah edged closer to Ben, kissed him and said, "Next July I will come to Winnipeg. If your parents approve and if you still want me, then if you ask me to marry you, I will say yes."

Ben was silent but deep in thought. Sarah gave him another gentle kiss and whispered in his ear.

"Ben, when we are married, I will give you all the children you might want. Maybe we could start with six."

They laid still and she put her hand in his. When it got chilly, they dressed and drove back to the Frank's home. They did not speak much, but an invisible bond had joined these two. They knew that love was both an ecstasy and an agony.

On Thursday morning Mirium noticed that something had happened to these two. Had they quarrelled? Had they done something of which they felt guilty? Isaac was not as perceptive. He said, "I can see that you seem bored. Well there is a lot of work in the garage and in the store warehouse.

You know what should be done."

All day they swept, cleaned, discarded, and rearranged. During the day they touched and an invisible communication passed between them. When the work was finished, Mirium had a fresh kugel for their supper. After supper Ben praised Mirium's kugel. Mirium reminded him that Sarah was an excellent cook. Each went their way to a refreshing bath and sleep.

Friday was Ben's last day with the Franks. Sarah suggested they drive to Yorkton. In Yorkton they walked in the malls and visited the downtown to see Croll's Department Store. The Croll family had been in Yorkton for many years. They were Jewish and Ben wanted to meet them. They went into the store and asked for Mr. or Mrs. Croll. A younger man came to meet them. They introduced themselves. Mr. Croll said he knew the Franks of Canora and quite a few families in Winnipeg- the Freedmens, Brounsteins and the Laimons. He didn't think he knew the Goldsteins. Ben asked if the synagogue was still active. Mr. Croll said they barely had enough members. Tomorrow was Saturday and he invited them to come. He would have Ben read the Torah. If they wanted to see the synagogue, it was on Betz Ave. They located the building. It was a small building from another era. Sarah said she would like to be married in a small synagogue. Ben said the ones in Winnipeg were quite large. They sat in the car and gradually got closer to each other. All the passions returned. They both said, "Not yet."

At the Frank's home Mirium told Ben to join them for breakfast. She and Sarah were going to make special latkes with cinnamon.

That Saturday morning Ben thanked the Frank's for their hospitality. He embraced each. Sarah walked with him to the car. He took her in his arms, "I love you Sarah. I cannot wait for next summer."

Sarah said good bye with a long and passionate kiss. She turned and went to the house. In her bedroom her pillow was wet with her tears. Why was love so painful?

For the rest of the year she did her school work with determination. In June there were no marks less than ninety. The class chose her to be the valedictorian. She spoke eloquently of courage, dedication, goals, and purpose. After the exercises were over she went home and began packing for her trip to Winnipeg.

Sarah roused from reverie. The air was so stuffy and the train was slowing down to change to the side track. She decided to walk to the end of the car and get some fresh air. As she stood on the narrow platform there was a sudden jolt and Sarah went tumbling down the railway embankment.

It was morning when she regained consciousness. Her entire side was bruised and she felt a gash on her head. She looked around. It seemed plausible that she had been thrown off the train.

Where was she going and who was she? She could not remember her name. She began walking down the track with her right ankle in pain. She came to a crossing. Should she keep going or go down the road? She chose the road. There must be someone not far on this road. She walked all day dragging her painful ankle.

In the evening she stopped under a spruce tree. She was so tired, but who am I? The next day was the same as the day before. There was some water in a rut. She washed her face and drank just a little to quench her thirst. The third day she kept walking, but thoughts about death in the forest crept into her injured head. Did hallucinations enveloped her mind? She saw gardens of flowers, young people in white dancing on the clouds. She dropped off into a troubled sleep. The next morning she felt a general body weakness and her ankle had swollen. Should she try walking or just sit and wait for death? That instinct to survive won the day. She kept on her tortured walk.

About noon she came to a clearing and there was a cabin. Was it real or just a mirage? The door was locked, but a cardboard sign read, "Key is under the block". Yes, it was there. She opened the door and the window shutters and went inside. Once inside she opened the cupboards. There were cans of beans, soup, meat, and large cans of flour and rice. Outside was a well, hay shed, corral, and a garden. Inside she looked in the mirror. Who was the girl with the dirty face and dishevelled hair? She washed, drank water, and then made a fire in the stove. Later she opened a can of soup. She wondered who owned the cabin and would they return and find her as an intruder? She didn't care. She wasn't going to walk any further. That evening she lowered the bedding, tucked herself in and slept.

Next day she ate, washed, and examined the surroundings more carefully. There was a calendar on the wall but she had no idea what day it was. On a paper she made an X each morning.

After six X's she heard an unfamiliar noise outside. There was a man on a horse leading a pack horse. The man spoke first, "Who are you?" She replied, "I don't know who I am."

The man was suspicious.

"What do you mean you don't know who you are? What is your name?"

"I don't know, I was thrown off a train and I came here after three days of walking."

The man seemed still puzzled and said, "The train tracks are at least thirty five miles from here."

When Sarah did not arrive in Winnipeg, Naomi Freedman phoned Mirium Frank. The Franks were frantic! Did Sarah get off at some stop? Was she worried about meeting the Goldstein family?

Was she forced? They contacted the CNR and then each station master where the train had stopped. No one knew anything about Sarah. Finally they asked the RCMP to put Sarah on a missing persons list.

During the weeks that passed there was no answer.

Randy Skogen was the forest ranger for the northern district of the Duck Mountain Forest Reserve. His job was to patrol the forest trails from April to November. He had a circuit with four cabins thirty miles apart. He would spend five days at each cabin. He would patrol two-ten mile trails for two days. The other three days he could choose his own duties.

"If you don't know your name and I don't know where to take you, then you will have to tag along with me for the next two weeks. I will have to give you a name. Since I found you in the forest, I will name you after a forest goddess. You will be Rhea! For a surname I will just give you mine. You are Rhea Skogen." When he first saw Rhea she was fairly good looking, about eighteen years old, but she was all scratched up as though she had fought a tiger. Having a girl around was new for Randy, but quite soon he found out she was no bother. She was pleasant and helpful and the days were no longer lonely for each. For his patrols Randy said she could go with him or she could stay in the cabin. She said she wanted to go along.

Randy put the saddle on the pack horse and they made the ten mile patrol together.

Rhea had made some bannock sandwiches and some tea for their noon lunch. The three optional days their time was pleasant for both. They picked wild raspberries and strawberries. They treked two miles through the bush to a lake where Rhea learned to cast and the fish were good. Rhea slept on the cot and Randy slept on the floor in a sleeping bag. They were falling for each other, but the mystery of who was this girl kept them apart. After a week they moved to the next cabin. Once again time went so quickly and their attachment to each other grew.

When they reached the home cabin Randy took Rhea in his old Jeep to the town of Swan River.

First they went to the RCMP station to inquire if Rhea was listed as a missing person. The reply was negative. Next Randy got a job for Rhea at the Flames Restaurant. She would stay with a widow relative of Randy's. Randy promised he would come and see Rhea at month's end. Rhea found the work pleasant.

She liked the staff of two waitresses and two cooks. They liked Rhea and she was so quick with numbers.

"Rhea, what is ten percent of $121.30?"

Randy did come at the end of the month. They spent time together-walking, talking, going to the show, and once he took her canoeing on the Swan River.

The next month Rhea went to see Dr. Patterson. She wanted to know something personal. Dr.

Patterson said her memory loss was due to damage on the section of her cerebrum. Dr. Patterson told Rhea that she had not given birth to any babies.

The following month when Randy returned, Rhea told Randy she had learned a bit more about herself. In their talks Randy had said he wanted a wife that liked nature. She wondered if Randy liked her. As they sat in his Jeep, Rhea leaned over and gave him a kiss. He responded with a kiss for her.

Rhea summoned the courage to ask, “Randy would you ever consider marrying me?”

Randy put his arms around her and said, “I am going to wait a year to find out who you are. At the end if there are no obstacles, I will marry you. I mean for sure.”

At the end of October Randy said his job was finished till next April. He was going back to his family in Brandon. He would finish his degree in Forestry at the Brandon College. Would Rhea like to move to Brandon? She wanted to be near Randy. In Brandon Rhea got a job with D.M. Accounting.

A Mrs. Meadows wanted to retire, so she became a mentor to Rhea. Rhea learned very quickly. On weekends Randy took her skating, hockey games, concerts, and there were just quiet times together.

In December at the RCMP detachment quarters in Brandon, Staff Sergeant Munroe told his Secretary to go through all the files and see that all papers were in their proper folders. In her non busy time Jean Nelson the Secretary followed orders. In doing the missing persons file she came to a picture and stopped. She had seen this girl somewhere, but where? She told the Sergeant about the find. They decided to put her picture in the classified of the Brandon Gazette. “Would this person contact the RCMP.”

About a week later a girl in the office came to Rhea’s desk, “Rhea your picture is in the paper.”

The next two weeks were hectic for Rhea. She asked for time off. She took the bus to Canora.

Her parents were overjoyed to see their daughter. Yet for Rhea/Sarah she could not remember them.

She received a dozen roses. The card read “To my love” from Ben Goldstein. She asked, “Mother who is Ben?”

A week later Ben came from Winnipeg. He took Rhea/Sarah to a high end restaurant in Yorkton.

In the dim light Ben edged closer and was going to kiss her. Sarah moved away. She could not make any connection. Further more she had Randy. Ben left the next day and asked the Franks to let him know when and if Sarah recovered. Her parents made an appointment for her in Regina. Dr. Kumar the brain specialist took a cat scan and told Sarah she had a lesion on the cerebrum. There was a slim chance that with surgery her memory would recover. Maybe some blood thinner might help overtime.

The psychiatrist Dr. Hemmings talked to Sarah. He said. "Hypnosis might work." Sarah said she would think about it.

At her parent's home, Sarah said she would not try for any cures. She was happy the way she was. She was going back to Brandon and she would get married to Randy. Her parents were extremely disappointed. In the Jewish culture when one left his faith, the parents would hold a ritual somewhat like a funeral. The meaning was that all contacts were to be severed. Her parents said they would not invoke this ritual, because Sarah was still their daughter. She was the only hope they had for any grandchildren. They said they would not go to the wedding. It would be too painful. However if she had children they would like to see them.

Rhea returned to Brandon and her job and she was going to hold Randy to his promise.

On Saturday June 6th was their big day. A small wedding would be in the park if it wasn't raining. Randy went to the forest and picked tiger lilies, lady slippers, and ferns. A florist made a bouquet from these wild flowers. It was a beautiful sunny day and a gentle breeze blew the scent of clover and lilacs over the small gathering. Margaret Braaten was the Celebrant.

"Randy Skogen, do you take Rhea Sarah Frank to be your lawful wife for as long as you live?"

"I do."

"Rhea Sarah Frank, do you take Randy Skogen to be your lawful wedded husband for as long as you live?"

"I do."

"I pronounce: Randy and Rhea are legally married according to the statutes of the Province of Manitoba. Randy will you now kiss your wife and let it not be the last one. You may now exchange rings."

Randy and Rhea's friends arranged a small outdoor reception. There was champagne and cake.

The Celebrant gave a short speech where she advised them to keep their love alive each day. Randy's friend got the garter and Rhea's friend got that unique bouquet.

Randy's parents arranged a catered banquet at the Ramada for about forty guests. There were the usual toasts and the guests kept clinking their glasses, so that Randy and Rhea were constantly rising and kissing. For their honeymoon they were going to the forest for a month. They would follow the same circuit when Randy first saw the bruised girl at the second cabin. I do not need to say more except to say that nature smiled on these two and love blossomed to the fullest extent.

POSTSCRIPT I hope you enjoyed reading the story. I am guessing that you want to know what happened to the principal characters. I will break protocol and spill the beans. The Franks sold their Canora property for half value and moved to an apartment in Winnipeg. They joined the Temple Beth congregation. Ben Goldstein got his degree and joined his father's firm which now is titled as Goldstein Goldstein and Harnon. He met a girl in his own congregation and they were married in the Temple Shalom Synagogue.

Randy got his degree in Forestry. He was appointed as the district manager by the Department of Natural Resources. Whenever he had a break, he always took Rhea on a nature trek. Rhea is still working at D.M. Accounting, sometimes part time and sometimes full time. A year after their marriage Rhea gave birth to twins. The boy was named Randolph Isaac. The girl they named Mirium Sarah. Rhea kept her promise. She and Randy took the one-year-old twins to see their grandparents. Isaac was his stoic self, but Mirium gushed profusely. She was sure the boy had many features of his grandfather. The girl was the image of her mother when Sarah was that age. The Grandparents asked that Randy and Rhea/Sarah bring the grandchildren as often as they could. They promised. When they got home and put the twins to bed, Randy looked at Rhea and grinned like the Cheshire Cat. Rhea was naturally beautiful, but now she had that special glow. You see Rhea was pregnant again. (Forgive me for sharing the secret).

4.
ESCAPE

JACK MUNROE AND SANDY GRANT FOUND ONE OF THE last parking spots in the Legion lot. The sound of music blared from the inside. They paid their admission, went in and joined the dancers. The drum beat a steady rhythm and the strobe lights, swept across the gyrating crowd. For the young dancers this was music at its best. When the music stopped the Band soloist announced, “Get your partners for a waltz.” The lead guitarist put down his instrument and picked up a fiddle. The melodic strains of the “Lara's Theme” filled the room.

Jack and Sandy did not have any lady escorts, so Sandy said, “Let's go for a beer.”

Two steps towards the adjoining room and Jack stopped! That girl sitting alone seemed familiar.

He approached her and said, “Myrna it's been a long time, would you like to dance?”

“I would love to,” said Myrna.

He put his arm around her waist and she slipped into his arms. She rested her head on his shoulder.

They glided in unison to the melodic music.

“I have heard that you have been dating John Jr., but where is he?”

“I guess he is in the other room, getting drunk as usual.”

"Myrna why don't you just dump him?"

"I can't."

"Why not?"

"John Sr. holds the mortgage on our farm and the house in town. He has told my father that if things went right, he would tear up the mortgage."

The music stopped and Jack escorted Myrna to the bench.

An usher approached them. "John Jr. is too drunk and is causing trouble. Should I call someone?"

"No, put him in the car and I will drive him home."

She turned to Jack, "Thank you for the dance and I will call you sometime."

At the McCain home, Douglas McDougal came out. He was the McCain's all purpose servant- butler, chauffeur, gardener, etc. After he guided John Jr. inside, he came out. "Thanks for your help, John Sr. will be pleased. I will drive you home."

John McCain Sr. was an important citizen and business man in the town of Bridgetown. There was McCain Motors, a Ford Dealership, McCain Lumber and Hardware, McCain Building with Bank of N.S. and a Medical Clinic on the ground floor and offices on the second. It was rumoured that he was the secret owner of the Blue Yak. He would not care to have that known, since he was the First Elder in the Presbyterian Church.

John Jr. was the only child of the family. The McCain's had built a modest fortune in the lumber trade. John Sr. had added to the assets. John Jr. was a disappointment. When sober he was a good worker and manager. However he had these drinking bouts which resulted in trouble: two drunk driving charges, four traffic infractions, etc. John Sr. pinned his hopes that if his son married Myrna Adams, she might put him on the correct path. John Sr. waited and hoped.

A few days later Jack got a call.

"This is Myrna, meet me by the Presbyterian Church."

He drove to the location. She looked around and got into the truck.

"Let's just drive to the edge of town. Jack, you know I don't care for John Jr., but what am I to do?"

"Myrna, I like you a lot and if you were free, we could be a number. Right now Sandy is inquiring about jobs in Halifax. If things work out for you and me, we could get serious. But we will have to wait." He kissed her gently then drove back to the church.

The following week Jack got a call from Sandy. "Meet me at the Blue Yak, I have some info about Halifax." Jack and Sandy were good friends for some years. After high school both went to Truro and took courses. Jack became an electrician and Sandy a carpenter. Now they sat in the Blue Yak, each with a beer. Sandy told Jack that Maritime Construction was building houses in a new subdivision of Halifax. He was sure both of them could get jobs. Jack said that he would get some things in order and go with Sandy. Before they finished their beer John Jr. staggered in. He saw Jack. He came to their table. "You SOB I hear you are trying to steal my girl."

"John Jr., you are drunk and I'm not trying to steal anyone's girl."

John Jr. sat at the bar and the bartender, Cam McKnee, put a glass of beer in front of him. He asked the bartender, "If some SOB was stealing your girl would you stand for that?"

Cam said, "John just drink your beer and don't make any trouble." John Jr. picked up his beer and went to Jack's table. "You're not going to steal my girl and you are an a-hole." He threw the beer in Jack's face.

The bartender came around grabbed John Jr. and pulled him away.

"Sit down on that damn stool and stay there!"

Cam walked over to Jack, "I'm sorry for what happened. If he wasn't John Sr.'s son I would throw him out."

Jack wiped his face and said, "He better not come here again!" The bartender brought two more glasses to Jack's table, "It's on the house."

At the bar John Jr. finished his beer, then said, "Give me another." The bartender asked, "Don't you think you had enough?"

John Jr. replied, "You're not going to tell me anything. My old man owns this joint and if I want I'll have him kick your ass down the road." Once again John Jr. picked up his glass and went to Jack's table. "I called you a SOB. What are you going to do about it?"

"Go back and finish your drink."

"You're not going to order me around." He swung the glass across Jack's face. Jack fell backwards. Then he pulled himself off the floor, picked up the chair and swung it at John Jr. John Jr.

fell back, hit his head on the bar and then fell to the floor. The bartender, Jack and Sandy bent to see the lifeless body. Sandy said, "let's get the hell out of here!"

Outside Sandy said, "Jack, if that bastard is dead, there will be real trouble. You know what John Sr. will do."

Jack said, "I know! I will disappear and keep in touch with you through my brother Scottie."

At the Munroe home, Jack said, "Mom, Dad, there has been an accident at the Blue Yak. John Jr. is dead and I'm involved."

Mom said, "Maybe you should surrender and the court will see it fairly?"

"No Mom. John Sr. is not going to accept his son's fault. He controls Bridgetown and it's going to be thirty years for me."

Jack's Dad asked, "What do you plan?"

"I'm going to disappear into the Gold Lake Wilderness. Sandy will get me a new identity and in a couple of years when things settle down, I will head to BC or the Yukon."

The family helped to gather supplies and tools Jack would need in the wilderness.

"Scottie will drive me to that abandoned Stewart farm on the edge of the wilderness. About once a month I will leave notes at that place." Tearfully Mom and Dad bade Jack a sad good bye.

When John Sr. was told that his son was dead, he called his lawyer Angus McLeod. "Come here at once."

When Angus McLeod arrived he was told the McCain plan. Angus went to each of the bar witnesses, who were there when John Jr. died. "This is the story when the cops ask you: "John Jr. was sitting peacefully at the bar. Jack Munroe was jealous that John Jr. had Myrna Adams as a fiancee. He grabbed a chair and killed him with several blows." Then the lawyer slipped each a fifty dollar bill.

Next morning Constable Prentice and Constable Hughes examined the scene and questioned the witnesses. They concluded this was an open-and-shut case of willfull murder.

A month later a preliminary hearing was held. John Sr.'s lawyer was there. There was no lawyer for Jack Munroe. So the Court appointed a law student from Dalhousie. Witnesses were called and each had the same story. The law student was suspicious. There were no grounds to challenge them since each swore to tell the truth. The session was short. The Magistrate said, "By the evidence presented this is an open-and-shut case. When Jack Munroe is apprehended, he will face a first degree charge of murder."

"God save the Queen."

Jack made three trips to carry supplies and tools about ten miles into the wilderness. For several days he searched for a suitable location to build a temporary home. He found a likely spot beside a flowing stream.

After the incident at the Blue Yak, the Mounties stayed on the case. They asked anyone and everyone if they knew where Jack could have gone. They asked Myrna if she saw Jack after the murder. They came to the Munroe farm with a search warrant and scoured every inch of the place.

"Mr. Munroe where is your son? It would be better if he surrendered. If he is innocent the Court will acquit him."

Mr. Munroe replied, "I don't know where he is. I know my son, if he felt he would get a fair trial he would be here. This I know, whoever paid off the witnesses is where you should direct your investigation."

In Bridgetown the search for Jack Munroe continued. John Sr. hired detectives to supplement the Police search. The witnesses who had perjured themselves were wondering if anymore money was going to come their way? If they came out with the truth they would face jail time for lying. Myrna and even Sandy were questioned, but there was no information. They did not know what happened to Jack.

In the wilderness Jack built a small cabin completely hid from the air. He and Scott communicated by hidden notes and always changing their place of contact. A year passed, and then two. Jack decided he would soon have to make a move. He asked Scott to see Sandy, and ask if he had papers for him. In town there were changes too. John Sr. lost interest in his holdings. He and his wife spent most of the year in Bermuda. In town some of the Blue Yak patrons began to talk. The story was that Jack Munroe was railroaded. A new Detachment head came to Bridgetown. Corporal Dick Newton heard the rumours. He took out the Munroe file and studied it. He asked the Division Head to send an undercover man. The town knew him as Ken Sanders. He posed as a Watkins salesman and as a regular drunk. He befriended the witnesses, and bought them drinks and asked innocent appearing questions. He wore a wire and collected all the evidence. When he had assembled all the necessary evidence, the Attorney General ordered a new preliminary trial for Jack Munroe. James McAlister, a well known criminal lawyer in Halifax heard about the case. He offered to act as Crown Prosecutor. He offered his services pro bono. He felt the judicial system needed to have its integrity restored. All the witnesses of three years ago: Cam McKnee, Nathan Boucher, John McKay, Brian McKnight, Alexander Melrose, and Gerald Miller were subpoenaed for a new trial. Cam McKnee was the first to take the stand. He repeated his sworn story. The Prosecutor had the court play the wire tape, then McAlister said, "Well Mr. McKnee what do you say now?"

"I am guilty."

The lawyers for the other witnesses advised a plea bargain. Each was sentenced to two years less a day for perjury. A further case against John Sr. McCain and Angus McLeod for malicious conspiracy was registered. Both pleaded guilty without trial. Angus McLeod was immediately disbarred and sentenced to two years. John Sr. escaped the reach of the law because he was no longer a Canadian citizen, but a citizen of Bermuda. A Civil case against McCain and McLeod was filed in court. Munroe's lawyer asked for $500,000.00 in damages. There was some bargaining, but both sides settled for $450,000. John Sr. McCain liquidated all his holdings in Bridgetown. New signs appeared on the former McCain buildings.

The community suggested that the former McCain Building should now be called the Munroe Building, but Jack declined. With the money Jack received, he spent the majority of it in a partnership with Sandy to form, "Munroe and Grant Construction". He offered to buy his parents a house in any town. They chose Wolfville. He bought the Stewart abandoned farm as a memorial of his time in the wilderness. He sent his brother Scott to Dalhousie to study Law.

After all this time he wondered about Myrna Adams. He inquired in Bridgetown, but no one seemed to know where she went after the BlueYak incident. He persisted and finally found her in Antigonish. She was a secretary there for the Dean of Arts at ST.F.X.University. He asked her for dinner. At first she hesitated, but then she agreed. The reunion went well and more dates followed. In Jack's arms and in his gentle manners she found security and love. Jack asked her to marry him. There was no doubt about her answer.

Sandy was introduced to Myrna's friend and they connected. A wedding date was set for June 15th 2000. It just might be a double wedding. When we choose a road to travel in life, we may never know what is at its end.

5.

A GRADUATION TO REMEMBER

THE CURTAINS PARTED ON THE STAGE OF THE AUDITORIUM. The flood lights came on. On the stage was the 1990 graduating class of Humboldt Collegiate. Standing at the back were twenty young men with fresh haircuts and dressed in tuxedos. Seated in front were twenty young ladies in gowns of various colors. The color and the lights enhanced the natural beauty of youthful faces.

In the lower portion of the auditorium, flashes from cameras sparkled like fire flies on a summer evening. There were parents and grandparents gleaming with pride. It seemed like a miracle that a scruffy little kid in grade one could in twelve years become so transformed. There were brothers and sisters also proud, but a little jealous. Then there were the would be lovers with visions of dates, engagements, and even marriages. Lastly were the citizens of the small city who came to see the pageantry and listen to the speeches.

The exercises this evening of June 30, 1990 were the apex of the events of the entire day. This forenoon, was an ecumenical service for the graduates at St. Michael's R.C. Church. Then in the late afternoon, was the banquet with its toasts and speeches. Now were the stage exercises.

The valedictory address was by Bonnie Lee Simpson What eloquence! What confidence!

Three other graduands also delivered messages equally well rehearsed. A grade eleven student gave a poignant speech of farewell. Then the Vice Principal handed out the scholarships. Next the Principal handed out the scrolls.

The keynote speech of this evening was by the Principal of the rival Scared Heart Academy.

The Principal was Sister Monica. A small headband and a cross on her business suit reminded the audience that she was a nun. Probably in her late twenties she projected a presence. Except for the insignia, she could have been a Hollywood Star. Her voice was mesmerizing. You could have heard a pin drop. She spoke of destiny and free will. It was a speech that everyone should hear periodically.

Whether the graduands heard it we cannot tell. There was so much on their minds this day.

After the speech the Master of Ceremonies thanked Sister Monica. He announced there would be one final portion of the the exercises. The auditorium seats were cleared, the graduands came to the lower floor. To the strains of music of a by gone era, the graduands performed the Grand March. Then were the brief dances with parents, fellow grads, and with their escorts. Quite a few girls were presented with flowers by lovers, friends, and parents. The proceedings ended when the graduands gathered in one group and a spokesperson thanked parents, teachers, friends, etc. She wished everyone farewell and reminded them to drive safely.

Bonnie Lee like so many other graduands drove home. Some just sat and reviewed all the events of the day. Bonnie Lee exchanged her attire for jeans, sweat shirts, and sports shoes. They were headed for a party. June Simpson said, "Bonnie I wish you wouldn't go."

"Mom, don't worry, I'll be alright. There will be mostly friends."

There was the sound of a car horn. "Bye mom, Bye Dad! I'm off, don't wait up for me."

Cathy Caldwell was sounding the horn.

The party was about a mile out of town in what once was a gravel pit. When they arrived the place was already full. There was rock music, beer, pot, and someone had built a fire. There were many, mostly men that Bonnie had never seen. Someone thrust a bottle of beer in Bonnie's hand. There was the fire, the shadows, the rhythmic drum sounds, and the gyrating dancers. This was Humboldt, but it could have been a scene of a ceremonial dance in darkest Africa. Bonnie took tiny sips of the beer and joined the dancers. A young man approached her and said, "Hi, take this and you will experience a nice buzz."

She didn't hesitate, she could handle anything. She downed the pill with a sip of beer. A few minutes later she saw colors, and the dancers appeared in funny shapes. She felt dizzy. She spoke to the man who had given her the pill. "I'm feeling really weird, would you mind taking me to my car?" He took her to Cathy's car and placed her in the back seat. She blacked out, but she still saw dancing figures and fire.

When the beer was gone and the fire was only embers, the disc jockey announced. "That's all!

That's it." Everyone headed for their cars. Cathy looked around. She couldn't see Bonnie. Where was she?

Did she go with someone and didn't tell her? When everyone was gone she went to her car. Bonnie was asleep in the back seat.

At the Simpson home, Cathy shook Bonnie. "Wake up you're home."

"Home? Where's home?" Cathy led Bonnie to the house. Inside, Bonnie was like a zombie. She walked past her mother and father without seeing them. She went straight to her bedroom and Jane Simpson followed. There was no waking Bonnie.

Back in the kitchen, she asked, "Cathy do you know what happened?"

"It was dark and I did not see Bonnie most of the time."

"Thanks for bringing her home."

In the morning Bonnie appeared bright and refreshed. "What happened to you last night?"

"Maybe I was just so exhausted from all the graduation events. I know I had one beer and then I conked out. Some nice young man took me to Cathy's car."

Bonnie Lee was the only child of Edward and Jane Simpson. Edward was the Principal of one of the Elementary schools. Jane worked as a receptionist and aide in the Medical Clinic. The Simpsons were not wealthy, but with frugal living they were able to provide their daughter advantages Girl Guides, music lessons, and summer trips to Europe and USA. They were also always supportive of Bonnie's school activities. Beside being an honour student, she was the leading player on the volleyball, basketball, and curling teams. Now she would be off to University.

During July Edward was shopping. He was looking for a good reliable car for Bonnie. He went to all the dealerships and used car shops. When Edward found three he thought would be suitable, he asked Bonnie to choose. She chose the Honda Accord.

About the third week Bonnie became aware that something didn't happen, that should have. Oh well, maybe all the excitement was too much. She made plans. She enrolled in a Pre-Med Arts program, next inquired about living places, and had to chose a dorm or an apartment with some other student.

August came and all the preparations were made. She liked the car. She had bought new clothes. There was still time for one week at Prince Albert National Park with her friends. The third week in August came and Bonnie knew! How could it have happened? She took her Mom into her bedroom.

"Mom, I think I'm pregnant."

"How?"

"I've missed two periods and I'm trying to recall. At that graduation party this man gave me a pill. I didn't even question or suspect anything. When he took me to the car and I passed out, did he rape me? I should have listened to you, Mom."

"Oh My Goodness!"

"Mom, maybe I should have an abortion?"

"Bonnie, your father and I are not religious, but we both agree that an abortion should be the choice only in the rarest of cases. I will talk to your father and we will decide how we should proceed."

The next day Jane Simpson took her daughter aside. "Your father and I think you should do both; carry on with your studies and have the baby."

"I can't do both."

"Oh yes you can!"

"How?"

"You can do one semester of the first year. You can take a leave. After delivery you should spend at least half a year with the baby. Then its' back to University for you. I will be there to help you. I can terminate my job. We can get by without my earrings. However I want you to understand that this will be your baby and not mine."

"Oh what a mess I have made of my life and what a shame for my family."

"No Bonnie, this is only a setback."

The plan was followed. Jane quit her job just before delivery. Edward was disappointed. He did not like to talk to others about an unmarried daughter who was going to have a baby. Bonnie completed the first semester.

On March 17th a 7lb boy was born. Bonnie named him Stephen Patrick Edward Simpson. Jane allowed Bonnie to do most of the caring — baths, diapers, feeding, etc. Bonnie became absorbed in motherhood. She found joy in being a mother. Jane was determined not to take over from Bonnie although the temptation was still there. Edward stayed out of the way, but whenever no one was looking he would go and admire that little boy in the crib. Sometimes the baby would hold his finger.

That little baby had captured the emotions of three people who cared and loved him.

The years passed ever so quickly. A pivotal year was 1998. Stevie was in Grade1. Bonnie had made the seventy mile trip from Saskatoon to Humboldt almost every weekend. She spent time with Stevie doing a thousand things. During the week it was Jane who mothered him. When he was hurt he came to her. He adored the two women who spoiled him. Yet it was Edward, his Grandfather, a surrogate father to whom he became attached. For Edward it was like a renewal of youth. He was nearing sixty, but with Stevie he felt like a young father. He made plans for them. There would be baseball, football, fishing, and hiking.

Another significant event happened that year. At the spring convocation of the U of S. The Dean announced: "Bonnie Lee Simpson, by the authority of this University I confer upon you the degree of Doctor of Medicine, cum laude."

The Chancellor handed her the portfolio that held the document for which she had worked for seven years. Bonnie Lee had specialized in Pediatrics and now she was headed for the General Hospital in Prince Albert, where she would intern for six months. Then she would take over the pediatrics from a retiring doctor. She would still make the trip to Humboldt as often as she could. She missed her son and with each visit he seemed to grow taller.

During all those years on the University campus, her striking attractive appearance got the attention of many young men. Who was this beauty they would inquire. They learned she was a medical student. Whenever there was an opportunity many a young man would approach her. He would introduce himself and ask if she would like to go with him for dinner, a dance, a party, or just lunch in the cafeteria. She always had the same answer for each: "I am flattered that you ask me, but you see I have a man in my life, slightly younger. However if you see me in the cafeteria, come and join me for some coffee."

After two years in Prince Albert she decided to move back to Humboldt. She would join a clinic and practice general medicine, but specialize in pediatrics. She wanted to be near her son as he grew older. Whenever they were together Stevie was so proud of his mother. She was so beautiful and she was a doctor.

Sometimes with the other boys in school, they would ask Stevie, "Who is your father?"

He would answer, "My father died a long time ago and my grandfather is my second father. For Edward, Stevie was the son he never had. June and Bonnie noticed that the two were inseparable.

The year was 2004. In southern Arizona and on the border with Mexico, Sergeant Lance Parker was instructing his men. "We have some inside info. The Mexican Cartel was sending some heavies and some "mules" with a quantity of marijuana and cocaine. We expect they will cross the border in Section Seven. We will place four on each side with search lights. After they crossed the border we will close in. Remember, some will be armed. Those boys are vicious." As expected on June 30th, the Mexican banderos crossed the line. Lance's men closed in. A gun fight ensued. The four banderos were shot, the six mules with the contraband were arrested. However, Lance Parker caught a stray bullet. He was dead.

At the Tucson Military Cemetery, men of his Unit carried the flag draped casket to its final resting place. It was unusual for there was no one to receive the flag. There were at least a thousand there to honour this hero.

After the funeral the Deputy Commander remarked, "It's unusual that there was no one from his family." The men who knew him, regarded him as a private person. There was no wife, no girlfriend, and he never mentioned his parents or home town. Men of his Unit were assigned to go to his apartment and make the final disposition of his effects. There was nothing unusual about the apartment. Clothes in the closest were neatly hung. There was a radio, TV and a few newspapers. They opened a brief case.

There was one item- a sealed manila envelope. On it was written: This envelope to be opened upon my death.

There was a written letter and a Will. The letter stated, "On June 30, 1990 I committed a crime for which I can never atone. I was a student at U of S, Saskatoon. On this day some friends heard that there would be a post graduation party in Humboldt. We drove there. We drank beer and we danced. I saw this pretty girl and gave her an ecstasy pill. She didn't feel well, and asked me to take her to her friend's car.

She passed out. I do not know why evil overtook my judgement. I placed her on the back seat and then I raped her. When we returned to Saskatoon, I could not believe what I had done. I was a coward and had committed a selfish act. I didn't want to spend my years in prison. I picked up all my things, left no trace and drove away. In Calgary I contacted a drug dealer I knew. He gave me an address. At that place for $1000 the man gave me a new identity and supporting documents. I headed as far south as I could — the Mexican border. The rest is history."

"My real name is Neil Stryker. My parents lived in Rosthern, Sask. I had no brothers or sisters. I ask for my parent's forgiveness."

The Will stated, *All my worldly possessions I give to the girl I had violated and to any child that resulted from my act. In the event that such a person and her issue does not exist, then I give all to the Orphanage in the town of Indian Head Sask.*"

Inquires were made. His parents were notified. The briefcase with the Will and a photo (Sergeant Lance Parker) was sent to Dr. B. L. Simpson Humboldt Saskatchewan.

Bonnie Lee shared the contents of the briefcase with her parents. The mystery was solved, but what a tragic end. They were shocked and numbed. What was there to say? The contents of the Will which was $215,000 they decided to put in trust for Stephen Patrick Edward Simpson. In her heart Dr. Bonnie Lee forgave the man known as Lance Parker for an act of evil and violence. Now Stephen when asked who was his father, would have an answer.

6.
FIRE AND FAITH

A. GENERAL STATEMENT

From the beginning of time fire and religion have been closely associated. In Greek Mythology the Goddess Hera gave birth to a son, Haephestus. Because he was deformed she left him on Mount Olympus. He survived and became the God of Fire. He had pity for mankind, so he gave them a gift which was fire.

In the Pre-Christian era Moses talked to God through a Burning Bush. Further, he asked that the Jews make sacrifices. In the Temple the priests burned animals. The smoke and aroma was to please God. In the Christian era the Church recognized there was God and also a rival who was Satan. The Church considered that heretics, challengers of the faith, old women labelled as witches, and persons possessed were servants of Satan. It was the Christian duty to cleanse the planet of Satan's children, so this was done by burning them at the stake. Thousands met that fate. You may say that was a long time ago.

Maybe? Two years ago in the Alberta election one of the candidates said, "Whoever believed that a woman has a right to an abortion should be burned at the stake!" Since this was not legal in these times, he promised that in the end they would burn forever in the Lake of Fire. In the story of Peter and Mary fire will be mentioned.

B. BACKGROUND NOTES

In the 1700's and 1800's ideas from the Enlightment spread through out Europe. In Russia some of these ideas took root. There were holy men who wandered and preached a new version of Christianity. One of these groups that grew were the Doukhabors (Spirit Wrestlers). Their core belief was that God lived within every sentient being. Therefore there was no need for Churches, priests, liturgies, icons, statues, etc. They accepted the Ten Commandments and The Beatitudes as a guide to Christian living. Their motto in one sentence was "Toil and Peaceful Life".

They were pacifists and vegetarians. They believed in the common purse and that living in communes was desirable. They also believed that spiritual growth was to be sought rather than materialism. Russian authorities considered them troublesome and pushed then to the edges of the Empire.

In an act of defiance on June 29, 1897 they burned all their guns. The Government of Canada needed settlers for the prairies so invited them. About 7500 came, settled in about fifty villages in three colonies.

In about fifteen years they cleared the wilderness into farming land.

C. THE STORY OF PETYA AND MASHA

It is 1917 and the people of the village of Smerenia (peaceful) are gathered in the Dom (home) for a sobranya (meeting). The

Dom was a central building for gatherings, orphan's home, and a guest house.

Men sat on one side and women sat on the other side. This evening Elder Ivan Vasilovich Rezansoff spoke.

"Brothers and Sisters we shall start with a prayer."

The Elder led the prayer then began a hymn. Everyone sang. Voices blended. Doukhabor's hymns were about their beliefs, etc. Sometimes a passage from a Russian Bible was read.

Elder Reznasoff said, "This evening we need to discuss What Should We Do? Brother Wasyl Michaelovich Konkin will speak first." Brother Konkin said, "Brothers and Sisters in Christ, this I believe and this I say — In 1897 Queen Victoria invited us to this land. Each soul was to get 160 acres. We could hold property in common.We could live as we always had in communes (villages). We would not have to serve in the military. We left the warm Caucasus and came to this land. It was wilderness. We toiled! Men worked on the railway. Everyone worked to clear the land. When we had no horses or oxen, our women hitched themselves to the plow. Now the Government has passed new laws. We can no longer live in villages. Each family has to live on a separate quarter section. We have to swear an Oath of Allegiance and our children have to go to English Schools. So what are we to do? We cannot go back to Russia. No other country wants us. So I say we should be as the grass. When the storm comes the grass bends, but it survives. A tree will be blown over and dies. So let us bend. Let's choose a homestead, move our houses on that piece of land. Our children can go to their schools, but we can teach them our way at home. May God be with us."

The gathering sang another hymn. "Brother Vladimer Ivanovich Salikien will speak." "Brothers and Sisters in Christ this I will say, yes Christ did say, "Man does not live on bread alone." As Doukhabors, we like Christ, should feed our souls. We have worked hard and for what? They are taking the fruits of our toil. Is that fair? Is that just? Yes, Christ said to turn the other cheek, but he also said we should seek justice, and be prepared to die for it. Let us not obey the authorities who are servants of Satan. Let us protest! We could burn a few schools! We could do more. Let us give the animals that worked for us their freedom. This Saturday those who believe in justice and in freedom, are invited to come with us to Kamsack, where we will walk on Main Street in the nude. They will call us Sons of Freedom. Yes, that is who we are."

The gathering sang another hymn. "We shall hear from Sergie Petrovich Kinakin." "Brothers and Sisters in Christ, I stand here today to say what our leader Petro Vasilovich Veregin has advised us to do. He has spoken to the Government, but they would not listen. Our Spiritual Leader has taken our joint funds and bought land in the Kootneys. There are blocks of land near Grand Forks, Brilliant, and Castlegar. He has advised us to go there. The climate is warmer. We can plant fruit trees. Already they have a jam factory. Some men can work in the saw mills, and some in the mines. We can live as a commune, have our gardens, and orchards. We will have a Dom where we can gather, pray, discuss, and sing. We have been Doukabors for 200 years and we can continue to Toil, love one another, and live in peace."

More hymns were sung. While the speaker spoke, the rest listened. They had pockets of sunflowers and this they chewed with dexterity. The shells covered the floor. At the end of the men's bench were Petya and Grisha. They were listening, but they were admiring Masha and Anuta on the other bench.

Petya whispered to Grisha, "I'm going to marry Masha." Grisha whispered, "If you marry Masha, I will marry Anuta." Across the room the girls were whispering and giggling. We could not hear what they said.

It is 1932 and many of the Doukhabors did move to the Kootenays. Petya and Masha did marry — the Doukhabor's way. Petya and Masha held hands and Grandpa Kinakin pronounced — "In the eyes of our families and in the eyes of God I pronounce you man and wife — one flesh. Remember that there is only one thing that will bind you as one, that is love."

Grisha and Anuta also were married. At this date Petya and Masha had three children — Petya Jr. twelve, Nadya nine and Doonya five. On June 29, 1932 the community gathered at the center and commerated that decisive day. They called it Peter's Day. The day they burned their guns.

On July 15th of 1932 in the Kinakin home Masha was rolling out the dough for pyrishki. Petya Jr. and Nadya were at the other end of the table copying from a Russian book. Masha looked out of the window. A car was coming very fast.

"Petya Nadya run and hide, the police are here." Petya hid in the wood pile and Nadya crawled under the bed.

"Mrs. Kinakin you keep breaking the law. Your children should have been in the public school.

Where are they?"

Masha stood trembling. She didn't say anything.

"Ok we'll find them." They did find them, and the children were handcuffed, and put in the police car.

When Petya Sr. came home from work he asked, "Where are the children?"

"They took them."

"How many times do we turn the other cheek? I'm going to see Grisha."

The next day Grisha got Petya six sticks of dynamite. Petya placed them under the police car. He lit the fuse. "Boom!" Car parts were flying in all directions.

Next morning there were more police from Nelson and Castlegar. They went from house to house.

"Tell us who blew up the police car or we'll throw you in jail." Most answered, "We don't know."

When it came to the Kinakin house Petya said, "Don't harass innocent people. I did it. Why? Your badge says, "Maintain the Right." Tell me, is it right to steal children and put them in prison?" It didn't matter. Petya went to jail. At this time there were quite a few men in the New Westmister Pen. There were women who paraded in the nude in Agassiz. There were hundreds of children in the New Denver facility.

Once a month parents were allowed to see their children in the New Denver Jail. It was a pitiful scene. Children on one side and parents on the other. Barb wire was between them. They reached through the wire to touch hands. Tears watered the ground by this fence.

As the years passed they realized that protests were futile. Children went to public schools. Nude parades and bombings stopped. The Doukhabor leader Peter Vasilovich Veregin, was on a train to Grand Forks when he met his death in 1924. Someone placed a bomb under the seat. Blame was pointed at the Sons of Freedom. The more logical answer was that the police set the bomb. The Sons of Freedom continued to defy the authorities. They refused to pay taxes. They refused to own property. They lived in shanties on Crown Land along the Kettle River. They called their village, Crestova (Christ's home).

EPILOGUE

What became of the Doukhabors? Like the grass in the storm they bent. They accepted materialism. They embraced education. Some abandoned vegetarianism. They would not bend on pacifism.

Petya and Masha lived to a ripe old age. They rest side by side in the Grand Forks Cemetery. Their descendents are many.

You may ask why I chose such an exotic topic or theme? You see, all the years we were in Saskatchewan, they were our neighbours and friends. One summer we drove to Mr. Fofonoff's farm. He was experimenting with fruit trees for the prairies. His wife asked us to stay for noon lunch. How could we refuse? We had fresh made borsch, perishki with butter, blini with honey and tea.

If you are in Sask. on June 29th, you might go to the National Museum at Veregin. There will be choirs- local and visiting. The women will be in their traditional dress. Their hymns tell the struggle to achieve peace. If you are hungry there will be thick slices of bread baked in clay ovens and slathered with butter. If you are thirsty there will be thick slices of watermelon. You will also hear when they took a stand, burned their guns, and refused to participate in war.

7.
A LADY IN WHITE

AT THE NURSE'S STATION A RED LIGHT ON THE CONSOLE flashed. Danielle Bishop responded.

"Olds Hospital."

"This is an emergency. We are at the Trochu corner. Person is unconscious and probably has broken bones. We're coming in."

Danielle looked at the chart, punched four numbers. The same message went out to Dr. Samuels, Dr. Gorski, Nurse Gates, and Nurse Johnson.

"We have an emergency. Ambulance coming in from Trochu. Person is unconscious and probably has broken bones."

The message would be repeated until all four answered. She received a call from Dr. Gorski.

"You might call Dr. Ward who has experience with broken limbs."

Danielle followed through.

Next she ran to a room marked private.

"Karen wake up, wake up. We have an emergency! Come quick."

She ran back to the station. The ambulance rolled in. Attendants transferred the body to the emergency table. Nurses and doctors half dressed came running in. Each went to a predetermined task.

One took the blood pressure, another checked the heart rate, another cut off the patients clothes, and another swabbed the bleeding. Dr. Ward came rushing in. He reviewed the vitals. Looked at the legs.

"This young man probably has a broken femur. Put a temporary splint on the femur. Put him on trauma protocol with a morphine drip. A nurse should be with him at all times. If there is a sudden change contact me at once. Tomorrow morning I want x-rays. In the surgery I want anaesthesiologist, another doctor, and two nurses. Get some sleep and see you in the morning."

During the night Nurse Gates and Danielle took turns with the patient. They now knew his name was Kevin Proctor. They watched the monitors. Danielle held Kevin's hand which twitched once in a while.

The next morning the team was there. Dr. Ward's prognosis was correct. The femur was set and a cast was placed around it. Dr. Ward said there should be monitors and periodic visits. He expected that Kevin would be in recovery about four or five days.

The Bishop family had a small farm between Carstairs and Didsbury. They had five children. The oldest four had already left home, married, and had children. Danielle was a late baby. She was a delightful and intelligent girl. She excelled in school studies and sports. For the Career Project she spent several afternoons at the Didsbury Hospital. She liked what she saw. After grade twelve she went to Red Deer and took a LPN course. She planned that if she liked nursing she would go back and complete two more years for an RN Degree. After Red Deer she wanted a job in the Didsbury Hospital, but there was no vacancy. There was an opening at the Olds Hospital for a Night Nurse- hours from eight pm to four am.

That is how she answered the call when Kevin Proctor came in as an emergency case.

After five days Kevin was discharged. That evening when Danielle came for her shift, a delivery person brought a bouquet of five roses.

The note read, "Thank you Danielle for your care. I was conscious when you held my hand. Love Kevin."

The next day a delivery person brought six roses.

The note read, "Danielle, I think I'm falling in love with you! Love Kevin." This was getting embarrassing.

The nurses and staff teased Danielle. "Danielle you've made a hit."

The third day the delivery person brought a bouquet of seven roses.

The note read, "Danielle, I'm still in love with you. Call me. 555-12XX

Danielle was quite aware that often male patients do develop a crush for some nurses.

She spoke to her mother, "Mom, what would you do?"

"You'll never know till you call him. This attraction may just wear off."

She was nervous when she made the call. Once Kevin answered her anxiety vanished. Kevin suggested that on Saturday he would take her to Olds College. They could walk the grounds and just talk.

Kevin brought her a bouquet of roses.

Danielle's mother later remarked, "That boy must like flowers or he is a florist just getting rid of unsold flowers." Of course she was teasing, for she saw in Kevin a man any mother would wish for her daughter.

At the College they slowly made their tour of the flower beds. There were two wedding parties taking photos. Neither said anything. Maybe suggesting a wedding would be too bold.

Kevin told Danielle that he had completed a farm mechanics course at the College. He offered to take her to the Pomeroy, but she said a sundae at the Dairy Queen would be fine. As they parted that evening, he did not kiss her and she wondered why? She needn't have worried, because they had another date, and another, and yet another. She was falling for this gentle farm boy.

On their fourth date he suggested they take all day Sunday and go to Calgary. She said she was a member of the LDS Church and Sunday services were important to her. A Sunday later he joined her and found that he enjoyed going with her to the Church. They attended single adult activities and had fun. The ladies at the Church began to whisper. What's with this couple? Are they married or what? No, but they were headed that way.

When winter came he took her skating and skidooing. If you were worrying, you needn't have because with each parting there was a passionate kiss.

When she was working, Danielle was eager for Kevin's next call.

When spring came, Kevin was busy with calving and then seeding. He still called her. He said he didn't have money for roses, but he would bring her dandelions as soon as they were out. Of course Danielle knew he was teasing. She loved his easy going personality. After the first week in May the seeding was over and Kevin came with roses.

He said, "Danielle, I cannot wait any longer. Will you marry me?"

Danielle was ecstatic, but she didn't want to show it!

"Kevin do you really love me?"

"Danielle you know I do."

"Alright I'll marry you!"

The news of an upcoming wedding spread like wild fire. Families first, then friends were looking forward with excitement. At the Church a bridal shower was being planned. Kevin's friends at the College and at Trochu were also planning. At the hospital her personality had endeared her to all. A committee was formed and everyone had suggestions.

Now that the whirlwind had been set in motion, final plans had to be set. Friday June 5th was for the bridal shower at the Church. Saturday June 6th the good old boys at the College and at Trochu would honour Kevin. Danielle worried a little because guys were unpredictable.

On Friday June 12th Pastor Eric Engel of the Evangelical Church would marry them. After Kevin became a member, then a year after that, they would be sealed for all time and eternity at the Calgary Temple. After the marriage ceremony there would be a banquet at the Rec. Center in Didsbury.

On Sunday June 14th the members of the LDS Church were preparing a surprise for the young couple. On Monday the Hospital staff had arranged for a banquet at the Legion. There would be music, fun, and a presentation of a large envelope. That envelope held more than you might have guessed. But it will be a secret. On Tuesday they would go south for a week long honeymoon. They wanted to stop and see the Cardston Alberta Temple. Then the rest of the week would be at the Waterton Park Resort.

On the day of the wedding June 12th, Kevin went to Three Hills to get his hair trimmed and to pick up some roses. Going home he thought of that crossing a year ago. It couldn't happen again. That semi surely could read the signs and yield. Oh My! He didn't. The semi went through and crashed into Kevin's car.

There were ambulances and police. The medics tried hard to revive Kevin's lifeless body, but it was no use. News spread and reporters came from Calgary, Red Deer, and Edmonton. This was a human interest story larger than life. At the family homes, in Didsbury, and in Trochu, grief and sadness was overwhelming.

The Bishop of the Church of Jesus Christ of Latter-day Saints and his councillors held an important meeting.

"You know two years ago we set up a Cemetery Plan. We bought two acres next to the cemetery west of town. The plan was that any member of the Church could be buried in the new cemetery. The plot would be free. After five years if there was no marker the Church would provide one. Should we offer the Proctor family the option of a plot?"

Kevin was not a member yet, but we expect he would be. Everyone agreed. The Proctor family was informed and they accepted. Kevin Proctor was buried in the new cemetery and his was the first grave.

As for Danielle her world had collapsed. Her deep love for Kevin, their plans, and the anticipated joy came crashing down. Even the promise of eternity with her Lord could not soothe her troubled spirit.

The Hospital gave her a two week leave. Her absence at home, at the Church, and at the hospital was palpable.

When she returned to work at the hospital, staff noticed the difference. Sometimes they spoke to her, but she would not hear. Her mind was somewhere else. Her infectious smile was no longer there. Her family and others noticed she was getting so thin. Was she unable to eat, or was she wishing for death?

A month after Kevin's death on July 12th, Danielle went to Kevin's grave. She laid a single rose on the earth. What she thought we will never know. After work at four o'clock in the morning she was driving home to Didsbury. At this hour usually there was no one on the road. We cannot know for sure, but a truck came from the east on the Bergen Road. It would seem neither saw the other. There was a crash! Someone coming from Didsbury came upon the crash and called 911. The police and the ambulance arrived. The ambulance took her to Olds. The emergency team tried and prayed. It seemed her spirit was reaching for another place. At six am her spirit left her body.

She was buried beside her love, Kevin Proctor. The Hospital staff remembered she had loved those roses Kevin had sent her. They ordered 200 roses and covered both graves.

Summer passed. In the fall colored leaves fell on those graves. Then winter came and covered both with a blanket of white. In the spring when the leaves on the trees came out, people driving by saw the graves a color of red, blue, and yellow. Who had planted crocuses and tulips on the graves? When June came and the seeding was done and the calves were born, friends of Kevin and Danielle remembered that a year ago, was their day that did not come to pass.

On Highway 27 and about 10 miles west of Olds is a farm yard with a sign that read:

"Welding and Fabricating-Morgan Bros."

On the first of July, Andrew Morgan got a call. "Hello this is Westeel Fabricating.

May I speak to Andrew?"

"Speaking."

"We have a problem at the shop. Two of our workers want to go back to the Philippines to visit their families for six weeks. We need your help. We know you and your brother are capable welders.

Would you come and fill in? We would give you top wages and a shift four to ten pm. What do you say?"

"I'll talk to my brother George and we will let you know."

They took the job. It would not interfere much with their own work. July 15th was such a hot day and at the shop everyone was sweating. It was a relief when quitting time came.

"George, let's stop for a cold beer at the Blue Yak." They had one beer and bought a box of six to drink at home. Driving home on 27, Andrew suddenly said, "hey did you see that?"

"What?"

"Those flickering lights on the grave yard, I will pull over." When the truck stopped they saw the light moving and stopping.

When the clouds parted and the moon shone, they saw a sight they would never forget! A woman in a white bridal dress was carrying a lantern. She would stop at each grave as if to read the words on the gravestones. Then she would move to the next one. The clouds moved and the moonlight was shaded. They did not see the woman now, but the flicker of the lantern light continued.

George said, "Boy what was that?"

Next day at the shop it was another hot day. At lunch break everyone was drinking water and wiping off the sweat.

Andrew spoke. "Last night at eleven we were driving home when we saw some lights at the graveyard west of town. There were flickering lights."

"Must of been fire flies."

"No! When the moon was clear of the clouds, we saw a woman in a white wedding dress. She was carrying a lantern and reading names on the gravestones."

"What kind of pot were you smoking?"

"You may not believe me, but I will swear on your Mother's Bible that we did see a lady in white."

"Ha! Ha! Another tall tale."

Mike Fisher who was from Torrington spoke up, "I've heard of this before. In Torrington we have an old gentleman. He is ninety nine years old and his name is Metro Ivanchuk. He said that in the old country and in Canada such apparitions do appear. The Lady in White is a bride who did not get married, because her man did not come. You see she is searching for her love. Usually she comes on warm summer days when there is a moon and clouds in the sky. When a gravestone is placed on her love's grave, she will find him. After that you will not see her again."

I do not know if this story is true or if it is just a myth. But I have heard that those who have heard the story, and whenever they are driving west of Olds on a summer's night, they will always glance to the left just in case they might see The Lady In White.

8.
EMPIRE

TWO HORSEMEN RODE THEIR HORSES TO THE CREST OF the hill. There they stopped. The older man, still lean and muscular sat in the saddle as though he had been trained in a riding school. The younger man with shoulders of a football fullback sat in a saddle more casually. They looked to the north at the green grass as far as the eye could see.

"Grandpa, with all the rains the grass is so lush that the calves will gain an extra 200 pounds."

They turned to the east.

"Tad, I've never seen such a good crop of barley. Look beyond the barley fields and you see the outlines of Cochrane. I worry."

Grandpa, "It looks like a bumper year, what's to worry?"

"Maybe not in my time, but in the near future those buildings and civilization will move farther and farther west and the land will not be the same."

They turned to the south. There in the valley below were all the buildings of Double Bar B.

Farther south were the ranch buildings of the Barton Boys.

"Tad, have you talked to the Bartons about selling?"

"Grandpa you know the Bartons. They'll put that big blue coffee pot on the stove. You have to drink about four to five cups of that powerful stuff before they'll talk business. I said we would offer them a good price for their half section ranch. They said an oil man and lawyers were there and offered them half a million. These speculators were planning to subdivide the land into one acre lots and sell them to the guys with deep pockets."

"We'll go there tomorrow. I think I can talk to them."

They turned to the west.

"Tad, those mountains remind me of the Carpathians where I was born."

"Grandpa, have you ever thought of going back at least for a visit?"

"I have. After the War I wrote letters, but there was no answer. Later I wrote to a priest in Krakow. He wrote back and said he could not find a trace of my parents or sister."

"Tad, you see that oak tree. When I came here Jim Balfour and I hauled water to keep four saplings alive. Out of the four one survived. It has adapted. Oak trees do not belong here, but this one just wanted to grow. Instead of growing up it grew sideways. Some of the branches are fifty feet long.

Some day I want you to bury me under that oak. I want to see the mountains and empire that spreads in all directions."

"Grandpa, let's ride back. I have a date in Cochrane with my future bride."

"Have you two set a date for the wedding?"

"Not yet, but maybe tonight Marilyn will name a date."

Tad changed to a business suit and drove to the Redford house.

Marilyn was at the steps waiting. "Marilyn, let's go to the Best Western."

"OK."

In the dining room a waiter brought the menu.

"Is there anything you would like?"

"Not particularly, you order for both of us."

The waiter came.

Tad said, "We'll have sirloin steaks well done, salad, and big bottle of chardonnay."

Marilyn seemed awful quiet this evening. She picked at her food. She barely took a sip of the wine. Tad told her of the grass, barley, and how it seemed to be a bountiful year.

All she said was, "That will be nice."

"Would you like to go anywhere else?"

"No, I think I'm just tired."

They drove back to the Redford house. Marilyn usually had a kiss for Tad, but today she said, "Tad, I've made a horrible mistake. I like you and I thought I was in love with you. Now I am asking you to release me from the promise I gave to you."

"What's wrong Marilyn?"

"I've thought about it. I would not make a good wife that you deserve. I've been at the Ranch. I don't like horses, cows, and all those natives."

"Have you got another guy?"

"I do. Tad, I have been meeting this Oil Executive from Calgary. I like him. There is nothing definite."

"Is it because he has a lot of money?"

"Not really, I'm sure there is enough wealth at the Double Bar B. No, it's not that. You know we talked about having children. Tad I don't like children."

"I'll wait if you want to reconsider."

"No! Please forget about me and don't hate me."

She took off her ring and handed it to Tad. She opened the door and left.

Tad was stunned! What had he done wrong?

In the morning Tad did not bother with breakfast. He just wanted to crawl into a hole and hide.

Grandpa called, "Let's go."

"Grandpa, I'm not in a very good mood this morning. Maybe you go without me."

"Did you and Marilyn have a spat?"

"No, it wasn't a spat, but we parted."

"Is it temporary or permanent?"

"It is permanent."

"Tad I have lived a long time and I have learned a few things. Tad sometimes women have a better instinct than us men. They know in advance whether a marriage will work a long time or not."

"Yes, but in the meantime a guy gets older and older. Then he settles into a pattern and becomes like the Bartons. Two old men scratching a living on a run down ranch, lonely, and waiting for someone to come, and share gossip, and that strong coffee. Doesn't sound like a future for me."

"You may be right, but we never know what tomorrow will bring. Sometimes setbacks are meant to strengthen our resolve or they may direct us in a new direction. On the Ranch we have had joys and tragedies. There were winters when cattle froze in the snow and summers when there was nothing but grasshoppers. I have buried a wife and a son at too early an age. But I've kept going! Now it will be good for you to just step back. Let's go and see the Bartons. I want you to look and think. I bet you will learn they do not have empty lives."

When they drove into the Barton's yard, John and Tom were digging a fence hole by the corral.

They saw the truck, dropped everything and hurried to the house.

"Come on in we'll have that coffee pot boiling in no time."

Tom put a cup of ground coffee in and filled the pot with water.

Tad thought *that coffee will be like used engine oil.*

John spoke up, "What's going on at that Double Bar?"

Grandpa answered, "The calves are getting fat, the barley is really filling out, and we might just have a wedding."

The Barton Boys both became alert.

John spoke, "Well holy shit! Don't you forget to invite us. We'll be there with bells on."

Tad looked at Grandpa, was the old man hallucinating?

Grandpa spoke, "I hear you boys were to that fancy retirement home in Cochrane. Are you thinking of retiring?"

"Yeah we was, we ain't getting any younger. Now we get that pension and if we sell this place, cows and all, we'll be on easy street. We went to look at the place."

"How did you like it?"

"Real good. We was thinking."

Tom interrupted. "I'll tell you about the tour. We was walking down the aisle and this woman just about knocked us down with her walker. The place is clean. They got four guys with mops going steady.

Now in one room there was four tables and people playing cards. One fellow younger than me was holding the cards, but two cards faced the wrong way. They must have a new game. In another room there was a woman playing the piano. She was singing, "It's a long way to Tipperary. Holy Jesus, I thought I was in the army again! There was some looking at the TV. The TV had a baseball game on. Some was sleeping,but there were two guys really into the game. This fellow yells at the TV, "throw it here you blockhead."

The other guy says, "He ain't got the ball."

"Well who in the blazes has it?"

"I don't know, maybe the umpire?"

"You got to be daft. The umpire doesn't have the ball except the one in his pants."

"That game was getting exciting, so I pulled out my pipe and stated filling it with tobacco.

That pretty girl tour guide said, "We don't smoke here."

So I shoved that pipe into my pocket. Our guide was going to show us the room. She said, "Our rooms are just right for single retired men." She opens the door and the resident is beating the wall with his cane. He is shouting, "Get out of here or I'll call the cops!"

Our guide says, "I guess I have the wrong room, but lets go into the cafeteria. We'll have some lunch."

She asks, "Do you want coffee, tea, or juice?"

John says, "Coffee."

She brought us a little plate with half a cookie. We wonder, where is the other half?

She brings in the coffee. I'm looking, their coffee is the colour of piss on a hot day. They must have forgot to put in the grounds. We say nothing. The guide brings us some papers.

"When can we sign you up?"

"Well, we got to sell those cows."

"You can't wait too long, because spaces fill up fast."

"We're used to waiting. In the spring we wait for the snow to melt; in summer we wait for the rain; in the fall we wait for the rain to stop."

We thank the guide for the wonderful tour. We get in the truck and go back to home. We put the coffee pot on the stove."

Grandpa says, "It is nice you had a good visit at that retirement home. Now Tad and I have a proposition. Since you are retiring, we'll buy your place. We don't need more land. We have 20,000 acres, but we don't like city folks putting up brick houses. They come on weekends and rip up the country with those ATV's, dune buggies, motor bikes, and jeeps."

John says, "Maybe we should think about this retiring."

Grandpa says, "Here's the deal. We pay you what you want, put it in a trust, and we give you an agreement that you can live here as long as you wish and raise cattle and whatever else."

John looked at Tom. "Sounds good to me."

"Is it a deal?"

"Yep! We's satisfied."

" OK whenever you are ready we'll go into Cochrane and sign some papers. Let's shake."

"We should have another cup of coffee, just to seal the deal."

Grandpa says, "You know boys if I drink another cup, I'll pee in my pants." The boys laughed.

"Yeah that could happen."

Grandpa says, "See you when you are ready."

On the way Tad said, "Grandpa, you had them eating out of your hands. How do you do it?"

"Well Tad you have to know your client and you have to speak their language."

Back at the Ranch Tad asked about a picture.

"Who is this Grandpa?"

Adam Cazimirsky was born in a village at the foothills of the Carpathian Mountains. His father was a Captain in the 15th Cavalry Regiment of Poland. At the age of eighteen Adam joined his father's regiment. Two years later Hitler's tanks rolled into Poland. The cavalry retreated and retreated. Horses were no match for tanks. Some retreated east to Russia. Others went south to Romania, Greece, Cyprus, and then England. There was no cavalry in England, so Adam joined the RAF. He became a fighter pilot.

He flew a Spitfire. Fighter Pilots escorted and guarded the heavy bombers that flew over France and Germany. There was a lot of close calls, but he was lucky and by the end of the European war he was Flying Officer Adam Cazimirsky. The Polish government wanted him back in Poland. He said he would come back, but first he had a boyhood dream to fulfill. He wanted to see the "Wild West" where the Cisco Kid, the Lone Ranger, Wild Bill Hickokm, and Mat Dillon controlled the bad guys. He flew to Canada and stopped in Calgary. The Polish Club helped him apply for a job. The Double Bar B Ranch was looking for workers. He was hired and Ed Balfour picked him up at a bus stop in Cochrane. Adam told Ed he wanted to work with horses. Ed realized this tall Polish pilot knew all about horses. He hoped he would stay on. However Adam's plans were to work the summer, fly back to Poland, join the Polish Air Force, marry a nice Polish girl, and raise a big family. He hoped he would be posted close to the Carpathian Mountains.

You might have guessed. The Rocky Mountains, wide plains and down to earth people captivated him. There was more. The Boss had a daughter. Betty was a pretty twenty year old brunette. She had a personality that was extraordinary. Adam fell for her, but he was hesitant. You see Betty had a decided limp. As a teenager, her horse stepped on a wasp's nest. Betty went flying. Her left leg was broken and the doctors couldn't set it properly.

In 1950 Adam married Elizabeth (Betty) Balfour. Two years later a son, Janos (John) was born.

At about the same time a Stoney, Eddie Smoke in the Tent, came to work for the Balfours. Smoky and his wife Mathilda raised a large family. Smoky was the expert cattleman on the Ranch. They lived in one of the houses on the Ranch property. They lived there for the rest of their lives.

After Adam and Tad got back from the Bartons, Tad kept busy trying to forget his failed experience with Marilyn Redford. At Smoky's house there was a car parked in front. Three days later it was still there. He decided to check if there was anything wrong at Smoky's house. He was about to knock when the door opened and there she was! She was about five feet nine inches tall, brown eyes, and very fine features. She was beautiful! He stood with his mouth open and then finally said, "I, I am Tad Cazimirsky."

"I know who you are. You're the Boss's grandson or whatever. Unless you want us out, I am here for July and August. My grandmother is almost blind and grandfather has severe arthritis. They are building a senior's home in Morley for us Stoneys. We may try to get them there, but they don't want to move."

"What do you do?"

"I'm a teacher at the Stoney High School. I teach English and Home Economics to Grade 9 and ten classes."

"Home Economics! Well I will have you come to the Big House and let you cook a gourmet meal."

"Not so fast Lover Boy! I don't cook for horny bachelors."

He laughed. This girl was a riot. Suddenly he had an idea.

He said, "I didn't mean to be so forward, I just wanted to ask if you would like to go with me to the Calgary Stampede?"

"You want to take an Indian girl to the Stampede?"

"Why not, I didn't see any labels on you. I just saw a pretty girl."

"Do you want me to wear feathers and a buckskin skirt?"

"I don't care what you wear."

"OK Lover Boy, I'll be ready."

Next day, when he came to get her, she had jeans, cowgirl boots, white blouse, and a white stetson. She was a knock out!

At the Stampede he had so much fun with her. He forgot Marilyn. Now he had this girl and hadn't even asked her name.

When they got back he said, "What is your name?"

"I thought you would never ask. I have two names. With my people I am Running Antelope. With your people I am Charlene Sinclair."

Next day he asked, "Would you like to go to a ball game at Okotoks?"

"Why not."

This time she wore a ball cap, tennis shoes, and jeans. After the game he took her for drinks and ice cream.

When he brought her home he asked, "May I kiss you?"

"Not so fast. You must first pass a test."

"What kind of test?"

"A fire test."

"What do I have to do?"

" We build a fire and spread the hot coals for ten feet. You must walk on those hot coals with bare feet."

"But I will burn my feet."

"Tough, you either walk or you do not kiss me."

Next day he took her to a concert in Red Deer.

When they got back he asked, "When can we do the test?"

"Tomorrow."

The next day he had the Ranch hands build a fire, spread the coals for the fire pit.

"When do I start?"

"I've changed my mind. If you burn your feet you won't be any good for any woman. I'll have another test for you tomorrow."

He was thinking this girl is playing me for a sucker. But he would go along for a while.

"As you know my name is Running Antelope. If you beat me in a race you get the kiss. Since I am a little weak woman I should have a twenty yard start."

"OK."

By this time there were spectators. This would be a 200 yard race and Smoky would say go. He had her! He had been a fullback in football.

"Go!"

She let him run past her, and then she put on the burners. He was left behind.

"Now you know who's going to be boss."

He looked so beat. She took him by the hand and led him to the bedroom of Smoky's house. She gave him a passionate kiss and hung on.

"Now I suppose you are thinking, when can I jump in bed with her?"

"I was not thinking that at all, but since you mentioned it, I would love to know when?"

"One of these days, I'll tell you."

Next he took her to the rodeo in Sundre.

"When?"

"You have to get permission from Grandfather and from Father Bouchard at the Stoney Mission."

"Two days later, he said "I've got permission from both."

"Fine on Sunday Aug. 24th we'll get married and then we'll see."

Before I tell you about the wedding, I will tell you about Adam and Tad. Adam's wife Betty gave birth to a son in 1952. Ten years later Betty died of breast cancer. The boy, Janos (Johnny) was ten years old. It was Mathilda, Smokey's wife that cared for him till he grew up. As a young man he took a Farm Mechanics course in Olds College. There he met Jean Singleton who was taking a Fashion Course. They married and they had a son Taddeus (Tad). When Tad was five years old there was a horrible accident on the Ranch. The Ranch bought some new round balers. One was causing trouble. Janos (John) went out to fix the problem. The power take-off caught his pant leg. The machine spun him around bashing him. He lived three days before he died. For a while Jean stayed on the Ranch, but she was not happy. She met Stan Staples whom she liked. She planned to marry Stan and take the young Tad with her. Adam Cazimirsky came to her.

"Jean I'm pleading with you. You were a good wife to John and a good mother to Tad. You are young and have many years ahead. I am glad that you have found a new love. I am asking that you leave Tad at the Ranch. Come as often as you wish. Take him on trips and holidays. We need Tad for the Empire. When he grows up he will have to manage and be a steward. There are 20,000 deeded acres and 10,000 more of leased land. There are also 500 head of cattle. Then there are buildings, machinery, and workers. All that was started by Ed Balfour and his wife Margaret. They were both Tad's Great Grandparents. It isn't the money, but the legacy of generations that toiled and built. Jean was reluctant but agreed. Adam hired a Filipino couple to care for Tad. Along with Mathilda they raised him to manhood. Tad completed courses in Business Management at the Olds College. Today he was getting married to a lovely girl, Running Antelope.

Now I am going to tell you about the wedding. The couple wanted to get married on Antelope Hill. Where they got the democrats and carriages I do not know. That is how the wedding party got to the crest of Antelope Hill. Father Bouchard performed the Catholic ceremony and blessed them with holy water. Chief Walking Stick of the Stoneys– performed the native ritual. The marriage song that was sung thousand of years ago. He blessed them with the smoke of sweet grass. They rode down to the yard.

There must have been a thousand people in the yard- ranchers, farmers, ranch hands, half the Stoney Nation, Barton Boys, Polish Club, Legion Club, and so many more. Ranch hands were roasting a fat steer and two pigs on a rotating spit over the coals. Three chefs with sharp knives were cutting off slices of roasted meat. There were tables laden with salads, vegetables, baked goods, desserts, ice cream, etc.

There were drinks- water, beer, pop, Polish Vodka, Scottish Whisky, and for the bridal couple champagne.

There were three lines for presentation and three lines for buffet. There were tables, but not enough.

Some ate standing, others sat on the grass. There was a large dance floor constructed. There was a band for the crowd. Fiddlers, two guitars, accordion, and a saxophone. They played Andy Desjarles and Don Messer tunes, there were Polish polkas, and tunes from the fifty's. Dancing and celebrating lasted till everyone was tired. For months, from Pincher Creek to Ponoka people talked about the wedding.

A year later Running Antelope gave birth to identical twin boys Edward Adam and Johnny Mathias. Two years later there was a little girl, Betty Jean.

The years kept rolling by. Two men were sitting on a bench watching their Great Grandchildren.

Two boys were playing catch and two girls were in the sandbox.

"Smoky its been more than fifty years since we were young and came to work on the Double Bar B."

After eight years since those two men rode to the crest of Antelope Hill and surveyed the Empire.

On June 2013 Adam Cazimirsky died in his sleep at the age of ninty three. He had in his last years arranged for his funeral.

This is my description of that day as I remember. Two wagons were proceeding up Antelope Hill.

In the first was a plain wooden box containing the body of Adam Cazimirsky. The second was for those who would have difficulty walking up the hill- Smoky and Mathilda, Barton Boys, Running Antelope with her four children, and others. Leading the procession was Tad. He was leading a black horse with an empty saddle and stirrups over the seat. On the pommel was a cap of a Polish Cavalry Lieutenant. Across the grave were some 2x6's on which rested the casket. On the casket were four caps- 1) Polish Cavalry 2) RAF Flying Officer 3) Deer Skin Band with an eagle feather 4) Grey Stetson.

First to speak was Bill Boyd of the Ranch Association.

"Adam Cazimirsky, you came to this land high in the saddle. Over the years you have been a man of distinction, integrity, and high moral character. You have been a true steward of the land. If there are ranchers and cowboys in heaven and we see one on a big black horse we will know it is you! Farewell, dear and trusted friend."

Next was Father Sirski of the Polish Club.

"Gospado Pomylo. Adam you have been a true son of the Polish soil. You have carried the best that is Polish and planted it here. We ask our Heavenly Father to take your soul into his bosom. In the name of Father, Son and Holy Ghost."

Then it was Allan McIntosh of the Legion.

"Adam, you have been a true brother. No greater love is there than that a man lay down his life for another. Lieutenant Adam Cazimirsky, Flying Officer Adam Cazimirsky, and Legion Brother, we will remember you as you fly high into the Blue Yonder."

Next was Chief Walking Stick.

"You came to this land. You respected the Great Spirit and its people, the Stoneys. We adopted you as our brother and gave you a name. To us your name is not Adam, but "Flying Eagle". When you soar into the Beyond, the Great Spirit will be there to welcome you!"

Eddie Smoke in the Tent (Smoky) was next.

He took some soil in his hands. The hats were removed. Smoky sprinkled the soil on the plain casket. "Ashes to Ashes, Dust to Dust, farewell good friend."

Last to speak was Tad.

"I ask that you remove your caps or hats, bow your heads as the bugler plays the "Last Post".

When the ceremonies are over, I ask that you stop at the Ranch yard for some refreshments and socializing. My Grandfather requested that as you are going down the hill, and the soil that he loved covers his body in eternal rest, a piper will play. You see when he came to this land he married a Scottish lass, Betty Balfour. She was his one and only love. The pipe music is to tell Betty that after so many years he is coming home to her."

As the mourners descended to the yard of Double Bar B. The sound of "Lament of the Isles" filled the valley.

That evening before the sun had set, Thadeus Cazimirsky and his love Running Antelope took their four children to face the hill.

Their mother said, "Children, on that hill is an oak tree. Under it's branches Grandpa's body rests.

In the summer the tree will shade Grandpa from the hot sun. In the winter it will keep the strong winds out and only the soft snow will be Grandpa's cover. Now look up, what do you see?"

"It's a bird. It is squawking."

" That bird is an Eagle. Your Grandpa's other name was "Flying Eagle". That bird up high is saying, "Flying Eagle" come fly with us."

"But Grandpa has no wings."

Not everything has wings, but they can still fly. Sometimes our eyes cannot see it, but you know it is there."

"Will we see Grandpa again?"

"Yes Grandpa will come. You may not see him but you will know he is here. Next spring when the wind blows from the mountains and you feel it on your face, that will be Grandpa. You may not hear him, but he will be saying, "I'm here and I will always be with you."

9.
QUEEN OF SPADES

IN THE POKER ROOM OF THE GOLDEN NUGGET CASINO were four men and one lady around the poker table. The game was high stakes Texas Hold'em. Two of the players had folded, so that there was only the dealer, one man, and the lady still in the game. The pot in the middle of the table was at least $6000. The lady had a full house in her hand. She was trying to guess what the man had. A flush or a straight would beat her. But he could be bluffing. He declared, "I raise and I call."

She met the raise and won!

Who was this lady? Her real name was Victoria (Vicky) Freeberg, but she also used aliases.

Their names were: Roxanne Wilson, Debbie Pearson, Lorna Gibson, and Cathy Graham. She wore a ball cap, shaded glasses, and casual clothes. She was very attractive and about thirty years of age. Her appearance seemed ordinary, but she was not. Under her loose trousers was a revolver strapped to one leg and a stiletto strapped to the other. On her bra was a pen, but it really was a two shot pistol. Vicky was a formidable gal. You wouldn't want to cross her up.

After Vicky won the pot the dealer declared the game over for the night. Vicky took her chips to the cage and cashed them in for cash and a cheque. A young man who had been one of the losers in the game said, “My name is Mike Van Dellen. Would you like to have dinner?”

For a moment Vicky was puzzled. What was his game? “OK,” she said.

“Should I pick you up at your room?”

“No, I’ll meet you in the Dining Room.”

The dinner was delicious. The talk was trivial. Neither revealed much of themselves. After dinner, she thanked him. He said, “Would you like to come to my room for a cocktail?”

“No, but thank you.”

“Shall I escort you to your room?”

“No, I would prefer that you would not.”

Why was Vicky so cautious? You see that at thirty, she had many experiences and had learned a lot about men and poker. Vicky was born in Lloydminister. Her father, Rev. Eric Freeberg was the Pastor of the Emmanuel Lutheran Church (Parish). She had an older sister, Glenda. Her mother, Karina was a typical pastor’s wife, supportive and helpful whenever the need arose. Quite often she played the organ and piano. She presided over ladies activities. In summary she was the perfect wife and mother.

Vicky did not fit in this religious family. She was vivacious and very intelligent. She listened to her father’s sermons, but inwardly she questioned.

Jesus was the Lamb of God, but on her Grandfather’s farm lambs were helpless. When her father referred to St. Paul who said, “Wives should submit to their husbands.”At home she looked up the word submit. What a bum deal for the wives. Although she disagreed, she did not contradict her father. After all, he provided for them and loved his wife and daughters.

Vicky had skipped a grade so she and her sister Glenda enrolled in the U of S at the same time.

Vicky found the University scene exciting and she participated in all the social events. She soon discovered that her enthusiasm disguised a certain naivety. She was invited to a Medical Students Frat Party. She anticipated a good time. Yes there was music, drinks, and pot. But there was something more.

Med student David Mulder took her to a room and raped her. She wondered what she should do? The next day she phoned David Mulder and asked him why he violated her.

David laughed, "You country bumpkin, that's what all the girls do."

She said she would go to the University Provost and maybe the police.

"Go ahead! You won't get anywhere."

In her mind she filed the incident for later resolution. She avoided further social events and plunged with a vengeance into her studies. After the first test in psychology Professor Campbell suspected that Vicky was cheating. She answered 100 out of 100 correctly. Two months later she repeated her perfect score. Professor Campbell took the case to the Department Head. They called in Vicky.

"We are quite sure you are cheating. Someone is supplying you with the test in advance. You will be suspended from this class."

Vicky didn't say anything. She realized she was mistreated and this was another bitter lesson.

She dropped the other classes, packed her bags and left for Regina. Vicky got a job just to cover living expenses. In her spare time she would go to the Casino and watch the games. She was so often at the Casino that the manager gave her a job. She advanced quickly and became the dealer in high stakes poker.

She met the high rollers. She received invitations, but she had learned her lesson. She found a friend in a security officer. He had been in the Special Forces, but he had broken some rules and was discharged. She asked him to teach her. On days when both were off they would drive ten miles out and he showed her how to shoot various types of guns, how to handle a knife, how to use chemicals, and how to set explosive charges.

During the two years that she worked at the Casino she met a variety of customers: Bkers, Lawyers, Native Chiefs, Promoters, etc. After the two years and a fair amount of earnings she began work at Richardsons Investment. Starting at the bottom, but with ambition she advanced to became one of the brokers. Once again she added to her experiences. Her next move was to Kelowna.

In Kelowna she opened an office, Okanagan Financial Planning. She joined the Black Mountain Golf and Country Club. In two years she had a clientele large enough so that she hired a secretary.

Periodically she would drive to the USA where she put her gambling skills to use.

It was on the last trip to Las Vegas that we first met her at the Golden Nugget Casino in a high stakes poker game. The reason she was wary about Mike Van Dellen coming to her room was due to the previous experience she had.

In Albuquerque she hadn't fastened the chain on her hotel room. While in the shower she heard someone enter. She quickly dressed and stepped out. The stranger grabbed her and threw her on the bed.

She was in trouble. It was survival time. She pleaded with the stranger on top of her.

"We don't have to be violent. I'll take off my clothes and you do the same and we'll do it properly."

He thought this was a willing chick. When both had their clothes off. She said, "Turn around and let's see what you got." He turned around and in a flash she plunged the stiletto just above the crotch. He doubled over.

"Who in the blazes are you? Call an ambulance."

She replied, "You may call me Queen of Spades and can call the ambulance yourself."

He left the room holding the gash. Vicky knew this meant police. She picked up her bags, went down the back stairs and she was off. She didn't stop until she reached Houston.

Returning to the Golden Nugget Casino she was at the high stake poker room. She suspected this would be her last day. The Casino monitors winners. After she had won the first pot of $6,000 two men came and stopped the game. "We believe you are card counting. Pick up your chips and leave. You will be on our black list." Vicky cashed in her chips, packed up and headed for her black Cadillac. She would head north and stop in Reno for a day or two.

Driving at the speed limit, she noticed a car catching up to her. She suspected hi jacking. The car pulled up along side of her and motioned for her to park. She obeyed and the other car parked in front, two men came out. She picked up the AK15 at her feet, opened the door and stepped out. "OK drop your guns or die!" One of the men raised his revolver. She gave him a burst at his feet. "Alright start walking down the road." They didn't argue with her. She shot a couple of tires and the gas tank. She turned her car around and headed back. Plans had to change. Vicki would head for San Francisco. She looked in her mirror and there was a blast and car pieces were flying in all directions.

Ten days later she was in Kelowna. She checked the business accounts. Then went to the Golf Course to meet new prospects. She also had a date with Albert Williams. Albert was an Estate Lawyer. He had been married with two children. Now he was divorced and looking. With everything in order, she told her secretary that she would be going to Saskatchewan. She had some unfinished business.

On No.1 Highway past Revelstoke, a semi veered to her lane and she almost went over into the ravine below.

She turned around and followed the semi. At Revelstoke the semi stopped at a truck stop. Vicky was beside his cab when he stepped out. A large bearded man with a tattoo descended. "You almost ran over me Sir!"

"Too bad. What are you going to do about it?"

"That depends on what you are going to do."

"I'm not going to do a darn thing, so get lost sister."

Vicky pulled the Glok 17 from behind her back. She riddled the truck with the full magazine of seventeen bullets.

"You damn bitch, who are you?"

"I'm the Queen of Spades and I have another mag just for you if you want it, sucker." He didn't have anything to say. Vicky got into her Cadillac and drove off.

Her first stop was in Lloydminister, where she spent two days with her parents and her sister.

Glenda was married and had two children.

Next she drove to Saskatoon where she made an appointment with Dr. David Mulder. At the clinic the doctor came into the room.

"What can I do for you?"

"I am soliciting funds for the Women's Shelter. Can we count on you?"

"My Accountant will look after charity donations."

"Dr. Mulder, this is a special request. I am here to remind you that some years ago you raped me at the Med. Student's Frat Party. So I expect that you will make a special ten percent donation from now till your career ends."

"You must be crazy. I'll call the police. This is blackmail."

"I don't think you will, you see I have this persuader." She pulled out the pistol and pointed it at him. "OK OK just leave."

Next she drove to Regina where she renewed contacts at the Casino and at Richardsons. She also mailed a letter to Dr. and Mrs. Mulder:

Dear Mrs Mulder, Your husband has agreed to make payments to the Women's Shelter. We thank him for his generosity and look forward to many years of help from him and yourself.

I remain, respectfully a former friend. She enclosed a playing card, A Queen of Spades She contacted one of her Biker acquaintances. She said, "I have a project with Dr. Mulder of Saskatoon. If he fails to make payments, I want you and some burly friend to drive to his home. Do some throttling in front of his home. Thanks in advance."

She made her way back, stopping at Casinos in Edmonton and Calgary. About six months later a note was pinned to the windshield of her car. The note read: "I know where you are Vicky. Two can play the game. Dr. D. Mulder."

The next move was up to Vicky. She took a deck of cards and dealt two hands one for each:

Vicki's hand was Ace, Queen, four, six, nine, Jack, Queen, the hand for Dr. Mulder was King, King, six, eight, six, King, Ace. He had three Kings and a pair and won. She wrote a note to Dr. D. Mulder.

"Before we kill each other, I am asking for a truce. I'll leave you alone, if you will do the same.

Other wise the next round will be for keeps."

Sincerely Vicky (The Queen of Spades) If you are playing the game sometimes you can raise and call, sometimes you can hold, and other times because of the cards you have, you fold.

If you are ever in West Kelowna and looking for a possible retirement home, you might see a home with an unusual insignia on the front door. It is a Queen of Spades. This is the home of Albert and Vicky Williams. If you peek around the house and into the back yard, you might see a little boy and girl playing in the sandbox.

10.
THE ROAD NOT TAKEN

ROBERT FROST WROTE A POEM BY THIS TITLE. HE TELLS of his walk on a country road in the woods. He comes to a fork and chooses. Later, he wonders what could have been, had he chosen the other branch of the road. Each of us face the same dilemma. We must choose, but even if we are satisfied with our choice, we wonder what would have been if we had chosen the other.

Two young ladies and a four year old boy were at a round up northwest of Sundre. The two ladies were Pat Hopkins and Joan Redford. Joan's son was Nathan Ryan. They were here at the annual round up of feral horses which were not protected. Joan was planning to buy a horse if one appealed to her. The horses that were in this large corral would end up three different ways: Some will be sold. Some would be released, and some would be sent to a slaughter plant. Why would a young lady want a wild horse? Many would have asked that question. Joan had been introduced to horses in her high school years. It was her dream that someday if it was possible, she would like to train and own a horse. When a filly came up for sale there was interest in several quarters. The horse had a black and white star on her forehead and one of the legs was white. She looked scruffy, her hooves needed trimming, and her tail was too long. The bidding was spirited, but in the end, for $100 Joan was owner of a wild horse.

She hired a trucker to bring this wild animal to her property.

The Redford family had lived in Olds for many years. John worked in the Coop store. His wife Susan was a stay at home mother. She was active in her Church activities and she was a volunteer for several causes. They had three daughters. The two oldest were married with families. Joan was the youngest. She took a Business Management Course and accepted the only position available. This position was with the Sundre Forest Products. Her personality and enthusiasm factored favourably with management and all the workers. In a firm with mostly men, Joan received much attention. She was attracted to one, a handsome trucker named Dan Harvey. One date led to the next. Both seemed to be headed one way. After a year of courtship, Dan proposed and Joan accepted. They set a date which was followed by a busy preparation routine. Dan seemed happy and Joan had stars in her eyes. A week before the date Dan said he could not go through with the marriage. You can imagine that Joan was devastated. To be rejected was the ultimate humiliation. Why did it happen?

When fifty percent of engagements and marriages fail, there could be many reasons. For some marriage releases the very best in each partner. For others marriage is viewed as the institution where one surrenders freedom for endless bondage.

Dan left for Ft. McMurray and said he would be responsible if Joan was pregnant. For Joan the next few months became difficult. However she recovered with the help of a friend Pat Hopkins, workers at the plant, her family, and her Church.

A boy was born. She named him Nathan Ryan. She kept her job and a Mrs. Herman in Sundre looked after the boy during her working hours. The boy was so likeable that Joan was completely captivated. Her parents also looked forward to each Sunday as Joan came to Church and spent the rest of the day with her parents.

Joan had a few dates with Constable Tim McKee, but a future with Tim seemed not practical.

So they parted as friends. One Sunday when Nathan was four, the Redfords stopped to talk to Jim and Ann Nelson. Jim said they were leaving their farm home and moving to Olds. Jim's plan was to rent the land and find someone for the yard site.

John summoned his daughter, "Joan maybe your dream can come true."

Jim sold the bigger machinery and some of the items that had been collected over the many years. Joan and Nathan moved in. Joan also convinced friend Pat Hopkins to join them. The place was well kept. The Nelsons left their two dogs, three cats, and about twenty chickens. This was the place that Joan brought her horse named Beauty. Joan spent most of the year getting Beauty to trust her.

Less than a year after the horse came to the farm, she gave birth to a foal, a little girl horse.

This was the year when two significant events happened. The first event happened the second day of the Sundre Rodeo. Clint, Frank, Josh, and Bill went to the bar to cap off the day. When the bartender announced closing time, the guys were just getting started. Josh said, "Let's go see those two gals on the road to Olds. Bill give them a call."

"They have an unlisted number."

"Oh well let's go anyway."

They drove into the yard and the dogs announced their arrival.

The girls woke up and peeked through the window. "This could be no good. Pat you phone the police and I'll barricade the door."

Clint said, "Frank I bet you can't ride that horse."

"Fifty dollars says I can."

"You're on." Frank climbed over the fence, took hold of the halter rope, led the horse to the railing and jumped on her back. The horse just stood. Frank kicked her side and fury broke loose.

Beauty began bucking and Frank went flying. On the way down her hoof struck Frank's head and knocked him unconscious. The others dragged him out of the corral.

"We've got to call an ambulance."

Before the ambulance arrived two police cars drove into the yard.

"OK, what are you doing in this yard?"

Clint said, "We meant no harm." The three were handcuffed and placed in the two cars. The ambulance picked up Frank. The guys were charged with trespassing, doing mischief, and attempted theft.

That same year Pat who had worked for Shell at the Harmattan Plant got married. Joan and Nathan were left alone at the farm house.

Two years later when Nathan was seven, there were two trained horses at the farm. Nathan had learned to ride.

That same year West Frazer Lumber Co. (the new owner) sent a new manager to the Sundre operation. Sidney Martin was about thirty five and had custody of his seven year old daughter. Joan had to show Sidney all the details of the operation. You can guess. Those two found each other.

The next time you see a truck laden with lumber going through Olds, remember that Sid and Joan are running the operation. Each has chosen the road that led to years of love and happiness.

"Never Give Up"

11.
TROUBLE IN PARADISE

"WHO DID ADAM AND EVE'S SONS AND DAUGHTERS MARRY?"

Paradise Valley is a typical Huterite Colony in Central Alberta. Like most other colonies it is engaged in agriculture: grain, beef, poultry, hogs, and vegetables. The Colony has sixteen married couples, eighteen singles over the age of fifteen, and thirty one under fifteen. The Colony manager is Jacob Hofer and the Preacher is Martin Hofer.

From the outside, the Colony seems successful and harmonious. However, there are murmurings and grumbles. Some of the men question Jacob's managerial abilities. Ten years ago he was part of a committee that made the Star City Purchase. The loan was too large and the interest rates were too high. The new Colony was forced to sell half of the land at a loss. Now ten years later both Colonies are struggling. There are no funds should a further split become necessary. Jacob admitted that there was a mistake. He said, "We were intoxicated by our past successes and over confident that we could handle any loan."

Jacob's wife Greta was the kitchen boss. The women that worked with her dreaded bouts of bad temper. Sometimes she would shout at the younger women, "Don't you know how to make kugel?" Jacob's family consisted of grown-up sons and daughters. Two sons went to the Star City Colony. Three daughters were married to men in other colonies. Only Abe aged twenty two was still living with his parents. He was the Machinery Boss. At home his mother nagged him, "Abe it is time that you should be married." Abe would reply, "Yeah, yeah I have looked, but no girl wants me."

Courtship and marriage in a Huterite community had defined limits. A Huterite must marry only a Huterite. Secondly, because only about twelve families form the base, one finds it hard to find a mate who is not too closely related. It is the boys who visit other colonies to find a mate. Girls will be the ones to move to new families and new colonies. Abe had visited four other Colonies, but either he was not attracted to a or the girl did not want his attention.

The Huterites have another ingenious way to promote marriages. Two or three times a year there is a selection day. A boy indicates he wants to marry and the Preacher presents him with three girls names who are willing to marry. When the choice is made and both parties agree then the marriage is on. It was at one of these selection days that Abe Hofer chose Delia Decker and she agreed. She had been passed over on three previous times, but Abe wanted to get his mother's nagging out of the way, so he was ready to marry any living thing.

A marriage is a festive occasion. Relatives come. There is plenty of food and chokecherry wine. Delia was excited and apprehensive. Her friends were happy for her. She looked gorgeous in her blue wedding gown. The Colony Manager who was her father in law assigned the couple to a new apartment. They would have a week's honeymoon, whenever colony work was slack.

This marriage got off on the wrong foot. Abe showed no interest or romance in his bride. In the evening when they were in their apartment, Abe sat silent. Delia was perplexed. Other women told her it would be quite different. What should she do? One evening she spoke.

"Abe why don't you love me?"

"Why should I?"

"Abe, I am your wife!"

"Wives like you are a dime a dozen."

"Then why did you marry me?"

"That was a mistake. I did it to satisfy my parents."

Delia went into the bathroom and cried. "Why am I being punished?"

Next evening Abe asked, "Is there any cake or cookies?"

She gave him a donut. He took one bite and threw the rest at her. She picked up the donut and threw it back at him. He got angry and slapped and kicked her.

The next day the women noticed the bruises on Delia's face, but they said nothing. Delia did not share her woes with the women.

A few days later Abe and a seventeen year old Paul Waldner were working in the machine shop. Abe gave Paul a sealed paper.

"Give this to your sister Sarah, and don't mention it to anyone."

When Sarah opened the message it read, "Meet me behind the chicken barn."

Sarah pondered, should she tell her mother about the message? She decided it would be exciting to have a clandestine meeting with Abe.

The next evening Luther Glantzer was taking some water to his new apple tree. He saw a woman running behind the chicken barn. Who was she?

The following evening Luther was going to find out. He quietly followed the woman around the corner. He saw Abe Hofer and fifteen year old Sarah Waldner in an embrace. He told his wife the juicy tale. Pretty soon the whole Colony knew the story of Abe and Sarah. Only Abe's parents, the preacher, and Delia were not informed about the affair, not yet.

On Sunday the school house was converted to a church. Desks were moved aside and benches became pews. This Sunday the services began as usual with scriptures and hymns in low German. Preacher Hofer announced that Brother Jacob Hofer had a message.

Jacob Hofer said, "Today I speak to you Brothers and Sisters with a heavy heart. If we are to walk in Christ's steps then our community should be harmonious. We all have different tasks, but we contribute to a common purse. No one is above another. Rumours have reached me that there is dissatisfaction with my leadership. I ask that you choose another manager. I will help him get started. My wife Greta also wishes to turn her duties as Kitchen Boss to another woman. Also there are rumours about my son Abe. I pray that we might heal misunderstandings and turn to God for guidance."

Preacher Martin Hofer said, "I ask that Abraham Hofer come to the front and explain why he is meeting Sarah Waldner behind the chicken barn?"

Abe came forward and knelt before the Preacher. "I have sinned and I repent. May God have mercy on me."

"Where is your wife?"

Abe looked around but did not see her. "I don't know."

"Have you ever beaten your wife?"

"Oh no Brother Martin, I would never do that."

"I will discuss your transgression with the Elder Committee. Leave this room and go and comfort your wife."

Preacher Hofer next said, "Sarah Waldner come to the front and explain your meetings behind the chicken barn."

Sarah started to cry and hung on to her mother.

Her mother said, "Go and confess your sins."

Sarah went forward and knelt. She was sobbing.

The Preacher asked, "Sarah did you study the scriptures that consorting with a married man is adultery? Should we stone you as the scriptures demand?"

"Please don't stone me! I will not meet with Abe again."

"We will discuss your transgression with the Committee. Now go to your parents and Delia, and ask for their forgiveness. You have shamed them and all the Community."

Delia waited till everyone was at Church. She was determined that she would not take any more beatings. She grabbed her coat and the few coins she had and went down the road. Three miles from the Colony, she rapped on the door of the Jackson's home. Mrs. Jackson opened the door and asked the woman to come in.

Delia said, "I need your help."

Mrs. Jackson saw what was the trouble. She went to the phone and dialed the police. "Here is a Huterite woman who has been beaten."

"We'll send a car at once."

Constable Hunter drove up with an unmarked police car.

He asked, "Delia who beat you?"

"My husband."

"What would happen if you went back?"

"I would be shunned by everyone."

"Why?"

"Because Huterites are not supposed to take their troubles outside the Colony."

"Do they treat all women like they have treated you?"

"Not all. Some husbands are kind and loving, but the scriptures say that women should submit to their husbands."

"We'll take you to a safe place for now."

Constable Hunter asked the Jacksons not to reveal that the police had taken Delia. Constable Hunter drove Delia to the Woman's Shelter in Red Deer. The Matron called Corporal Bradley who handled these types of cases. They let Delia tell her story. They assured her she was safe. They also informed her of options.

Back in the Colony Abe did not find Delia in the apartment. Oh well he wasn't going to worry about her. What was on his mind was who squealed to the Preacher about his affair with Sarah. There would be a pay back.

The next day Delia did not come to the kitchen. Greta went to their apartment but Delia was not there. Next she told Jacob about the missing Delia.

Jacob went to the machine shop and asked Abe, "Where is Delia?"

"I don't know."

"She is your wife and you don't seem to care."

Jacob rang the Colony bell. All available persons came to see what was the emergency.

Jacob said, "We are missing Delia, so put aside your work and search." They searched till dark.

Next day the search went out further. This was repeated the third day.

On the fourth day Jacob phoned the police. Corporal Bradley came in his cruiser with lights flashing. Jacob Hofer and Martin Hofer met the Corporal.

"Where is Delia's husband?"

"In the machine building."

"Get him out here!"

When Abe came the Corporal asked, "When was the last time you saw your wife?"

"Maybe Saturday or Sunday."

"This is Thursday. If you cared for your wife you would have notified us sooner, or maybe you don't want anyone to find her. Did you kill her?"

"No."

"Did you beat her?"

"Oh No!"

"Let's go to your apartment." There the Corporal examined the place.

"You know if you killed her and hid the body, it would be better to confess."

"I didn't kill her!"

"We'll send a finger print and blood expert. I saw some drops on the floor. The rest of you keep looking, especially where a body could be hidden."

He got in his cruiser and drove away. He looked in the rear view mirror and smiled. *That will give those sanctimonious liars something to think about.*

The following day the Corporal returned. "We found your wife, but she has been beaten. Abraham Hofer you are charged with assault and battery."

He put the handcuffs on Abe and drove away. Jacob and Martin were shocked! How could a Huterite do such a crime?

Jacob and Martin drove to Red Deer to their lawyer. He arranged for bail. A trial date was set. On the way home Jacob exclaimed, "How could you cause so much trouble, you dumkopf!"

The charges were withdrawn. A lawyer was assigned for Delia. He informed the Colony that Delia was seeking a divorce and a settlement. Abe said, "But I have no money!"

"That's not a problem, the Colony will pay for you."

The Colony Elders were assembled and the decision was made that Abe should leave the Colony, get a job and support Delia. After he had fulfilled his obligations, he could ask to be readmitted.

Delia adjusted to the outside world with difficulty, but she succeeded. She missed the Colony life but as time passed the departure became just a memory. The Paradise Valley Colony returned to its' normal routine, penitent and wiser.

12.
THE MARIA PANCHUK STORY

I TAKE YOU TO THE VILLAGE OF UKOSTAV IN THE WESTERN Ukraine. In 1939 the village was under Polish Control. The population consisted of a few Jews, sometimes Gypsies, a few Poles, but the majority were Ukrainians. In the fall of 1939 Hitler and Stalin divided Poland. The village came under Soviet control. The authorities wanted all the small holders to pool their land into one collective block with an industrial pattern. Some accepted the plan. Others were bitterly opposed to the plan and the Bolsheviks.

In 1941 Hitler decided he wanted the USSR. His armies marched in on a massive scale. Some of his troops moved through the village. The anti communists welcomed the German Army. The Wehrmacht were followed by the dreaded SS. With the help of informers they identified Jews, managers, and communists. All were herded into the Strilchuk home. The doors were closed and the house was set on fire.

Maria Strilchuk was a ten year old girl who escaped death because she was with her maternal grandparents. For the next four years, 1941 to 1945 Maria was a fugitive. She never slept in a bed nor did she eat at a table. Her relatives and others helped her, but never openly. If the SS were near she would go to the forested hills two miles away. There she was protected by the

Partisans. The Partisans were on the Soviet side. Their activity was to disrupt German movement of supplies. The SS hated this "terrorist gang". They were shot on sight. During those four years Maria had to be wary of any informers of the SS, roving gangs and soldiers of either side. They would not hesitate to rape a young girl.

After the SS burned sixteen people in the Strilchuk's home the villagers wondered who would take the Strilchuk's land. It turned out to be the Dubinsky family. The finger was pointed at the Dubinskys for being the informers. One summer night the Dubinsky's barn and the family home went up in smoke. It was suspected that the Partisans were paying back.

In 1944-45 the Soviets drove the Nazis into a retreat. Maria was now safe and she found work in the reconstituted collective farm. Those who had helped the Nazis (Germans) retreated and escaped to Germany and Austria. From there they came to Canada, US, and Australia. They were protected because the Soviet Union was our presumed enemy so anyone who was anti Soviet, no matter their past activities was welcomed. Now seventy years later Western countries decided to make a show by putting their ninety year old "criminals" on trial. We Canadians wanted to wash our hands of the blood by protecting war criminals.

In 1925 Nick and Ann Panchuk with three children immigrated to Canada . They had some acquaintances in the Swan Plain area and so they settled on an abandoned homestead. They had few resources, but they bought cows and chickens. Nick did some carpentry and in the winter worked at Larson's sawmill. Slowly the family got on its feet and the farm and family made gains. The children went to school. In time the two older girls married and raised their own families.

In 1951 the Panchuk family consisted of the parents Nick and Ann and son Michael, who was now thirty years old. The parents wished that Michael would find a wife, but thus far it didn't happen.

They wrote a letter to relatives in Ukraine mentioning that they were concerned about son Michael. A letter came back and it read, "There is a twenty year old girl who lost her family and had no dowery or property. She might be a candidate." The Panchuks wrote back with an offer. They would pay for her passage. The costs would be forgiven if she married Michael. If she did not choose to do so, she would work and pay back the costs to the Panchuks.

So in 1952 Maria came to the Panchuk home. She married Michael and this Maria Strilchuk became Maria Panchuk. The marriage exceeded expectations! Michael and Maria fell in love and everyone smiled. The young couple moved into the main house while the parents settled in the smaller house that had been used as a summer kitchen.

Then tragedy struck. Michael got sick. Doctors weren't sure what the cause of his decline. Today we might suspect pancreatic cancer. Before their first anniversary Michael died.

After the usual period of mourning, Nick and Ann spoke to Maria.

"Maria, you have been a dutiful daughter and you have brought hope and joy to our hearts. Now you must make a decision about your future. It is not proper that you should be tied to two older people who are in declining years. You are still young with a long life ahead. If you wish to go back to Ukraine we will pay your fare. If you choose to marry someone we will support you in any way we can."

Maria did not hesitate to give her reply.

"Mom and Dad, I came here with a satchel with a few clothes. I had nothing else. You took me in and I benefited from your kindness. Your family became my family, your son became my beloved husband, your Church became my Church.

My only decision is to stay with you and help until the Lord decides to take you to His bosom."

Before five years were up both Nick and Ann went to their eternal rest. Maria was now alone. Her sisters-in-law said, "Maria you have not added much to this property. You should go back to the Ukraine, where you belong."

At first Maria was about to agree, but her neighbours spoke to her.

"Maria by law this farm is yours." Maria did not want to create animosity so she agreed to a compromise. The assets would be sold and the proceeds would be divided three ways. After the sale was concluded Maria had no home, no farm, no job, but she had a bit over $5000. Friends suggested that in Norquay a small hospital had been opened. She followed their advice and got a job as a kitchen helper.

Three years later she moved to Canora where she was a kitchen helper in a larger hospital. She had moved because there was a larger community of Orthodox believers, her new adopted Church. Whether Maria had opportunity or desire to marry we do not know. We know that Maria remained single. Her life was full. She liked her work at the hospital. She enjoyed the fellowship with her Church friends. There was more. A few years in Canora she missed the relationship with the soil. She bought a small house with a substantial garden space. In the winter she had TV, radio, and needle work. In summer it was her passion to grow vegetables, flowers, and fruits. She became an expert in horticulture so societies called on Maria to be a judge and to speak to members. Her neighbours spoke kindly of Maria. Quite often she would be in bare feet tending to cucumbers and glads. With a smile they spoke of Maria as the barefoot saint. She resented being called a saint. She would say, "What saint would go to the store in rubber boots and dirt under her finger nails?"

It was at one of those horticulture shows that I first saw Maria. She was in her senior years yet she exhibited a presence of a lady in midlife. So that summer when she was eighty eight, we decided to pay her a visit and talk to this lady. We were told that she was not difficult to find on Shewchuk Avenue. You would know which was her house. When we walked to her front door and knocked, a woman in kerchief, running shoes and a hoe came around the corner. We introduced ourselves and asked if she would tell us about her story.

She said, "Oy, Yoh, Yoh!" I was just a poor girl who came to Canada." She sensed that we were disappointed. She said, "Come I will show you my garden. The dahlias are especially beautiful." I need not describe this oasis of beauty and bounty. Everything was just a bit more luscious. If she talked to her plants I was convinced they listened. We thanked her for the tour and were just about to leave. She said, "You must come inside, I will make some coffee. Come, Come." Before she scurried to her small kitchen, she set some pastries on the coffee table. As we munched mini cinnamon rolls we looked around. There was just enough furniture to make the small room cozy. On the wall were four pictures: Jesus, Mary, an orchard scene, and a wedding photo. Along one wall was a bookcase filled with ribbons, plaques, statues, and pennants of prizes she had won over the years. There was a framed certificate Maria Panchuk, Citizen of the Year and there were letters from the Governor General, Prime Minister and Premier congratulating her on her eighty eight birthday. The coffee surpassed any that we had at Tim Hortons or Starbucks.

She told us her story. When she recalled the sad episodes tears would form in her eyes. After the account of her life, two cups of coffee, and all the pastries, we needed to leave. It was with regret that we could not stay longer with this exceptional lady.

When we got to our car, we looked back and saw Maria was wiping away the tears.

From time to time as I listen to world events or when spring comes, I remember Maria.

Here was a woman who held no public office, she did not head a committee, she had faced adversity like most of us never will. Yet she faced life on her own terms, filled with joy and hope. When the Lord calls her for eternal rest, He will not mind if she is barefoot and has a packet of seeds in her apron pocket!

13.
A WALK IN THE WOODS

I AM GOING TO THE WOODS TODAY. I AM ANXIOUS TO SEE my friends this first of May.

Years ago another farmer bought the woods that I wanted. He did not turn these woods into cultivated land. He does not know that I walk on his property. The leaves are out and the early plants are about to bloom. When I step into this sanctuary of nature, I will walk silently and reverently.

First I must look down at the ground for morels. If there are some I will pick them for a spring feast. I don't think my neighbour would mind. I don't see any. Maybe it is too early. When the land was covered with groves of trees everyone was a mushroom hunter. Mushroom picking binds a family together. Each can contribute. Off to my right is an old brush pile. Years ago others were burned, this one survived. Last year a duck made her nest in the tangled branches. The duck is a symbol of a mother's sacrifice. She plucked the soft feathers off her own breast to make a warm nest for the eggs she laid. By chance I saw where she led her brood to water almost a mile away. I think kindergarten teachers have copied the duck. "OK children, Johnny will hold this end of the rope and Sally the other end. Everyone will hold on. At the street we will look both ways. At the park we will play some games."

Some smart alec whispered, “Yeah some crummy games.”

“After the park everyone will hold on to the rope and we’ll walk to the library. There we will draw and paint. Then I’ll show you how the computers work. At the end I have a special treat for you!”

One girl whispers to another, “I think it’s candy.”

One boy whispers to his buddy, “I bet it’s some apples she and her husband can’t eat.”

I’m not going to check that brush pile. It will only frighten her if she is in there.

Some thirty yards ahead is one of the landmarks of the woods. Years ago a big old popular tree died, but it remained standing. Woodpeckers found the wood just right and hollowed out a nesting place. I’ll just wait and see if there is anyone there.

My wait proved fortuitous. Out of no where she came with a worm in her beak. Four little heads popped out with mouths wide open. This situation always intrigued me. Four hungry mouths and one worm. “Who gets the worm?” I’ve searched the scriptures to no avail. I’ve read science books still no answer. I think our PM should form a committee with a large sum of money to answer the question.

“Who gets the worm?”

My view is that the mother knows best. She stops feeding the big one and gives the worm to the smallest. That’s how our society works. Our Mother Government takes from the rich and feeds the poor.

Right beside the path I notice something new. There is a patch of blue bells. They weren’t there last year. I stop by the spruce grove. All the squirrels stop chattering. Some cones were falling down. I believe this is the time for young squirrels to learn how to hold the pine cones.

The path ends at the old farm site. It is seventy years since anyone has lived here. The floor of the house had caved in. The roof on the barn looks like a saddle. I’m here to check the barn wall. For years swallows have come to build nests of mud and grass and fastened them to the wall. How do they do it without any glue? They are not here yet, maybe soon. That flight from South America is a long way. Over there by those trees is a broken down granary. I know who lives there. It's my enemy– my adversary. Those bandits with dark masks will be up to no good come September. I'm sure they have a calendar. First of September they will go almost a mile at night, sneak into my garden and go straight for the corn. Last summer I had gone out to pick some for my supper, but they beat me. They had raised havoc. I had a good notion to call the police. If those bandits were human and I had called the police, this is how events would have proceeded.

"RCMP Kamsack Detachment."

"This is Mr. B. at the Assinaboine Crossing. I want to report a crime."

"What's the crime?"

"I had an invasion! There is vandalism, terrorism, and theft."

"Do you know who the criminals are?"

"I don't know their names, but they have black masks."

"What did they vandalize?"

"My whole corn patch! Without the corn I'll need the food bank!"

"You know we're busy now. We want to nab a lady in a van who is speeding and not observing the traffic rules."

"Look here flatfoot. I'm a tax payer. There has been a theft and I expect action."

"Mr. B. do you think the thief is a person or something else?"

"That doesn't matter, a theft is a theft and a thief is a thief." Constable Mike Davis and Constable Ruth Miller arrived at the crime scene three hours later.

"What do you want us to do?"

"I want you to get the thieves and put them in the clink."

"Sue, take a picture of the crime scene. We will report your request to the Sergeant."

"Just remember, you may think I'm some hayseed, but I have important contacts."

When they got back to the station they probably had a good laugh, Cuckoo Bill is up to his antics.

Two weeks passed. There was no response. I phoned the CBC reporter and told a good story. I said in the Pelly area there is rampant crime. Grains, vegetables, gasoline, batteries, and cattle are stolen. The thieves are laughing at the residents. Farmers are getting a vigilante group ready. All are armed with shotguns and rifles. The RCMP are told if they can't do the job, they should get out of the way. Next day CBC evening news featured, "Crime and Chaos in the Pelly Area." The following day in the House of Commons Question Period, Mr. Speaker rose.

"Mr. Speaker, the world knows that there is no law and order in the Pelly Area. What is the Government going to do about it?"

Mr. Trudeau rose.

"Mr. Speaker, The former government had eight years to fix the problem. In cooperation with the middle class we are going to fix it."

"Mr. Speaker, once again, what is the government going to do?"

"Mr. Speaker this government is going to solve the problem. We will compensate all middle class residents for any losses."

"Mr. Speaker, once again, throwing money at the problem is not solving it. I ask for the third or fourth time. What is the government really doing?"

"Mr. Speaker, I repeat and repeat that we are going to help the middle class and all who have been oppressed by the previous government. We are approving an Action Committee, Mr. Bellgarde from the Indigenous People, Mr. Sinclair from the Royal Commission, Mr. Campbell from the Metis

Association, and Miss Gordon from the Indigenous Women's Group. They have an unlimited budget, and two months to make recommendations."

"Mr. Speaker, again for the fifth time, what is the prime minister personally going to do?"

"Mr. Speaker, Sophie and I and six Cabinet Ministers and their spouses will fly to the area and meet with the middle class people of the area."

"Mr. Speaker it never fails, but the Prime Minister and his government always closes the barn door after the horse is gone."

The Speaker rose and said, "This is all the time allotted for Question Period today. Go and resume your work for the people of Canada."

Back at the farm there was action. A florist delivered a huge wreath. The card read, "TO ALL OUR MIDDLE CLASS FRIENDS IN PELLY WE ARE WITH YOU"- Government of Canada.

Then two police cruisers drove in. From the second cruiser the Constable opened the door and a dog bounded out. They went straight to the corn patch. "Okay Justin do your job." He told me that Justin was the dog's name. Justin made circles until he found the one trail and off through the woods they went. The second constable followed with a rifle, just in case there was a fire fight. Justin ended up at the pile of boards and scraps at the abandoned farm. He barked as if to say, "Here's the criminal!"

The Constable shouted, "OK, you down there, surrender and come out with your hands up." There was no reply. The second Constable said, "Should I send a few bullets his way?"

"No, not yet. I'll contact the Sergeant."

The Sergeant said, "Do not shoot the suspect. We want him for questioning. We need to get you some tear gas. If we don't have any here, I'll contact Yorkton or Regina. Just stand guard."

Three hours later a small plane was circling above the farm. Finally he landed on the road. Another Constable stepped out with six canisters of tear gas and then he was off to the crime scene.

"Okay for the last time come out or we will act with lethal force!"

There was no reply. The Constable pulled the release trigger and threw the canister in the cavity below the scrap pile. There wasn't much of a noise, but smoke drifted out. Then they came one, two, three, four, bedraggled, confused, and scared racoons. They ran in four directions. "Should we shoot them?"

"No, its not legal to shoot a fleeing suspect."

The Constable with the dog said, "Good work Justin, you've done your job. Here's a wiener for you."

The Constables headed back to the yard. I asked, "Did you get them?"

"Yes we got them. The case is solved and closed. Further investigation will be secret. You are not to mention this to anyone and that is an order. We thank you Mr. B."

They got into their cruisers and drove off. There was a cloud of dust for a mile. I think those bandits moved to another farm two miles away. I remembered a saying, "He who laughs last laughs best."

Now I'm back to my walk in the woods. I've almost completed the circuit. Before me is a meadow covered with shallow water. I removed my shoes and socks. Then rolled up my pant legs. I walked through the warm water and my thoughts went back to many years ago. In the evening Mother would say, "Wash your feet before you go to bed." This did not mean a tub or basin. We ran to the slough waded in the shallow water. It may not make sense because going back the feet would get soiled again. But Mother was right. The lesson I learned at her knee was- "Don't go to bed with dirty feet."

My walk in the woods has ended. Everything seems right with the world. I didn't pick any mushrooms, so I'll just open a can of beans, fry some eggs with a handful of green onions. I hope that you get a chance to walk in the woods. If you will do so, it will give you a new perspective on life.

Good Night Cuckoo Bill

14.
THE FEUD

"VENGENCE IS MINE SAITH THE LORD."

A Saturday in mid June Rita and I had been to the College garden. It was a beautiful day. The sky was blue with fluffy white clouds. A gentle breeze made the day perfect. The young tree swallows were learning to fly. To the south the Canada geese were announcing that they had a family. The seeds Rita planted a month ago were now green plants. Rita was in a ebullient mood.

Before we left the College grounds I said, "Rita, park the van and let's see the roses." There were two reasons for stopping. I did want to see the roses, but I also saw the placard that read — "Wedding on the Grounds." We walked slowly along the walkway and a wedding program had just started. There were probably seventy guests. At the front was the wedding party. I learned later that the principals were: Dr. Don Campbell, a physician at the Wild Rose Clinic and Patricia Dunbar, attorney with the Martinson and Harder firm. The marriage ceremony was conducted by Rev. Fr. Pat O'Neil. He was followed by another celebrant, Rev. Donna Evans of the Anglican Church.

I thought of the line that was often used to describe the bride's wedding attire- "Something old, something borrowed, something new, and something blue." That phrase applied to the entire ceremony. Here were two people like others for thousands of years who had decided to be joined together. Here were two celebrants cooperating. Ceremonies were usually held in churches, but this one was in the beautiful outdoors. What about something blue? The sky was blue. The bridesmaids had light blue gowns. If you were observant the best men in tuxedos had blue bow ties. The garter now hidden was probably blue.

The total scene spoke of love, hope, and promise. The groom's father rose to speak.

"Dearly beloved, we are here to celebrate a special day for Don and Patricia. It is also a special day for both families. This is what we had hoped for when they came into the world as babies. Also significantly I call on our two families to lay aside more than over a century of animosity."

Patricia's mother rose to speak. "Rev. Father Pat and Rev. Donna, we are appreciative of your contribution for two blessings are better than one. I also echo the message of Tom Campbell. Let us bury for good the misunderstanding that has plagued our families for too long."

By this time Rita and I had walked far enough away so that we did not hear what followed. Rita's friend had served at the reception that same evening at the Evergreen Center. She catered to ninety guests: Relatives, friends, associates, etc.

Rev. Donna Evans pronounced the blessing. The menu for the reception was especially delicious. As guests arrived they went to the head table and exchanged greetings with the married couple. They presented gifts and envelopes of money. Contrary to custom Don and Patricia did not choose an exotic honeymoon. They had just bought a modest house on 51 Ave. They were excited about choosing furnishings. More importantly, here were two people in love.

After that episode at the College, I forgot to check the roses. However, I was intrigued by the mystery of what had kept these two families in a hostile relationship for more than one century.

I asked the LDS church to help me trace back the genealogy of these two families. They were able to go back to the 1500's, but I stopped at 1850 when two men of that name had come to the Ft. Pelly area to work for the Hudson Bay Company. This Trading Post was less than a mile from our former home in Saskatchewan.

At the Ft. Pelly Post the first week in August was a special time. Traders from outlying posts and natives brought furs and hides. At the Post they would trade for tea, sugar, cloth, knives, guns, traps, etc.

The annual event began when Mac McDernid got out his bag pipes and played several tunes. Two or three days were set aside for socializing. There might be letters from the old country. There were dances and rum, enough to make one merry. The Post Factor (manager) had to be careful. He did not want a riot and bloodshed. The dances were for young and old. Males on one side, the females on the other side. Music by two fiddlers and a Metis beating on a hollow log. There were pattern dances and there was jigging. Young men had their eyes on the girls and vice versa.

A part of the week involved the missionaries. They would marry couples and they would christen babies. The mothers were very astute! "What do I get if you baptize my baby?" The missionaries did have gifts. It might be a baby blanket, a cup, beads, or some other object.

During the 1800's, poor young men came from England and Scotland to serve a seven year contract. In 1850 Neil Campbell and Bruce Dunbar came to the Hudson Bay Company. In the following year they were part of the August celebration. Another feature of the August celebration was that young men and ladies got to meet each other. This year John Maclise and his Saulteaux wife from the Hibernia post brought their sixteen year old daughter Susan to the celebration. At the dance Neil and Bruce saw a variety of girls, but they were attracted to

Susan Maclise. She had inherited the best features from each of her parents. She was a bit taller than the average. Her face was a lighter tone. Her eyes sparkled. She was dressed in a tartan skirt, red blouse, and on her feet were beaded moccasins. All the men wanted to dance with her. Neil and Bruce danced and proposed, "Be my wife?" To each proposal she gave the same answer, "Talk to my father."

It would seem that girls were auctioned, but there was and is a simpler purpose. Every father wants his daughter to marry a dependable, respectful, and kind husband. Fathers do not like fly by nighters, gigolos and bums.

Bruce's offering to John Maclise was a Hundson Bay blanket. Neil offered a Hudson Bay blanket and a pound of tea. Neil was offered the hand of Susan. The next day Fr. Leduc married the two. Bruce did not keep silent or accept the outcome. He said, "Neil, I know you did not have the money for the tea. You probably stole it from the warehouse."

"Are you calling me a thief?"

"If the shoe fits, wear it."

"You know Bruce, we can settle the lie you uttered. We can settle with knives, wrestling, or fight to the death."

"I don't want your death to be on my conscience. But know this that no Campbell will ever cast a shadow over my doorstep."

"That's fine with me. I will always remember the lie and accusation. We will never have anything to do with your clan."

So this is how the feud started. Hate and animosity began. The next year Bruce married a Saulteaux girl. Both Neil and Bruce chose to remain in Canada. Both raised large families. However the quarrel was never forgotten. It festered down through the generations. When the Campbell's home burned, Dunbars spread the news that the Campbells set it on fire to collect insurance. When the Dunbar's boy drowned, the Campbells said it was God's punishment for the sins of the Dunbars. And so it continued. Many forgot what was the cause for the original dispute. No one would believe that a pound of tea could cause such hard feelings and would last for so long.

We come full circle today and with that wedding at the College Rose Garden. Dr. Don and Patricia met at several social functions and attraction was mutual. Patricia was smart, elegant, and a prize. Patricia saw the young doctor as handsome, polite, and a man she wanted as a life partner. I am sure that Rita and I wish Don and Patricia many years of happiness and a home full of children.

15. TWO SUMMERS AT DARWIN POND

DARWIN POND IS MUCH LIKE OTHER PONDS. IT HAS water, grass, various plants, and shrubs. It is the same yet it is different. It has a log with one one end in the water and the other end on the land. Its residents have experienced a transformation. The pond was part of the Olds College Wetlands Project. Dr. W. Allison wrote an article about the project and it was published in Scientific American. Dr. Suzuki read the article and added a compliment. He said the project was a wonderful model of conservation. He also said it deserved an elegant name. Some residents of the pond thought they should name their home Suzuki Water Park. However there were many objections. They said Dr. Suzuki preaches a fine speech about conservation and climate change, but he does not practice it. In other words he was a hypocrite. So the Pond residents considered other names. They settled on Darwin in honour of the great naturalist, Charles Darwin. Some of the people did not like Charles Darwin, but the Pond residents dismissed their opinion. They said their religion was superior to the people's religion. They believed in the Great Creator. They did not know what she looked like, but they believed in

The Golden Pond in the Great Beyond. They admired all her creations. They celebrated special events such as births, marriages, and even deaths.

When a Pond resident passed away after a long or short life, they took the body and placed it on top of the five foot high ant Castle. They said at night two white birds came down and took the body to the Great Beyond. Others disputed this version. They said it was two brown bats that carried the body to the Great Beyond. There were sceptics who said that at night the ants would come out and dissect the remains and recycle them. So there was doubt as to which version was correct. There were rumours that Benny the Bat knew the truth, but he was so antisocial. He slept during the day and flew around at night. He preferred not to talk to anyone.

There had been a great transformation in the Pond community. The residents changed. They were kinder, more cooperative, and they helped each other. There was such a good atmosphere that some referred to the place as Harmony Pond. Yes, it was harmonious now, but it wasn't so before.

It all started in the summer of the year 2016. Everyone was going about their duties, somewhat in a selfish way. Fredie the brown frog was bored and said he remembered the Spring Jamboree when all the boy frogs sang their love songs to the girl frogs. He sang but his song sounded like a squeak. One girl frog told Fredie, "No girl frog is going to come to you if your song is a squeak. How will she know if you are a frog or a mouse?"

Fredie pondered. How he wished he had a voice like Bill the bullfrog — a song that sounded like thunder. If only he had such a voice, then all the girl frogs would come to him. He determined that he would practice the seductive low sound. He thought he would get better results higher above the water. He climbed on the log and made a great effort. All that came out was a loud squeak!

Someone heard it. It was Anabelle, the ant. She came to the other end of the log.

"Anabelle, oh it is you. I hardly recognized you. Your antennas are white and I see you have lost one leg. What happened to you?"

"Fredie, hard times have come my way. I am at death's door. When I was young the ant bosses made me a Queen. All I had to do was lay eggs. Now my egg laying days are over. The bosses said I was of no use and a burden. They told me to leave the Castle or they would throw me out. So here I am, a hungry old ant."

"Don't they have a place for seniors in the Castle? Isn't there a food bank?"

"They have stored food, but it is for the winter and for the workers. There is none for me. I steal a little as workers carry food to the Castle. There are a few kind workers. Today one gave me a dried mosquito. I have been talking about my woes. Why did you squeak?"

"Anabelle, I have been so lonely. I want a wife. Will you marry me?"

"I am flattered by the proposal, but Fredie marriage would not work. You spend time in the water and I am a land being. I am too old for you. The residents will say, "There goes Anabelle the cradle robber. If I am not gone to the Great Beyond and you need advice just give me a squeak or a whistle." She wandered off on her five legs.

The next time he got on the log the squeak sounded like a gentle croak. Jimmy the Grasshopper answered, "Fredie what gives? Do you have a stomach ache?"

"No Jimmy, I am so lonely I want a wife. Would you be my wife?"

"Fredie, that's ridiculous. I'm a vegetarian and you eat bugs. Our life styles are different. I'm a free spirit. I love the good life. You don't catch me sitting on a log hoping some female would come along. If I want a girl grass hopper all I do is give a click and they come. Good luck Fredie."

Next day when he gave his croak, Walter the water beetle heard it. "Fredie don't you know what time of the year this is? I was just about to catch a water spider for dinner when you scared him off. Where are your manners?"

"Oh I'm so sorry Walter, but I was lonely and I hoped to call a girl frog, but none came. Walter would you be my wife?"

"You've got to be kidding! Do I look like a frog? We water beetles know who's male and who's female. It is only the low life they call people, that are confused. We don't have gays. Don't ask me such a stupid request again."
"Walter, I apologize."

"Apology accepted. Next time don't scare my dinner away."

The croaks were getting better. Millie the country mouse heard it and came to the log. Fredie looked and she seemed familiar, yet she had changed.

"Millie, at first I wasn't sure if it was you. You have changed. I see you have put on weight."

"Weight? My eye! It's that bum Mickey. He got me pregnant. He swore on a pile of sunflower seeds that he loved me and that he would be there if I got pregnant. Where is he? He's probably gallivanting and getting other girl mice pregnant. But what is with you Fredie?"

"Millie, I am so lonely and I want a wife. Would you be my wife?"

"Fredie, that would be adultery. But when my eight are on their own and if I can be free of Mickey, I would consider. I might join a mouse convent and if not, I'll call you. But remember I will not be fooled again with that "I love you" stuff and she ambled off.

One afternoon Fredie was dozing when beside the log was a loud splash and Maggie the mud hen came out of the water.

"Maggie what are you doing on this side of the pond?"

"I was chasing a minnow, but it swam under the log. Fredie you look so downcast. What is the matter?"

"Maggie I am so lonely. I want a wife. Will you marry me?"

"Fredie it is nice of you to offer, but marriage might not work. We mud hens hunt under the water and sometimes we cannot tell what we are chasing. What if I was chasing a minnow and caught you instead? They would call it attempted murder. For us, frogs are considered jail bait. Freddie I like you, but you can see why I must decline." Maggie disappeared under the water.

Fredie wondered why girl frogs were not attracted to him. He would ask his cousin, Leo the leopard frog. He swan over to where Leo hung out.

"Leo why am I not attractive to the girl frogs?"

"The answer is simple. You are so brown you have no spots."

"How can I get some spots?"

"You might try Jimmy the grasshopper. He is always spitting that brown juice all over the plants.

Fredie scurried over to the shore. "Jimmy, Jimmy, Jimmy!

"I heard you the first time. Why are your knickers in a knot this time?"

"Jimmy, I need spots on my back. Can you help?"

"Sure, lay on the sand. Do you want big spots or little ones?"

"How about some of each."

Jimmy sprayed Fredie's back with that foul smelling brown gunk. Fredie could not wait. He was going to swim to the other side where the girl frogs hung out. No one was saying any thing. Fredie asked, "How do you like my spots?"

"What spots? I don't see any." Fredie realized the spots had washed off. He swan back to the log, dejected as ever.

Next day he went back to see Leo. "Leo the spots washed off. Your plan did not work."

"Well I'm not a magician. I have another suggestion."

"What is it?"

"You have to change your voice. You should take singing lessons."

"But who gives singing lessons on this pond?"

"You might try Joe the red-winged blackbird. He is a real good singer."

Fredie found Joe swinging on a cat tail.

"Joe can you teach me to have a singing voice?"

"I don't know Fredie. We could try. We will start with the scales. Listen carefully as the key changes: Doh, ray, me, fah, soh, la, te, doh. Now you repeat."

Fredie could say the words, but they were all one key.

"Fredie, go back to your log and practice. It might help if you put a pebble in your mouth when you say the scales."

Fredie practised. He swallowed a few pebbles and a few fell out of his mouth. After a week he went back to Joe. He recited the doh ray me scales. Joe just shook his head.

"Fredie it's no use. Sometimes you cannot make silk purses out of sow's ears. Try something else. I don't have time right now. I've got my eye on that yellow-winged beauty." Then he flew off.

The next day while Fredie was practising his croak, another resident came to the log. It was Gertie the garter snake. She said, "Fredie, I was basking on a warm rock when you woke me. What are you doing croaking in the middle of the day?"

"Oh Gertie I was practising my croak, but I'm getting no where. Gertie I am so lonely. Would you be my wife?"

"Fredie, you can see we are not a match. You are so brown. I want a husband as colourful as I am, green, yellow, and black."

Fredie swan back to the log — "Guess I am a loser no matter what I try." He stayed awake all night. He would change plans. He would announce to the Pond residents that from this day forward he would be a bachelor.

Before he could make the announcement, he saw Serena, the shrew at the other end of the log.

"Serena, I haven't seen you for a long time. Where have you been? You look so pretty. Your nose is longer."

"I've been far away. I heard rumours that you were looking for a wife."

"Yes, would you be my wife?"

"I will consider it, but I see some obstacles. I hate water. I am much too fast for you. How would it look if I ran ahead and then waited for you to catch up? The residents would say, "There goes Serena dragging her husband behind. That would be embarrassing."

"I don't want to embarrass you and I could practice hopping faster."

"No, it just wouldn't work," and off she disappeared.

Fredie decided now to make his great announcement. He squeaked and croaked until all the residents were at the log.

"My dear friends I have come to announce that I will be a bachelor forever."

Anabelle was first to respond. "Fredie you have made a hasty decision. Let us think logically."

Millie replied, "Yes let us think logically. Anabelle you are the wise one. Do you have a plan?"

Jimmy interrupted. "I object, I am sure grasshoppers are smarter than ants. Ants just work, work, work. Now grasshoppers live the good life, no work and lots of fun. Now who is wiser?"

Millie spoke again. "Jimmy, you are always showing off and presenting your hare brained ideas. Anabelle, tell us your plan."

Anabelle stood up on her five legs.

"My friends, thank you for your support. My plan is this: First we have to organize and we will need a ceremonial king. Who do you suggest for a king or president or prime minister?"

The residents looked around and said, "We think Bill, the bullfrog could make a good king. He is big and fat and he has a thunderous voice."

"Good! Now we must have some rules."

"What rules?"

"I can think of a few:

1. Members shall not kill or eat other members
2. Members shall not steal from other members
3. Members shall not poop on other members space.
4. Members shall not commit adultery with other members.
5. Members shall observe the Season Rule our Mother Creator handed down to us. We might come up with more rules."

Then the residents clapped and cheered. "Anabelle you're the wise one."

Anabelle then said, "We have the rules. We will need a judge should someone break a rule or two. Who do you propose for judge?"

The residents looked around and unanimously pointed to Mike.

Anabelle said, "I declare by unanimous vote that Mike the muskrat will be the judge."

Serena the shrew spoke up. "We have an organization, but how are we going to find a wife for Fredie?"

Anabelle said, "This is my plan. We will all go out and search as far as we can. When the moon is full again we will come here and report. Hopefully, someone will find a wife for Fredie. So good luck and start searching."

When the moon was full they were all there, but it seemed no one had found a mate for Fredie. Anabelle said, "It appears that we have failed, but we will have your report."

One by one they reported that they had tried, but could find no wife for Fredie. Walter's report was different. "I couldn't find a frog mate, but I found this green stick. We could give it to Fredie and he could pretend it is his wife."

"No No! They shouted, a green stick would not do." Anabelle was about to declare that her plan was a failure, when out of nowhere appeared Serena. She had a brown girl frog beside her. "I apologize for being late, but travelling with a frog is a slow process. I have brought Fanny from a far away pond. She wants to see what Fredie has to offer." Fredie's eyes doubled in size. Was this a jackpot just for him?

"Fanny, come to me. Let's not waste a moment. We can go straight to our honeymoon."

Fanny spoke up in her pleasant, girlish voice: "Before I commit, I want some guarantees."

Anabelle said, "Walter get a lily leaf and put it on the log." When this was done, "Fredie you must put your stamp on this leaf declaring that you will never abandon Fanny as long as you live."

"What do I do? I promise a hundred times."

"Spit three globs and then leave your hand print in each glob."

"OK, my prints and promises are there. Come on Fanny let's be off!"

"Fredie, I must have a formal wedding. This day is one to observe properly."

"A wedding ceremony, how can that be done?"

Anabelle spoke up, "Yes we need a formal ceremony. We will need a Reverend. Who looks like a distinguished Reverend?" The residents all talked at once, but all agreed that Leo, the leopard frog should do the honours.

Leo stepped forward and said, "Fredie and Fanny you will be at the water end of the log. Now Fredie do you promise that Fanny will not be hungry the rest of her life?"

"I do, I do."

"Do you promise you will protect Fanny from all enemies?"

"I do, I do."

"Fredie do you promise to observe Mother Creator's Season Rule?"

"Fredie hesitated. He wasn't sure what the rule was. What is the rule?"

" The rule states that mating shall be at a certain season. All year sex is not for us. It is for lower life which we call humans."

"What if I am brimming with desire?"

"The rule must be obeyed. If you are so weak minded then find an old cat tail and pretend it is your partner."

"Fredie didn't like the rule, but there was no alternative. He said, "I promise."

"Fanny, do you promise to manage the food supply with care?"

"I do."

"Fanny do you promise that on cold nights you will cuddle and keep Fredie warm?"

"I do."

"Do you promise to observe Mother Creator's Season Rule?"

"I know it will be difficult, but I promise."

"By the authority granted by this assembly I pronounce you bound to each other forever and no exceptions. To consecrate this event, hold each other and slide off into the water and come out on the other side. This will signify you are leaving your past life and now emerging into a new life, clean and fresh."

Anabelle summarized the great event. Jimmy grumbled, but he rejoiced also that there had been a miraculous event. Fredie and Fanny found an old blackbird nest at the edge of the pond. They rearranged the grasses and made it their home. During the summer they kept their promises. When the cold weather came they borrowed under their home for the long winter sleep.

In the spring of 2017, the days became warmer and the ice on the pond melted. Fredie and Fanny woke from their sleep. They were hungry. Hunger was forgotten, as they heard the first love calls. Spring Jamboree was here. Fredie and Fanny did not need to look for a mate, they were already a pair.

Two weeks later Fanny whispered in Fredie's ear, "Fredie I have a secret to tell you."

"I bet you caught a large mosquito."

"Fredie you are so droll, my secret is that I'm pregnant. Aren't you excited?" Fredie didn't know what to do or say.

"Fredie in two weeks you must help make a special nest for our new babies." Fredie did as he was told and Fanny deposited the babies in this slimy bed. Fredie was puzzled. There must be some mistake. Those black balls did not look like frog babies.

"Fanny those can't be our babies."

"Fredie you don't seem to know anything. There will be a change in two weeks." Two weeks later Fredie saw little ones swimming. They had no feet and had a tail. Once again Fredie wondered, *Was Fanny having an affair with some salamander, or toad?* Fanny reassured him that all would be right in another two weeks. Later they saw the babies and they looked just like their parents.

"Hallelujah! What a miracle," exclaimed Fredie.

He was the proudest father in the pond. In the years that followed Fredie and Fanny looked forward to Spring Jamboree and the family that came after. There were many brown frogs in the pond who traced their ancestry to Fredie and Fanny.

When the time came, Fredie and Fanny knew they would leave this earth and Darwin Pond. They fell into an eternal sleep. The residents put their bodies on top of ant Castle. The next morning they were gone. I would like to think they had been taken to the Great Beyond and Mother Creator.

Some summer evening when the million stars are out, look for a twinkling little star far away. I want to imagine it is the Great Beyond. I also imagine Fredie and Fanny are on Golden Pond swimming side by side. They are ever together and ever in love.

16.

THE FUTURE IN THE BRAVE NEW WORLD

THE YEAR IS 2025 AND TWO SPACESHIPS ARE CIRCLING the planet Earth. They are observing the features of the planet. Ship #1 called the Vector was commanded by Commander Thor. Ship #2 Orion, was commanded by Commander Zora. The spaceships had come from the planet Casa in a distant solar system. The voyage from Casa to Earth had taken one hundred earth years.

The Casians had superior technology a hundred years ago. They knew what was happening on the planet Earth. They knew of the wholesale slaughter in which humans engaged. They suspected that before long humans would destroy the planet.

The purpose of the voyage was to see if they could help the Earthlings avoid total destruction. They had arrived, but were they too late? What they saw was destruction. The cities were lying in ruins and unlivable because of the nuclear contamination. They saw people fighting for food and water. There was chaos everywhere.

Who were the Casians? They, like the humans on Earth had evolved over a billion years. Their evolution had taken them to a higher level. Physically they were similar to humans. They were five feet to six feet and weighed at about 150 lbs. They had no hair and their eyes were larger. Their skin was shades of ivory. They were superior in several ways. Their intelligence measured 250 to 300. Their life span was 250- 350 years. They could communicate telepathically. Their technology was far superior. They could travel through space for years in perpetuity. Their high intelligence and genetic manifestations created individuals who were compatible to change and whose code of behaviour made them a superior society. They viewed the Earthlings as victims of their own evolution. Their aggressiveness, lack of empathy, and killer instinct was fine when they were struggling for survival. Now the same genetic capabilities were leading them to self destruction. The second genetic flaw was that their intelligence was inferior so that they could not differentiate always what was real and what was fantasy. Thus they were prone to manipulation by others. These flaws resulted in the chaos and destruction that the Casians observed from their spaceships. Here and there were communities that had organized themselves for survival. It was almost like going back to the middle Ages.

There were vestiges of advanced technology, but there was no one remaining who knew how to operate, create, or repair. What could the Casians do for these humans? To them the answer was obvious. To change society you must first change the individual. This meant basic change.

In the Casian world, life begins as it does on the Earth. A sperm is united with an egg cell, where as the Earth process is haphazard, the Casians is designed with a purpose. All undesirable traits are removed from the genes. Desirable traits are installed. Then the sperm and egg are united to form an embryo. There would be a bank of women who would volunteer to carry the fetus until birth. Others would contribute to the raising of the baby until he/she became a unique individual. In the process if errors were detected then the fetus was aborted.

"Marriage was by design also. First, there had to be a marriage of minds. A male and female would petition a Council for permission to have a physical union. There would be tests and interrogation. Divorce and same sex marriage were prohibited. Any breach of the rules and the individuals would be banished into space.

In politics rivalry was replaced by competence. A Council of Wizards chose who was to be Head of State and this was reviewed every three years. There were no political parties. For those chosen it was a duty and not an ego trip.

In Economics, the Casians recognized that individuals were not equal in abilities, although they were designed to be as equal as possible. The ablest were allowed to keep the rewards for superior performance. There would be no wide variations in rewards. There were no welfare cases. Everyone had to contribute.

Recreation activities followed a similar pattern. You chose — sports, music, fine arts, etc. A special fund to finance programs was created by the wealthiest Casians. In sports the emphasis was on mental ability rather then on brute force. As for religion, it did not exist in the Casian society. They reasoned that others such as Earthlings had religion to compensate for insecurity, lack of knowledge, etc. For the Casians there was no afterlife- heaven, hell, etc. Religion on earth rested on tradition, and supernatural. For the Casians life existed until the body could no longer reproduce vital parts. Death came to all at some time. It was viewed as eternal sleep.

The Casians recognized that their society limited the amount of free will each individual might want. This was not a problem because they were designed at birth to follow certain paths. For Casians intellect, genetic design, and a societal plan kept them advancing. There were no wars because the killer instinct was eliminated. Their marriages were intellectual first and intimate second. Their children were not necessarily from their own genetic source, but they were still treated as though they were. They made the most of their life on the planet because there was no other.

Why have the humans nearly destroyed the Earth planet? We could trace the cause about a billion years ago when they evolved with a selfish gene and a killer instinct. The problem came to a head in the year 2018. The President of the only superpower decided to exert his authority and force changes. This angered people within the USA and abroad. They showed their disapproval in the November elections and the many protests. The President's party lost the House of Reps in Congress. His actions would be curtailed for the next two years when the Presidential elections would be held. He summoned his closest ministers to do a post mortem. They said if he was to win the next election in 2020 he would have to create a diversion abroad. The President decided to act on their advice. First, his staff would bombard the US population with propaganda. Tell the people that North Korea, Russia, and China were out to destroy the USA. He issued ultimatums to these countries. They refused to bow. He took military action. US bombed the crap out of North Korea. The USA through NATO began border assaults on Russia. He ordered his navy to stop all ships going to China and Russia. China responded by asking the US President to reverse his actions or they would use their nuclear weapons. Both sides sent their missiles and there was mutual destruction. When the Casians arrived the Earth was almost totally destroyed.

Fifty miles from the ruins of New York City, three generations of the Jefferson family were huddled in their cold house. The house belonged to James and Sally Jefferson, a couple in their fifties. Also in this house were Thomas and Sandra Jefferson. They had been on their honeymoon when catastrophe struck. They could not go back to their job or apartment in New York because of radioactivity and there were no homes or jobs to go back to. They had a two year old son Benny, who was suffering from several ailments.

This evening Thomas and Sandra were going to a meeting at their Shepherdville Community Center to hear from the casian visitors. Commander Zora addressed the assembly. "I have presented you a vision of our Casian Way. I have also stated that your way is headed for total destruction. You must choose."

"We have heard you," replied the Assembly Chairperson. "Your Casian Way sounds like Communism and Atheism. We have rejected those ideas in the past and so will likely reject them now."

"I do not understand why you would choose destruction of humanity and your Earth planet."

"For us Earth people, our lives here whether long or short is not important. Our Earth is also not important, whether it exists or not. This place we call Earth is a temporary place. When the end comes we can escape to our desired destination."

"Where is this desired place?"

"When the end comes our escape will be to our gods, our myths, and our supernaturals."

"Thank you for your courtesy. We Casians hope you will find your Utopia."

The following morning the residents of Shepherdville heard a roar and earth shook. They went out to see. Two spaceships rose and the disappeared into space.

on jobs to go back to. They had [illegible] years to [illegible] [illegible] [illegible]

[illegible] [illegible] [illegible]

[illegible] [illegible] [illegible] Commander [illegible] [illegible] They [illegible] [illegible] have destroyed [illegible] [illegible] destruction. You have chosen [illegible] the Assembly and general [illegible] [illegible] [illegible] the past and so will likely [illegible]

I do not understand why you would choose destruction for humanity and your Earth planet.

[illegible] Earth people, our lives here, whether long or short, [illegible] important. Our Earth is also not important, whether [illegible] [illegible]. This place we call Earth is a temporary place. [illegible] [illegible] desired [illegible] [illegible] [illegible]

[illegible] our body [illegible]

[illegible] [illegible] [illegible] you [illegible]

[illegible] [illegible] [illegible]

17. SERGEANT IAN MACPHERSON OF THE RCMP

SGT. MACPHERSON SAT AT HIS DESK SCANNING A POLICE circular. He was the commanding officer of the Mayerthorpe Detachment. His eight officers had their assignments so he was not particularly busy. His Secretary was busy typing reports. It was one circular that held his attention. "Murder and Abduction in Hudson Hope." What was so special? These events occur everyday. For him this was special. Hudson Hope was his boyhood home. He had his mother still living in the town. He had been there the previous summer and there were always rumours. This was new. His mother had not mentioned the murder in her last letter. He asked his Secretary, Helen Peterson to get the particulars of this case. Ten minutes later she handed him a typed sheet. Ryan Black had shot Mohammed el Sahib and then abducted his Mohammed's wife. He was now on the run with a warrant for his arrest. Why did this case weigh on his mind? Maybe it was that he had been coasting towards his twenty fifth year pension and retirement. Did he want to do something significant before he handed in his badge? Or was that monument reminding him of four young constables who had lost their lives at the hands of James (Jimmy) Roszko. He saw a parallel between Roszko and Black of Hudson Hope. Both were career criminals. Both had an obsessive hate for the mounties.

Oh well, the officers at Hudson Hope would arrest Black without any problem. So he dismissed his concern but his thoughts kept coming back to his own life in Hudson Hope.

The Census of 1951 listed one MacPherson in the town of Hudson Hope. His name was James MacPherson, male, age 27, single, nickname "Jack". He had a house in the town. His occupation was guide and trapper. He probably was a descendent of the earliest MacPhersons who settled in this area. The journals of Alexander MacKenzie mentioned Dugald McPherson as one in his exploration party in the 1700's.

Beyond the census we could say more about Jack. He was a jack of all trades, a guide, trapper, prospector, trader, rancher, etc. He could handle horses, a truck, and a Cat. He could build you a house. He had inherited a house and small ranch. Ranch life would keep him tied down so he sold it. He worked only enough to meet his basic needs. So he spent time in the foothills prospecting for gold and other minerals.

In June 1951 Jack was ten miles north of town to see his friend Hector Fortin. Hector had horses. Jack was arranging a venture for some tourists who wanted to see the mighty Peace and the land of valleys. So he and Hector would partner up and make some money.

Hector was an interesting character. He may have been Metis or maybe Dene. It didn't matter. He was honest and generous. He had a houseful of kids of all ages. Hector was easy going so it was his wife Margot that had to keep some order. Which she did! When they were getting out of hand she used her French or Dene commands that would have made a sailor blush. Hector enjoyed her colorful expressions. Hector and Jack agreed on their joint venture. Margot settled the kids and made some tea. There was bannock and jam to complete the lunch. Jack was headed for his battered 1948 half ton, when out of the pasture rode two girls. He had seen the younger one before but the older one just paralysed him. His eyes widened. He could not move. She was Margie Fortin, age eighteen. She had flowing brown hair and eyes that twinkled. Her smile was infectious. Jack forgot about going home. Conversations followed and even a date for a show in Hudson Hope was arranged. Where was Margie all these years. The ten miles back to Hudson Hope seemed to fly. Jack had changed course in mid stream of his life.

Margie Fortin had so captivated Jack that one might have wondered if she cast a spell over this mature and experienced man. No. Margie was flesh and blood and this was just a characteristic of a smart young lady. For the past two years she had been at St. Xavier Residential School where she was completing her grades eleven and twelve education. Most of the students at St. Xavier were resentful. They hated the School and they hated the Sisters of Service who were their teachers and guardians.

Margie was not one of them. She thrived in this jail like setting. She liked the discipline. She liked the structured life. She was determined to absorb as much knowledge that the School could offer. Her attitude endeared her to the Sisters. They went out of their way to mentor this talented girl. Sister Monica taught her how to read music and how to play the guitar. Sister Justina introduced her to the classics. Sister Bernadette taught her about fine art and crafts.

Before she left, one of the Sisters said, “Margie you are so talented, you have a maturity beyond your years. You would make a super Sister. Please consider taking the vow.”

Margie replied, “Sisters, I thank you for all you have gifted unto me. At this time I cannot consider the Sisterhood. I do not have the calling. I would like to go to University, but my family has no money. I will go back to Hudson Hope and try to get a job. I hope to save enough to pursue my dream.” The day she left St. Xavier, the Sisters gave her gifts and everyone was in tears.

"Margie we will pray for you each day." Margie said, "You have opened my mind and my heart. I will always remember."

After that first date a stream of dates followed. Residents of the town had a saying, "There goes the 48 Ford and it knows it's way to the Fortin ranch."

Before Christmas arrived the two were married. Father Dalaire performed the ceremony. It was a marriage some would say, "Made in Heaven". The wedding was simple because there was no money. Margie and Jack settled in the old MacPherson house in Hudson Hope.

Then came the children. Ian was first and a year later there was Laurie. Then the doctor advised that more would be risky. Because Jack's work took him everywhere in the region, it was Margie that became the principal parent. The discipline she knew at St. Xavier she adopted as her rule for being a mother and a mentor. She reviewed their school work each day. They had to do some physical work at home. There was time for leisure but it was limited. When free time appeared, it was to music practice and the classics. Ian and Laurie often referred to their mother as "the slave master". All she needed was a whip. But in truth they loved their super Mom.

Ian and Laurie treasured July and August of each year for the golden time Mom created. She would take a horse and cart and later an ATV and go ten miles north west to a cabin on Whisky Creek. Jack had built this cabin for his trap line work. During the long daylight of these two months they lived face to face with nature. They caught fish and smoked it. They picked berries and canned them. They picked mushrooms and nuts and dried them. They cut wood for the winter. They tanned hides. There was time for swimming. When the day's work was done they would make a smudge to keep the mosquitoes at bay. They might read the classics. They might play chess and quite often they picked up their instruments and played. It might be a Don Messer dance tune or it might be a Mozart Sonota . When the two months ended each one was richer. They had a tan and were brimming with health. They had partaken of the treasures that Whisky Creek offered. Through the classics and music they had been in the great cities and the cultural halls of the world.

In later years Ian and Laurie brought their children to the cabin on Whiskey Creek, hoping that the magic of earlier years could be repeated with their children. It was no use. The first day they explored the new surroundings. The second day they were bored. The third day they wanted to go home. The chapters in our lives are personal and cannot be repeated or transferred to anyone else.

Ian had always wanted to be a Mountie. After grade twelve he was disappointed when his application was not accepted. He pursed a second choice Law. After two years came an acceptance. Ian dropped his Law studies and was off to the RCMP training center at Regina. Laurie chose the Commerce field. She married another accountant. They had four children. In the business section of Edmonton you will see an office with a plaque that reads (Patterson and MacPherson Accountants) At the graduation ceremony in Regina in 1972, Ian was one of the new constables. He looked so handsome. He was six feet tall. In his serge jacket and polished boots he made so many proud. Jack and Margie were there. Hector and Margaret were there. There was Laurie and so many others.

Ian's first posting was to Vegreville. He was assigned to the traffic detail. When the first serious crash happened he had to go to the hospital to get the statements. In the trauma room was a very attractive LPN. She was the nurse assigned. Ian could not get his eyes off this girl. Her badge name was Karen Kindratsky.

In the days that followed he thought of Karen and how could he meet her in a social setting. He had no trouble confronting a 300 lb biker, but to ask this girl for a date was too difficult. So he tried to dismiss her from his thoughts but it didn't work. Meanwhile he had traffic duty.

There is a story still told in social circles about an incident involving Constable MacPherson. One afternoon he stopped eighty year old Mrs. Derkach.

"Mrs. Derkach, you have broken the law. You went through a stop sign."

"Constable, I looked both ways there was no one. I'm sure I stopped."

"Mrs. Derkach you have to come to a dead stop, not a rolling stop."

"Did I?"

"Yes you did. I don't know whether to send you to prison or give you a thousand dollar fine?"

"Constable, I am at your mercy."

"Mrs. Derkach, this time I will give you a warning, but you must obey every law in the land. If you don't I'll throw the book at you."

"Constable, I will thank you for your mercy and I will obey every law in the land." This incident with Mrs. Derkach marked how Ian responded to others. He remembered that his Mother had said, "Ian, in life every decision you make should be tempered with common sense, humility, and all the wisdom you can muster."

A few days later Ian had to respond to a domestic dispute. Mrs. Howard had a dispute with her husband Gordon. She said Gordon and his family were just one step above their ape relatives in Africa. Gordon did not like that reference, so he gave his wife Delphine the fist. Constable MacPherson heard both sides and admitted that Gordon was provoked, but a fist was not appropriate. He charged Gordon with assault.

It happened that the following day there was a Bingo session in the Borshchiv Hall. Between games there was gossip and opinions. John Bender was heard to say, "Mrs. Howard deserved the fist and that Constable MacPherson is just a pig." Mrs. Derkach got out of her chair, all four feet of her. She walked over to six foot John, grabbed his shirt front. She said, "Look here you louse, one more bad word about Constable MacPherson and I'll bash your head in with a rolling pin. If that isn't enough I'll take those two things you have between your legs and use then for baseball practice!"

The Bingo players dropped their cards and everyone burst into laughter. Even John had to laugh. The story got out to the Detachment and any time some member complained, there would be a response, "never mind calling a lawyer, just give Mrs. Derkach a call!"

The next day there was a serious accident. Constable MacPherson was at the hospital and the same attractive LPN was there. This time he threw caution to the wind.

"Karen I would like to meet you in a social setting. If you give me your phone number, I will call you."

"That would be nice. My number is 556-01XX."

When they met as a pair they liked each other. Their backgrounds were similar, growing up in a rural environment. Dates were followed by engagement and a marriage. The wedding brought diverse groups together: Ukrainian and Polish families from Mundare, and Scottish and Dene families from Hudson Hope.

In the years that followed there were children, Mariette, James, and Bonita. Every three or four years there were moves. Three Hills, Brooks, Ponoka, Ft. St. John and Lloydminister. The moves were hard on Karen and the children. There were new homes, new schools, and new friends. It was difficult to establish deep relationships when you were always moving. Wherever Constable MacPherson was stationed he established a reputation for being a cop who was disciplined, thorough, and fair. There were stories at each place.

In Ft.St.John they tell the story of how Corporal MacPherson solved a theft crime. Someone had stolen a snowmobile. Corporal MacPherson was assigned to the case. His first move was to talk to known thieves. He found Tim Paxton and Angus Weaselhead at the bar.

"Gentlemen, I have a problem and I know you can help me."

"Oh we're always glad to help!"

"Have you heard that a snowmobile has been stolen?"

"No Corporal, this is the first we hear about it."

"Have you any ides about who might have stolen it?"

"No! We have no idea."

Corporal MacPherson saw Angus's eyes dart. He said, "You know if you are lying I would have to charge you for obstruction of justice."

"We would never lie to you. We respect the police." Then Tim spoke in Dene. "Angus, we have to move that machine from Kadar's garage."

The Corporal smiled. "Gentlemen you have been very helpful and I hope to see you again soon."

The thieves did not know the Corporal could understand Dene. The Corporal and a fellow officer met the thieves at the garage.

Before the move to Mayerthorpe Karen said. "Ian, we have to talk. Twenty two years ago the fire of passion and a purpose brought us together. I have no regrets. Those years were purposeful. We raised a family and I was by your side as a partner and helper. Now we are at crossroads. The fire of passion has dimmed and the purpose has been fulfilled. Our children are on their own. You will be taking your retirement and my role will be the housekeeper. If you do not choose another career, we will be doing as thousands of other retirees are doing. There will be trips to Arizona, golf games, visits with children and grandchildren, reunions, social groups within clubs and churches. For many who want an aimless leisure life that is a dream fulfilled. I want something different. I want to complete my medical training. I want to help the sick, the injured, and the helpless. Ian, I am not going with you to Mayerthorpe. I want a permanent separation and I want a fair settlement."

Ian was not taken aback. He knew that the union was now a union of convenience. He said. "Karen, I loved you twenty years ago and I still love you. I recognize the truth of your words. Over the years it was my career and the Force that had the priority. You had become a servant rather than a partner. Although I know it will be a loss for me, I want you to be happy and fulfilled. The settlement will follow your request. There was a hug and a kiss and the two parted. Each went their way.

At Mayerthorpe, Sgt. MacPherson could not let go of the Hudson Hope murder case. Whenever he had the time, he had two files before him. They seemed so similar. *Could he in his final year in the Force, prevent a tragedy?*

James Roszko was the youngest in his family and small in stature. He was probably bullied in school. His defence was to become aggressive and threatening. When fists weren't enough he chose knives and a gun.

Sgt. MacPherson looked at Roszko's long record of so many charges, so many convictions, and so many acquittals. In the community he could get his way, but in prison he would have no gun. In his last stay he was beaten up several times. He vowed he would never be in prison again. He also vowed the cops would get a pay back.

The last episode started as a commonplace event. He bought a truck but after one payment he paid no more. The Dealer wanted payment or the truck. Jimmy would give neither. He hid the truck. The Dealer asked the RCMP for assistance. "Get the truck or charge him with theft."

The Sergeant in charge sent two officers to Jimmy's farm home. They waited for Jimmy to show up. At midnight the

Sergeant sent two more. They waited for Jimmy but he did not show.

Jimmy told Art his so-called friend, he would get even with the cops. On the way back to the farm with Art, Jimmy got out before his place. He crept to the back of the machine shed where he had a hidden rifle and ammunition. He waited. In the morning one of the officers decided to check the grow up at the back of the shed, when he appeared in the doorway he got a bullet. Another officer rushed to drag him away and he got a bullet. The third officer radioed for help, then he crept to the fallen officers and started shooting. Jimmy got him too. The fourth officer thought if he crawled he would not be a target. Unfortunately Jimmy got him too. Reports say a police bullet had grazed Jimmy's arm. He knew how this was going to end and so he took his own life.

Sgt. MacPherson knew there was miscalculations that led to four young men losing their lives.

Could he do something to prevent a similar tragedy at Hudson Hope? He knew that Ryan Black had vowed to get even with those who sent him to prison. The case of Ryan Black troubled Sgt. MacPherson. Finally he took action reluctantly. He called Superintendent Susan Milford.

"Hi Ian, I was expecting a call from you."

"How did you know?"

"Ian, we were in the same graduation class in Regina so many years ago. We have been following each other's careers. I can guess what this call is about, but I want you to tell me."

"Susan, each day I see that monument to the four Mounties. I don't want another Mountie dead. Here is what I am requesting. I want to set up a small task force. Besides myself, I want one Mountie who knows this terrain and who has a dog partner. I could also use an expert tracker. I want aerial surveillance until the case is closed."

"Ian, I'm going to grant your request, but with a heavy heart. In two years I will have my retirement party and I want you there alive."

"Thanks Susan, and I'll keep in touch as the exercise proceeds."

Two years ago Mohammed had bought the convenience store. With some part-time help and with the help of his sister, the business was a success. A year ago there was a break-in and the camera showed Ryan Black as the thief. Mohammed testified and Ryan was given a year in prison. He vowed he would get even with that Arab. At the same time Mohammed's sister completed grade twelve and was off to University. Mohammed advertised for help. A Dene girl, Francine Crane had also completed grade twelve and she needed a job and applied. Mohammed and Francine were compatible in work. They also were attracted to each other. Before the year had passed they were married.

In school Ryan was bullied and he had no friends. Only Francine was friendly. He concluded that Francine had a crush on him and so he considered her as his girl. But she had disappointed him. While he sat in prison she married that Arab. As soon as he got out he would settle some scores. He would make Mohammed's life miserable by increments. He would steal Mohammed's ATV and drive it into the lake. Things went wrong when the Arab came out with a bat and so Ryan shot him. Now he was on the run. The game wasn't over yet. He had to beat Roszko's score of four dead Mounties. He had abducted Francine. Maybe she would willingly be his lover and cooperate in his grand plan? Francine was uncooperative and she was a nuisance. He could still use her as bait or as a shield in a fire fight. Why weren't those stupid cops not combing the woods for him? Maybe he couldn't get four at one time, but he could pick them off one by one. Why weren't they coming? He had set camp fires to attract them.

Sgt. MacPherson set up his Command Center in a cabin five miles east of Hudson Hope. From Prince George came Constable Pat O'Neil and his partner Thor. From Whitehorse came Cameron McKay and Roy Abbot, an aerial pilot.

He provided his info to Corporal Prekaski, Commanding Officer at the Hudson Hope detachment. Corporal Prekaski brought any info to the Command Center. Sgt. McPherson rented a travel trailer and parked it at the camp grounds. He spread the word that he had retired and was now looking for an investment, maybe a hotel or restaurant. Each morning he had breakfast with his mother. During the day he wandered around town meeting old acquaintances, etc. In the evening he would go to his trailer. At midnight he would go to the Command Centre. He and the other two officers practised going silently through the woods. Sometimes they would go three, four, or five miles. From the aerial info, the heat source was north-east of Hudson Hope. There were camp fires set each day in the quadrant.

About eight miles from Hudson Hope, the pilot detected a faint source of heat daily from the same location. This was there in the following days. Twelve days after the exercise started, the night was dark and muggy. Sgt MacPherson said, "now is the time and let's hope for success."

They were dropped off three miles from the objective. Silently with night goggles, moccasin feet, and guns drawn, they crept to their objective. They found Ryan asleep with a rifle beside him and a rope from his leg to Francine. A hand covered Ryan's mouth. Other hands put cuffs on hands and feet. Francise who was frightened was released.

At District Court in Ft.St.John, Judge Mellon said, "Ryan Black, your record speaks for itself. You have taken an innocent man's life for no reason. Society cannot have you in its' midst. I sentence you to thirty years with no parole." The gavel came down and Ryan Black was taken away. Judge Mellon asked for attention.

"Citizens, I want to commend Sgt. MacPherson and his team for a task done to perfection! Society is indebted to men and women like them who do their duty on our behalf. Congratulations and thank you."

The Clerk said, "God Save the Queen." The gavel came down again. A chapter of human history had come to a conclusion.

Sgt. MacPherson commended his team members. Thanked them, wished them many years of satisfaction in their careers. There were handshakes, hugs, and tears as they parted.

Before he left, he went to see his mother. "Mom I'm going back to Mayerthorpe. I will make some changes, but I will come to see you from time to time." His mother did not ask any questions. She hugged her son and said, "I am proud of you and I will always love you."

Word of the Sergeant's mission reached the Mayerthorpe detachment. They wanted to shout a victory hurrah, but they knew that he was a humble hero. The first call was from Susan Melford.

"Ian congratulations on the success of your mission. I have to confess there were tears of joy when I heard you were safe. I expect you at my retirement party."

"Thank you Susan, you gave me the opportunity to do my duty. I will be leaving the Force, but I will be at your party."

Sgt. MacPherson wrote several letters: One to the Personnel Department of the RCMP he requested to retire at the end of the year. The second to the University of Alberta College of Law he applied for admission to complete his Law Degree. Third to his former wife Karen, that he had decided in a career change. He also wished her well in her career. At the end of the year and on the last day as an officer of the RCMP he assembled the members of his staff.

"Fellow Officers, it has been an honour to be your Commanding Officer. You have honoured the badge that you wear. When you accepted the badge it was a promise to "Maintain the Law". I know you will do so for the remainder of your careers. I have one last request of you. It is advice I learned from my mother, "To serve mankind is a noble purpose. Remember you are not God. In every decision you make, temper it with common sense, humility, and the best wisdom you can muster. Farewell and best wishes."

There was the usual farewell. Members from all the places he served gathered money for a suitable gift. Besides the money there was a gift of two books embossed in gold and a golden gavel.

The books were the Criminal Code of Canada and the Bible. Citizen Ian MacPherson drove away in his Ford Mustang. A chapter in a man's life had ended. A chapter in the annals of the RCMP also ended. Well done Ian MacPherson a good and faithful servant.

Elipogue In the story Jack is given a minor role. Yet he is a noble character. I like to think this way. Margie drove the car but Jack put the gasoline in. Someday someone will write of Jack's adventures in the Rockies, the valleys and streams of the Peace Country.

When the Ryan Black incident happened Jack had passed away three years earlier. Hector and Margot have also passed away. Their fourteen grandchildren have scattered to other parts of Canada and the USA. I'm sure they treasure with fondness their parents. Although very poor, Hector brought laughter and joy. Margot had a difficult task with fourteen rambunctious kids. She kept them fed, clothed, and schooled. When they became too rambunctious she settled the group with choice words in three languages.

Five years after the event, Karen had completed her medical studies and more. She is one of the Senior Surgical Nurses at the Edmonton General Hospital. When not in the operating room she has her friends, her cat, and the freedom to do want she wants. Ian was accepted in the College of Law. He graduated and was admitted to the Bar. He specialized in Criminal Law. His office is in downtown Edmonton. The sign reads: MacDonald MacDonald and MacPherson. Lawyers, Barristers, and Solicitors. Neither Ian nor Karen have remarried. They get together periodically to discuss work and their children and families.

For me the most memorable character is Margie. She saw in the Residential School what others could not see. She married an honest common man. She did not curb his free spirit but recognized and embraced it. To her children she brought the world. Today she lives in the MacPherson house in Hudson Hope. The house could use some repair, but it isn't the building, but the lady who intrigues us. Knock on the door and who is there? A tall lady. Her skin is a bit darker and there are wrinkles. Her hair is a mixture of black and white firmly set in two braids. It is the eyes and smile that say she is genuine and you will never forget her once you have met her. You might expect her voice accented in the guttural tones of her Dene heritage. You would be surprised. Whether she speaks in English or French you would think she was educated at Oxford or the French Bourse. There is a constant stream of visitors who are treated warmly. They seek her advice in many fields. She has been dubbed the "Oracle of Hudson Hope". She had been urged to move to a larger center but she declines. "My work is here."

18.
THE PICNIC

IT WAS A SCENE REPEATED A THOUSAND TIMES IN A thousand places. It was the last day of a school year. The teacher would hand out report cards and encouragement. That was the scene at Deer Meadow School and Miss Morton was especially in fine spirits. It had been a good year and in two weeks she was getting married.

She said, “Students it has been a successful and a good year. You have made my task pleasant and easy. Before I hand out the report cards, I am announcing two happy events. First, you have all passed. Secondly, I am getting married in two weeks.”

Schroeder whispered, “I heard her guy is the gas jockey at the Coop.”

Before the cards were handed out Peppermint Patty and Sally walked to the front. “Miss Morton, the class wishes to thank you for being the best teacher and we wish to congratulate you and wish the best in your marriage.”

The girls handed Miss Morton a huge bouquet and a box neatly wrapped and decorated with ribbons and bows.

“Miss Morton this gift is to be opened at your bridal shower.”

The two girls knew what was in the box, but the rest could only speculate. There were all kinds of guesses: Maybe it was a make-up kit?. A year’s supply of diapers, a rolling pin, a leash, a frying pan, and so the guessing went on, as Miss Morton handed out the cards.

Before she left she said, "Thank you so much! I will treasure this day forever." Tears streamed down her flushed cheeks.

"Class I have some more good news. The Principal has said I will move to the next higher class, so I will have you as my class next year."

"Good Grief, Miss Martin for another year."

"It's Miss Morton and not Miss Martin."

By now you have noted that this scene is familiar. It has been seen a thousand times by thousands young and old. The students peered into their own cards, sighed relief and then wanted to know what grades others had achieved. Someone spoke up.

"Lucy,what grade did you get?"

Lucy smug as ever replied, "An A+ obviously."

The other girls bunched in a group looked at each others grades. They were A's.

Patty asked, "Linus what is your grade?"

"I received an A as well."

The other boys compared grades. Most had B's. They turned to Charlie, "What did Miss Morton give you?"

Charlie replied, "I got a lousy C-."

Lucy said, "Charlie, you are never going to be an astronaut with a grade C-."

Then Charlie said, "I will work harder, do my homework and you can count on me to get an A+."

Snoopy and Woodstock giggled at Charlie's prediction." Snoopy was next to speak. "I did not get a report card."

"That's because you are a dog and dogs don't get report cards." Snoopy hung his head and put his paws to cover the tears coming from his eyes. Sally said, "Now you have hurt his feelings."

Woodstock spoke, "Don't feel sad Snoopy. I will make you a report card."

"How can you do that? You're not a teacher and you have no paper."

"I will make Snoopy a report card out of grass."

"What a joke!"

"If the girls in Hawaii can wear grass skirts, I can make a grass report card for Snoopy."

The Peanut class ambled outside. It would be an hour before buses would take them home. Sherry said, "the other classes are having year end picnics." "Why don't we have a picnic?"

"Yah! Yah! Let's have a picnic."

"Where could we hold it?"

"How about at the swimming pool?"

"No, there is too much yellow stuff in the water."

"How about the College Rose Garden?"

"You can't make a fire there."

"How about at the golf course?"

"No, you have to be a member and a golfer."

"What about in Centennial Park?"

"No, there will be too many people there."

So suggestions were made and rejected.

Lucy spoke, "Obviously we cannot choose a place. Maybe we should forget the whole thing?"

"No! No! A picnic is a must."

Woodstock perched on Snoopy's head. "OK Snoopy, what do you say?"

"I say the picnic should be at Dogpound."

"Is that supposed to be a sick joke?"

"No, Dogpound is a great place. There is a store, ball diamond, picnic tables and there is a stream near by."

Charlie said, "Snoopy you have saved the day!"

"How are we going to get there?"

Peppermint Patty spoke up, “My Father knows everyone important in town. I am sure he will help us to get to Dogpound.”

“Hurray for Patty and Mr. Sanford her dad.”

“We’ll need an organizer. I’ll be the organizer, said Lucy. Sherry you get the wieners. Sally you get the buns. Pig Pen you get the mustard and drinks. Charlie you get the fishing poles. Woodstock you get the worms. Snoopy you get the wiener sticks. Be here tomorrow at ten sharp and I mean sharp.”

The next morning at ten, a battered old school bus painted gray drove into the school yard. Who was the driver? It was John. It was a good choice. John was a gentleman and a good driver. Everyone piled in and they were off for Dogpound!

The first event was the ball game. Lucy insisted that she would be the pitcher. Pig Pen would be the catcher. It was a dusty place and he was already dirty. Woodstock would be the umpire and scorekeeper. The one who covered most bases would be the winner. Snoopy had the advantage. It was hard to pitch him strikes and he kept stealing bases. In the end it was Snoopy who was champion. His prize was a fishing rod. Some complained that Snoopy was just an opportunist.

Next was the fishing event. Everyone, including Snoopy had a fishing pole. Linus said, “Woodstock, Where are the worms?”

Woodstock hemmed and hawed. Finally he admitted that he found three worms, but temptation was stronger than the promise, so he had eaten the bait.

Patty said, “Maybe a piece of marshmallow would serve as bait.”

No one was catching anything. There wasn’t even a bite and then surprise! Lucy exclaimed, “I’ve got something.”

Everyone stopped to watch. “Pull it on shore.” Lucy did. Out of the water came an old boot.

Snoopy grinned, “That should make good boot steaks.”

“You are so droll Snoopy.”

John had fired up the pit and it was just right for the wiener roast. Everyone had two wieners. Snoopy asked if he could have more.

"No, No! Everyone gets just two." Snoopy turned to Woodstock, "Give me your wieners and I'll help you find worms. My nose is especially sharp these days."

Snoopy had two extras, but there was disgust. "Snoopy you are a fraud and a cheat. I hope you get a good stomach ache."

John announced, "I've spoken to the storekeeper and there will be an ice cream for each of you."

"Hurray and thank you John."

It was time to go back. Everyone found a seat. Girls chose the front seats and the boys preferred the back ones. John turned the key. There was a grinding noise and a back fire and they were off for Olds. Charlie noticed that there was no one sitting with the Red Head. He was off like a flash.

"May I sit beside you?"

"If you wish."

Peppermint Patty said, "Charlie you are a regular skirt chaser."

Charlie smiled. For once he wasn't a loser.

The day wasn't over for the guys at the back. They decided to make noise imitations. They would moo like a cow. Bark like a dog. Snoopy said it was a poor imitation of a bark. Then he made a noise of a siren. John was sure a police cruiser was following so he pulled to the side of the road.

"Snoopy, it ain't funny!"

The bus rolled into the Deer Meadow yard. When he turned off the key there was a bang and a cloud of smoke. Yes, the picnic ended with a bang. The Peanut Gang said the picnic was a success and everyone had a good time. Snoopy burped as if to agree. Charlie was in Seventh Heaven. Just to sit beside the Red Head girl was for him the prize of the day.

19.
DANNY AND LEE ANN

MOUNTAIN VIEW COLLEGIATE AND THE ADJACENT College are alma mater to more than a thousand graduates. Students who walked the halls of these institutions were from rural and small town communities. Their culture was rooted in nature, the land, Christian values, and hard work. Besides the studies many of the students formed enduring friendships. Some even found their life partners in this setting.

In 1990 two students of very different backgrounds came together in friendship and love. George Proctor the Science teacher had drawn up a seating plan. By circumstance and chance he placed Danny O'Keefe and Lee Ann Chan side by side. The attraction was mutual. Good looks and smiles were a good introduction, but it was the compatible personalities that formed a lasting bond. For two years classmates always observed that those two seats were reserved for Danny and Lee. On one occasion Danny asked Lee, "What are you doing on Saturday?"

She would have liked to reply that she was free and anxious to go with him, but there were obstacles in the way. Danny and Lee Ann knew that their budding romance could not go any further because their families were so different and would not approve. The head of the Chan family was Michael, the Loan

Officer at the Mountain View Credit Union. His wife Daria worked as a receptionist for a dentist, Dr. Rose Choy. The oldest daughter Susan was beginning her studies in veterinarian medicine. Lee Ann was planning for a pharmacy career. The youngest was David who was thinking of computers. The most important member was Micheal's mother May Chan. A few years after her husband's death in China, she came to head the Chan family in Canada. She had inherited money, and she could speak English, and drive a car. In the Chinese culture all important decisions were deferred to the eldest. May Chan had the last word.

The O'Keefe family was headed by Andrew O'Keefe. He and a partner, Steven Dunnigan were owners of the A&S Electric. Andrew's wife, Madeline worked at the hospital as a LPN. The oldest, Martha was married to Jed Parsons. They had a child Barry. The second son was Jeremiah who had begun his novitiate at St. Thomas More Seminary. He was aspiring to be a priest. Next was Danny who wanted to be an engineer. After Danny was Scott. The youngest was Barbara. The O'Keefe family were very devoted to the RC Church. They attended all the masses and observed all the sacraments. Andrew was Grand Knight of The Knights of Columbus. Rev. Fr. Damien Sullivan, the parish priest was a very frequent guest at their home.

After graduation in 1992 Danny and Lee Ann went to the University of Calgary. He choose engineering and she choose pharmacy. Grandmother May Chan went with Lee Ann and lived in an apartment close to the University. Danny and Lee Ann had no dates, but once a week they met at the Arts cafeteria. They often talked about their future. Danny asked Lee if she would convert. Her answer was no. Further he asked her if both stepped away from their culture and beliefs would she marry him. The answer was probably. After two years into their courses each consulted their mentors. Danny talked to Fr. Sullivan.

This was his statement, " The R.C. Church began with Jesus. We are tolerant of other Christian sects, but do not recognize their authority. We do not approve of mixed marriages. We are sceptical of conversions for convenience. Danny my son, think carefully about your choice. Pray for divine guidance and may God Bless You."

Lee Ann Chan went to her Grandmother for counsel.

This is what she said, "The Chinese civilization is one of the oldest on earth. Thousands of years ago the Chinese left behind their Gods and their myths. They kept some of their superstitions. For guidance, the Chinese refer to the wisdom teachings of Lao Tse, Confucius, and Buddha. To chose Danny as your partner would be like going back to the Dark Ages. At first he will treat you like Royalty, but when he gets tired of you he will look for another woman. You are not going to be a winner if you choose Danny."

Danny and Lee were disappointed that their families showed so much objection to their marriage plans. They decided to focus on their studies. Two years later both graduated with distinction and they had jobs. Danny with Suncor Energy as Project Manager. Lee Ann had a deferred job at Rexall Drugs. Both were now independent and they decided to ignore family objections and get married. The families remained silent, neither congratulating or objecting.

It was Martha Parsons (O'Keefe) and Susan Chan that got together and decided to do something. They went to each family and said, "It is silly and shameful the way we are acting. We are feeding on our own prejudices. We should rejoice that Danny and Lee Ann have found love. Both families decided to change their attitudes. They would hold an engagement party at the Evergreen Center and show approval to the young couple. To the party they invited relatives, friends, neighbours, etc. They found a Caterer to prepare a lunch. They engaged some Entertainment. They even considered releasing two doves, but it would cause a commotion at the Evergreen Center. Irene Dugan brought her large Irish harp and sang a number of Irish love songs. From Calgary four teenage girls from the China Club dressed in colourful tunics performed violin music– Ode To Love by Mozrat and Handle's Ode To Joy, plus a few more classical tunes. Danny and Lee Ann came in holding hands. Lee Ann was dressed in an expensive Chinese gown.

Danny said, "I give you this engagement ring as a token of my love."

Lee Ann gave Danny a little book that had inspirational quotations.

She said, "I give this as a token of my love for you for now and forever."

Parents and others came to congratulate the couple. Some brought cards, flowers, and candy. The lunch was delicious and everyone felt uplifted.

A week after the engagement party May Chan announced that she wanted to go back to China for a visit before her relatives and friends passed away. She wanted Lee Ann to accompany her as a helper.

She said, "We will be back before the end of June and there will still be two months before the wedding." Danny was not particularly pleased, but he accepted the plan.

Two weeks later, Danny tried to contact Lee Ann, but there was no reply. He asked the Chan family to establish contact. They also failed. The end of June came and Grandma and Lee Ann had not returned. What happened? Danny and the Chans contacted the Consulate in Shanghai because Lee Ann was a Canadian citizen.

The Consulate was obliged to find out what had happened. A week later the Consulate contacted the Chan family. This is what they reported, Lee Ann was working for Hwang Ho Pharma and Grandma Chan had died two weeks earlier. In questioning Lee Ann, she did not remember or know anything about Canada. She did not know of any family in Canada. She did not know of any prospective fiance.

At the end of September Danny flew to Shanghai and met Lee Ann. She did not recognize him as anyone she knew. She was polite, but perplexed. There was even a dinner date. Danny speculated that maybe she wanted to be out of the engagement. He also left her a number of photographs and returned to Canada.

Lee Ann was puzzled. The person in the photograph looked like her but it could have been a double. At work she asked whether anyone knew about memory loss. One of the employees mentioned a hypnotist who was able to manipulate willing subjects. There was one other mystery that had no answer. Why couldn't she remember those missing years? Did her Grandma have something to do about her memory loss? Why would she? On her days off she began to go to Chinese herbal/medicine stores. Did they sell something that would cause a memory loss? Most stores did not know much about such a medicine. She found a store where the young owner said we do not have such a compound, but I will ask my Grandpa.

"Grandpa come here. We need you." A very old man shuffled from the back. He said that he remembered that there was such a compound, but he would check. From the drawer he pulled out a tattered old book and began to leaf through it. Yes there was a compound that would induce hypnosis.

Lee Ann asked, "Is there a herbal compound that would restore memory?"

"Yes, there is."

"Does your store sell any of these herbal compounds?"

The young man replied, "No, but you might try some of the other stores."

For the next two weeks she inquired in quite a number of herbal stores, but no one carried those medicines. She went back to the store with the old Grandpa.

She asked, “Do you know where these exotic herbal medicines come from?”

“I seem to remember that they come from a place in the Himalayas.”

At the Consulate she asked for assistance. She wanted to go to where the exotic herbs were grown. The Consulate provided her with a letter and suggested a person who knew Chinese and Tibetan languages. This trip would be very costly, but her Grandma had left her a fortune.

With her companion she began the trip to Tibet. They travelled by boat, bus, and train. They finally reached Lhasa. At the main monastery they asked to see Dalai Llama. He agreed to see them. He was very interested in Canada and he sympathized with her memory problem,. He appointed one of the monks to accompany them to the Shang La Valley where there was a monastery that grew exotic herbs. The trip might be three or four days. She hired a porter and two yaks. She would always remember that trip to the Shang La Valley. It was a trail along a mountain side. There were cliffs above you and cliffs below you. Sometimes they had to clear rocks off the trail. In places the trail was only four feet wide. After four days, There it was! Down below was the village and on the opposite bank was a Tibetan monastery. They arranged for accommodations in the village. The following morning they began a trek to the monastery.

At the Monastery they rang a bell. After a while a monk in Saffron robes came and asked, “How can we help you?” They told the monk the nature of their mission. He replied, “That would be Sun Duc, and I will go get him.”

After sometime the monk called Sun Duc came to talk to them. After they told him what they were after, he replied, “Yes we have that herbal plant. We grow about thirty plants that are not found anywhere else in the world. We store them in a cave attached to the monastery and we sell them to the

China trade. Do you want Stargrad that is designed to restore your memory?"

"Yes we do."

He put his finger on the table and they put a fifty yuan note on the table. Then another fifty was placed. He kept his finger on the table until four fifties were there. He picked up the money and said, "I will go get that herbal medicine for you."

After a long while he returned with two jars. From the large jar he withdrew five pieces and put them into the smaller jar. "When you decide to take the medicine follow my instructions precisely. A very light breakfast or lunch and a fast for the rest of the day. You will steep each piece and drink it before noon. On the third day you will begin to see a change. On the fourth day your former memory will have been restored. If it hasn't, use the fifth stick."

Lee Ann and her helper returned to Shanghi. She took the herbal medicine and recovered her memory. After she recovered her memory she decided to return to Canada. She put her matters in order: job, apartment, and her banking.

After Danny's trip to China he concluded that Lee Ann wanted to get out of the marriage. He went back to his work and his schedule of two weeks at the Oil Sands, one week in Calgary and one week free. Quite often in his free week he went back to his family.

The O'Keefes traditionally held a Christmas party for their closest friends. Father Sullivan had a plan. A young woman named Marilyn Stevens had joined the Congregation. She had taken a position with the Martinson & Harder Law firm. He asked the O'Keefes if he could bring Marilyn so that she could meet some new people and the family. They agreed. At the party Farther Sullivan was looking for one special person. When Danny came in, Father Sullivan took Marilyn by the hand and approached Danny. "Danny, I want you to meet a special person. This is Marilyn Stevens. She just joined the

Law Martinson & Harder. Marilyn, I want you to meet Danny O'Keefe, King of the Oil Sands."

Danny was not particularly looking for a girlfriend, but he found Marilyn intriguing. She was attractive, perfectly dressed and she had a lot of self assurance. Marilyn found Danny handsome, with a pleasant personality and success written all over him. What followed was more dates, dinner parties, a choral concert in Didsbury and a trip to Calgary to watch the Christmas Carol. In the weeks and the months that followed the romance grew and by July they decided to get married.

In August Lee Ann sent a note to her family. "I'm coming home!" After she returned, word spread and Danny heard that she was back. Marilyn knew about Danny's former engagement. She told Danny, "Lee Ann was your promised fiancee, and if you wish to go back to her, I will withdraw the promise you made to me."

Danny did not reply. A sense of guilt overwhelmed him.. He had made a solemn promise and now he had failed.

Lee Ann's family asked what she intended to do regarding Danny. She said, "It would be up to Danny to make the move."

Father Sullivan conducted the wedding of Danny and Marilyn. When he came to that part of the wedding service which said, "If there be anyone who believes this marriage should not proceed let him come forward or forever hold his peace."

In the audience all heads turned to the door. Why? Did they expect a beautiful Chinese girl dressed in a gorgeous gown to come down the aisle? No one appeared and the anticipation fell like deflated balloon. There was disappointment but also relief. A year later Danny and Marilyn had a little girl. Marilyn suggested they call her Lee Ann. Danny said he had enough guilt.

Lee Ann decided to resume her pharmacological studies at the University of Alberta in Edmonton. After two years she received her doctorate. She was now Dr. Lee Ann Chan

Professor of Pharmacology. During those two years she made many friends and was happy in her state of life. She began a special project. She was collecting material to write a book called, "Folk Medicine".

When Madeline Susan O'Keefe was five years old her mother Marilyn, told a friend of a special incident. She was sitting in the living room watching television when she thought she heard a sob coming from the bedroom. She opened the door and saw Danny on his knees sobbing, "Lee Ann, where are you?" Quietly she closed the door and left that moment for Danny.

EPILOGUE

Sometimes a love is so profound and tragic that its' story lives on forever and ever.

20.
PRESUMED DEAD

THREE MEN SAT IN A LOUNGE OF THE HOLIDAY INN AT Hinton, Alberta. They were there to discuss their annual fishing trip to Skookum Lake. There was a doubt that the trip would take place, because two of them were having marital problems and the third was planning to drop his girlfriend. After some talk they decided to go ahead with the trip. It might be enjoyable and palliative.

On his way to get his geology degree Bill Stadnyk pinched every penny that came his way. Once he earned his degree, Energy Companies were eager to hire him. He had more money, but he still kept his parsimonious ways. The first cheque he earned he married Jennifer Power. The couple had two daughters, Sherry and Penny. Five years after his graduation, financiers called him to their suite at the Palliser Hotel.

"We are forming a midsize Energy Company. We will provide the capital and we want you in. We will start with giving you a bundle of options. You will be the Second Vice President and you will be the Operations Manager. You will be paid cash or given options."

Once Bill got his position as a corporate man, Jennifer thought she should reflect the style of a wealthy corporate wife, driving a Cadillac convertible instead of an eight year old

Honda. Her girls should be wearing designer clothes, instead of discounted clothes. Bill responded by saying, "Personal achievement is more important than looking for ways to spend someone else's money."

Behind his back they called him cheap, a scrooge, and sometimes even a jerk. Jennifer planned that if she couldn't get more money through the front door she would just buy the things she wanted and put them on the credit cards.

Bill said nothing, but just went to the card companies and put a limit. When she came to pay for some items she wanted, the transactions would not go through. It was so humiliating. She was being treated like a shop lifter.

After one of these incidents she was thinking, *Maybe a divorce would solve her problem, but she dismissed the idea. She wanted a well that would not go dry.*

One summer day she went to Samson's Furniture to look at some end tables. There were no customers and the salesman had gone home for the day. So it was just her and the manager, Craig Winston. They talked about furniture and then they spoke of their woes. Craig said his girlfriend dumped him after he bought her a $1,000 engagement ring. Jennifer said her husband treated her like dirt. After this encounter there were more clandestine meetings. This progressed into a full blown affair. They realized this could not go on. The plan was that she would file for divorce and strip Bill of his wealth, then marry Craig.

The next time Bill came home Jennifer said, "Our marriage is going no where I am not happy and I want a divorce." Bill replied, "I know I have been a poor husband, but it was not with intent. I have an emergency up north, give me a week and I will cooperate with you."

"You better keep your word!"

Bill took his suitcase and left. He didn't go up north. He went to a hotel and called his lawyer.

"I want you to transfer any cash into options that cannot be redeemed for seven years. I'm willing to pay support for my two daughters. I'm not sure about Jennifer. My parents helped to buy the house. Jennifer contributed nothing financially. After the divorce put the house up for sale. She can keep the car."

When her lawyer began a discovery he knew what was up. Jennifer talked to Craig. Both did not want to wait seven years. They would accept the divorce on Bill's terms. A few days later Bill called his old friend, Nestor Timryk. He told him his story. Nestor wrote a letter to the Samson's Company, that Craig Winston was having affairs with a number of married women. There were scandals and trouble brewing.

The Company called Craig. He said, "There was only one affair."

The Company said, "One is too many. Scandals and rumours are bad for business. You are fired! You have caused damage already there will be no severance pay."

Craig called Jennifer with the news. "I have no job and no money. I'm going to Edmonton and if something turns up I will call you."

Jennifer had no money either so she went job hunting. She got a part time job at Tim Hortons and the Ramada. As she was scrubbing toilets at the Ramada she mused, "*Why have I been punished? I've been a good wife. It's all Bill's fault,that jerk.*"

Mike Morisey began his career as a Cat driver. He was good. Next, he borrowed some money and bought his own Cat. He began to win contracts and his one Cat, became Morisey's Construction. With money in his pocket he had a fling with Cathy Jones and Cathy said her daughter Susan was his. He agreed to support his daughter. Then he went on to marry Teena Darfur and they had two children, James and Brittany. At the time of the meeting at the Holiday Inn he had lost a major contract. Half of his equipment was idle, but still costing money.

His wife berated him. "You have money for someone else's child, but not ours. What kind of an operator are you? If you don't turn this around I'm leaving!"

Douglas Copperfield had graduated with a Science degree. His interest was in environment and conservation. He got a job with the Department of Natural Resources. He had money and a girlfriend Megan McLeod. A marriage was in the offing. He took her to Richardson's Jewellers to look at some rings. The Jeweller set out a number at various prices:$200, $500, $1,000, $3,000, and $5,000. Douglas was prepared to spend $500. When it came to the $500 ring he asked Megan, "How do you like it?"

She replied, "It's so cheap and so tacky."

Douglas was deflated. In his mind he thought if the ring is cheap, he must be cheap. This girl was not going to be for him.

Section 2 Tom Gates was a drifter. He had come from New Brunswick and stopped at Hinton where he fashioned a lifestyle that satisfied him. In the summer he worked at construction. In the winter there was UI/EI. He was always on the look out to make a little extra money. He lived in an old trailor in the section of Hinton that the residents called London. If Hinton's London needed a king, Tom was a good candidate. He also had an old truck. The police did not like Tom and he didn't like them. They were sure he was supplying the dry Indian Reserve 461 with liquor. They could never catch him. There were rumours that he was a fence for stolen goods. When a radio was stolen an informer suggested it might be Tom. They searched his property and they found a radio in the dumpster in the alley. In defence he said that radio was not on his property and he knew nothing about it.

They saw a deer hide in the back of his truck and charged him with hunting out of season.

He said, "It was road kill and I picked it up at the side of the road and if they looked they would see no bullet holes in the hide."

They charged him with driving with a broken tail light.

In defence he said, "I was driving to the garage." The mechanic corroborated Tom's story.

One evening the police were patrolling the strip where girls of the evening made a living. They spotted Tom's truck. He picked up a girl and they followed. He stopped at the A&W and the girl got out. He just had given a girl he knew a lift to the restaurant.

This London of Hinton had a community center. It was "Bull Moose Tavern". In the Tavern you could get a coffee, sandwich, a beer, and some bootleg liquor. There were two pool tables and three card tables at the back where you could play five dollar limit poker. The Bull Moose was where residents exchanged information and made deals. Tom became interested in an old timer. Pierre Fontaine was a trapper. Pierre said, "This is my last year in the bush. I am going to get my old age pension. I will live in London and enjoy life."

Tom wanted a change and he thought a trap line might be the answer. He said, "Pierre take me as your partner for the winter. Teach me to trap, hunt, and fix skidoos. In the spring after we sell the furs we just might make a deal."

He enjoyed the winter with Pierre. He learned much. He even learned to speak French and Beaver. In the spring Pierre asked, "Are you going to buy my property?"

Tom's response was, "Let's make a swap. My trailor and truck for your trap line and property." The deal was sealed.

Normally Tom would be going out there in October, but he was eager to try out some new ideas. He hired a person with pack horses to take some heavy materials to the cabin. He also hired a float plane to take some extra materials including some grain, six hens, and a rooster. He spent the summer building fences and sheds. He was planning to bring some goats the following year. In winter he was on the trap line and spent evenings skinning and preparing pelts.

In May of the following year a float plane took him out and he sold his furs. He returned to his cabin and bought those three goats. He was satisfied he had everything except a companion, preferably a female. He couldn't think of any woman in London who would like to come to live out there in isolation. He thought a native girl might be more willing.

In the Indian village of Beaverton were two families that came each June to a summer camp one mile from Tom's cabin. Moses Samson and his wife Livia had six children. The oldest Francine was fifteen. Jonah Keeper and his wife Agnes had four children. The oldest was fourteen. They would spend June to mid August catching fish, smoking it, tanning hides, picking berries, and mushrooms. Everyone enjoyed the shallow waters of Crooked Lake.

In mid June Tom decided to pay a friendly visit to his neighbours. He took a dozen eggs and a bottle of whisky. The eggs were for the women and the whisky for the men. After much conversation Tom said, "Moses I'm looking for a girl to be my wife."

Moses said, "No wife here."

Tom responded, "What about that big girl there?"

Moses said, "She is only fifteen."

Livia interrupted. "Thirteen."

Tom said, "Thirteen is too young, but fifteen might be okay."

Before he left he said, "I will come again maybe the girl will get older. I think her father will get some money."

"Good, and you bring some whisky next time."

Two weeks later Tom was there with some eggs and the whisky. He did not mention anything about a wife, but the two families were anxious to hear what he had to offer. Finally he said, "Is Francine getting any older?"

"Yes, She is fifteen but almost sixteen. How much you pay?"

"Fifty."

"Not enough."

"Seventy five."

"Not enough."

"One hundred."

"Not enough."

"That is all I got!"

"Maybe you have something else?"

"Alright it will be a hundred and a shotgun."

"Good, Francine will make you a very good wife."

Francine bundled up a few of her meagre possessions and followed Tom. The older women had talked to her and said, "It wouldn't be so bad to be Tom's wife even if he was twenty years older."

At first Francine was shy and bewildered. Soon she became interested in her new home, the chickens and goats. She opened up and Tom was pleased. She could do so many things. She could cook, clean, sew, look after the animals, and cut wood.

For Christmas he said they would go into Beaverton. They made the eighteen mile trip with a skidoo and a sled. Francine was happy to see her family. Livia and Agnes took Francine aside and told her what was going to happen. They prepared a bundle of flannel, blankets, baby clothes, and bottles. They also said that when the pains started Tom should come and get one of them. Irrespective, Livia said she would come about the middle of March and be there.

Section 3

It was the summer that little Moses was one year old that a horrendous tragedy occurred. Bill Stadnyk, Mike Morisey, and Douglas Copperfield hired a pilot, Darrin Tower to fly them to

Skookum Lodge. The take off was successful and the Cessna 172 headed North. Just over Crooked Lake the engine faltered and the pilot tried to land on the water. He was unsuccessful and the plane plunged into the forest that separated the Indian Camp from Tom's cabin. People in both places saw the crash and the flames emerging from the trees. Moses told his two older sons, "Go see what happened!"

They returned with pale faces and in shock. "The plane is burning and there are three people trapped. One man is on the ground and he may be dead."

"Run and get Tom Gates!"

When Tom arrived he saw the scene. The man on the ground was badly injured and had lost lots of blood. Tom ordered Moses and Jonah to get two poles and with a piece of the air plane they made a stretcher. They carried the injured man to Tom's cabin. They made a make shift bed. Tom cleaned off the gash and set the broken leg as best he could. He forced a couple tumblers of whisky into the stranger. "Moses and Jonah you are going to hold this man down while I do some sewing." He poured some whisky over the gash. Then with a needle and common thread he sewed the two parts together. He told Moses, "Livia and Angus should make Indian medicine and Maxine should come help Francine."

The women came and applied a poultice of something like green mud. They wrapped it with a cloth. The two younger women cared for this survivor for days. When he was delirious they would apply cold towels. They fed him poached eggs and broth. After a week and a half he became conscious and began to regain strength. They learned his name was Douglas Copperfield. He wanted to inform the authorities that he was alive.

Tom said, "It is impossible, there is no radio."

When the two families returned to Beaverton, they would took Douglas with them.

When the flight to Skookum Lake did not arrive, there was concern. Search planes flew over the route from Hinton to Skookum Lake. After a week the conclusion was that the plane had gone down and all the men were PRESUMED DEAD.

In August Douglas and the two families returned to Beaverton. A plane came to take Douglas to Hinton. Before he left he said he would be back the following June and hold a grand picnic with all the people.

Following Douglas's return another plane carrying two investigators and a reporter named Chris Thornton came to Tom's landing. They investigated the crash site and picked up the remains.

The following year the people at the summer camp and at Tom's cabin kept watching for a plane. Towards the end of June the plane came in and everyone rushed to Tom's landing wanting to help. There were boxes and crates to move up to Tom's yard. He had anticipated a wiener roast. Tom had the fire pit ready. The fire had been started and when the coals were still hot two older boys were assigned to do the roasting of the wieners. They handed the roasted wieners to Livia and Agnes who had the buttered buns ready. Everyone had as many hot dogs as they wanted and there was a lot of pop. The speciality was ice cream. The older girls had the honor of scooping the ice cream into the cones. Everyone could eat as many as they wanted as long as the ice cream lasted.

When everyone had enough Jonah announced, "Now that you are full to the top it is time to shake it down. Grab your partner for a square." There were enough people for two separate squares.

"Bow to your partner and circle.

All to the center.

All back where you were-swing. Once again do it right. You will dance all through the night.

Single file circle left.

Now to the right.

Boys to the left girls to the right-circle-meet your partner-swing Lets do it again Single file to the right. All men left Meet your partner swing Couple one do your thing Circle once-circle twice-hawk stay in, birdie fly out Circle-birdie stay in-hawk fly out-circle and swing That's it. That's all."

Doing the square dance was not strange to these people, because they held weekly dances in the assembly room at school. In between the energetic square dances Moses and Jonah would play slower tunes. Jonah on the banjo would play and sing "O Susannah" and everyone was transported to the South and cotton fields. Moses would play the "Red River Jig" and they were transported to the Red River Colony and the settlement of Metis pioneers.

After everyone was tuckered out, Douglas Copperfield spoke, "You are the people that saved my life, I will be forever grateful. I wish to say that all of you from this day forward are my dearest friends. I shall try my best to come and visit you each year at the end of June. My pilot is urging me to go, but I have one last task."

He opened some boxes and drew out small gifts for each of them. For the men he gave pipes and pouches of tobacco. For the boys he gave jackknives. For the girls he gave comb sets, beads, and scarfs. For the four women who cared for him, he gave a little more — skirts, blouses, beads, sashes, and scarves. For the little ones there were toys.

"Now I say good bye until I come to see you again."

He and the pilot walked down the hill to the landing. Tom urged everyone to sing "He's a Jolly Good Fellow". Everyone watched as the plane taxied, gained speed, and lifted off. All the watchers experienced a feeling of regret that he was leaving.

After the visit of the investigators, the names of the three who perished, were now officially declared dead. It was stated that Douglas Copperfield was the sole survivor. After the death of the three, there had to be some legal follow up. The pilot Andrew Sexton, had no estate and his girlfriend moved on, got married and had a family. Mike Morisey the contractor, left behind some debts and the Company had to declare bankruptcy. There were no funds to distribute. His survivors went on to find jobs and new mates. Bill Stadnyk left a considerable estate and his mother Mary was the Executor. She mailed cheques to his daughters until they reached eighteen. His daughters showed no interest in connecting to their father's family. Mary established a scholarship fund for those aspiring to study geology. The biggest monument to Bill was in the town of Smoky Lake. The little Orthodox Church was getting run down. Mary had it dismantled and a beautiful new church was built. It was consecrated as Saint Basil Ukrainian Orthodox Church. There was a plaque that stated this Church was erected in the ever lasting memory of Bill Stadnyk. The Church had all the features of an Orthodox Church– except something new in the vestibule. To the right and to the left were dioramas. To the right was a pioneer homestead with a pump jack and a derrick in the distance. The left diorama showed Bill Stadnyk pointing to three big storage tanks on a hill. The name Neptune was printed on each. As part of the memorial to Bill, Mary set aside funds for an annual requiem mass to be held at the date of his death. After the service the Priest and the Cantor led a procession to the grave of Bill Stadnyk. With kudilla and holy water they blessed the grave site. "God Have Mercy, God Have Mercy, God Have Mercy and take Bill Stadnyk's soul to your bosom."

The procession went back to the Church and the Priest announced there would be a meal for everyone at the Smoky Lake National Hall. This tribute was repeated in the following years. There was still considerable funds left and they were discussing about building a recreation center in memory of Bill Stadnyk.

Section 4 Fifteen years ago I Chris Thornton, was with the investigators at the Crooked Lake air plane crash. Now I am working for the Edmonton Journal and my vacation will begin in a few days. I said, "Maggie, this year we are going to alter our vacation plans. I have a mission and obsession. I want to go back and see the people and place of fifteen years ago."

"But you promised we would be going to Saskatchewan."

"I know, but there will still be time to go there."

"Alright this time, but I don't want you to be flirting with brown eyed girls."

"I will be the model of propriety."

I drove to the Hinton air strip. Two float planes were bobbing in the water. To the man at the first plane, I said "do you ever go to Crooked Lake?"

"As a matter of fact I'm going there in four days."

"Can I be a passenger on your flight?"

"No, I already have a passenger. I have reached the limit of freight. But go to the office there, that other plane may be free that day."

At the office the lady had her headphones on. She was talking to a pilot somewhere.

She took off her headphones and said, "I'm sorry to have kept you waiting, but what can I do for you?"

"I want to go to Tom's landing at Crooked Lake."

"Yes we can take you there on the second plane."

"How much will it cost?"

"Three hundred and fifty. You can take 500 pounds of freight."

"Can you suggest articles of freight that would be appropriate?"

"Go to the pilot of the second plane and he may have a suggestion."

As I approached the pilot, I stopped there was something familiar.

The pilot laughed and said, "You are not the first one that has seen something familiar about me. I am Jeremiah Samson, Son of Moses Samson."

"Jeremiah, what a surprise! You will be taking me to Crooked Lake and Tom's landing and would you suggest some articles of freight."

"Up there they need everything. You can take flour, sugar, beans, rice, salt, and Tom Gates is always building something so bring a lot of nails. It will be picnic day and some nice treats will be appreciated."

Four days later two planes landed and taxied to Tom's landing. There was all kinds of excitement. It was picnic day. What was the second plane for? I recognized very few, but I did see Tom Gates. He aged and had white hair. I also noted that Moses Samson and Jonah Keeper with their wives had been brought to the picnic site on ATV's. There were also four new couples.

I asked, "Where is Francine?"

One of the children shouted, "Mom, someone wants to see you."

The last time I saw her she was a gangly fifteen year old. Now she was mature and still slim.

She wore slacks and a blouse. She had a beautiful smile as she approached me. We talked about her family and she pointed out her children.

"There is Moses almost sixteen and taller than his father. Desiree is fourteen, Maxine is eleven, Joshua nine and Sammy is eight."

The picnic followed the same pattern as in other years– wiener roast, a dance, and gifts. Moses and Jonah played the same square dance tunes, but the majority of the dance was given to new musicians on electric guitars powered by batteries. There was a girl drummer. There were new dancers who were just as excited with the new tunes.

I had a chance to talk to Tom Gates.

He said, "Up to now the children were doing home schooling, but this fall they would go to Hinton where they would take regular schooling. Francine would be going with them. It's going to be lonely for me, but I might ask one of the Samson boys to spend the winter with me."

As the sun was setting, the pilot Jeremiah Samson urged me to go. It had been a good day and my mission was complete. I was quite impressed with the close relationship of Douglas Copperfield and the people of this community. There was so much love and gratitude. What I had witnessed was an affirmation that — THE SUN WILL RISE TOMORROW.

* * *

Change is the constant. Whether it is an individual, a group, a nation, or the world. Change marches in the footprints of time. Periodically the pace is interrupted by episodes of triumph as well as tragedy. The story you have read presents unique characters. Despite changes and obstacles, they march with confidence into the future.

21.

SHANGHAID

"GENTLEMEN MAY I JOIN YOU?"

"There are no gentlemen here, but if you buy a round, you may take the fourth chair."

"Bar Keep, set us four."

"My name is Colin Masters."

The other three introduced themselves.

"And where be you heading?"

"I'm going to Port Hawkesbury."

"Port Hawkesbury? I heard there is no one there, but one old fisherman."

"Well it's not very big, but my family lives there and I have a lady friend."

"Well if I had a lady friend I would live anywhere, The Arctic or the Tropics."

"I'm wondering if you know of any boat heading north east to Port Hawkesbury?"

The three men stared at each other as if they knew of no boat sailing north east. One of the new friends shouted, "Hey Jack our friend needs a way to get to Port Hawkesbury." No one immediately replied.

Another customer said, "There's a mail boat going north east at midnight."

"Jack, another four. Our friend has time till midnight."

One eyed Jack Blackmore, was the owner and sole operator of the "Jolly Roger", a seedy saloon on Harbour Street. His place would not win awards for cleanliness or decor. It didn't matter. His customers were sailors off ships that anchored in Lunenburg. Jack kept order in his place by the use of salty language and his fists. One time when there was a free for all and chairs were flying the police arrived. Jack said, "Look here, with one eye I can't tell who is who. I may just flatten one of you. So stay away. I'll handle things my way."

"Colin, where are you coming from?"

"I've been two years a sailor aboard the Graf Spitzbergen. It is one of the newer ships- sails and engines. I got tired of shovelling coal and unfurling sails. I'm going home to marry my sweetheart, Barbara McNeil."

"You Black Guard of this scurvy place, our friend is going to get married. We should send him to Hawkesbury in a proper fashion!"

At that moment a sailor came in and handed Jack a note. The note read "4". Jack knew what that meant. He fixed four drinks and came to Colin's table. "These drinks are to celebrate a coming wedding and they are on the House."

After a while the four got drowsy. Four sailors came in and escorted them to a boat and then to a schooner. This was a shanghai as neat you would ever see.

The three masted schooner was named "Grey Dolphin". It was a whaler and all set to sail for the southern seas. Captain Ned Melroe gave orders. "Raise anchor, unfurl the sails we're off to the sunny south." Colin had got as far as Lunenburg and now he was on board the Grey Dolphin headed south.

Two years ago in Port Hawkesbury Jack McDonald spoke to his red haired daughter.

"Barbara my dear daughter, you should marry Angus Stewart. He is an iron worker and he has his own shop. Marry

Angus and you will not go hungry and there be many bairns healthy and strong."

"Father, I have talked to you before about Angus. Yes he is a good man, but my heart is on one Colin Martins."

"Barbara, this one you call Colin is as poor as a church mouse. I will not have you marry a penniless vagabond."

Jack McDonald called Colin and said, "You are not my choice as husband for my Barbara. But I will not stand in the way of a head strong lass. But to you I say you better have some green in that purse or I will not permit her to marry you." That is how Colin after two years at sea was at the Jolly Roger in Lunenburg harbour.

The Grey Dolphin had a crew of thirty. Captain Ned Melroe was master. He did take his turn at the wheel but most of the time he was in his cabin, drunk. Navigation was left to his niece Debra March or the second mate, James Smith. The first mate was Igor Stroganoff also referred to as "The Mad Russian". Igor was as wide as he was tall. His arms were like telephone poles ans fists like the hams of a large hog. He gave orders and kept order. There was no insubordination or back talk. Anyone who tried, did it only once.

The first stop was in the Bahamas. They took on drinking water and a few provisions. They were also caught in the tropical doldrums. The sails were limp and there wasn't even a breeze. After a week, a wind came and the ship moved. At Rio they took on six casks of rum. At Buenos Aires they packed barrels of beef and salted it. Then south to their destination. They knew when they had reached the hunting waters when Jimmy in the crow's nest hollered, "There she blows!"

Everyone moved into high gear. Four boats were launched with four men in each. Fires were lit. Men would harpoon a whale. It would drag the boat until it played out. The whale carcass was secured so it would not sink and then towed to the mother ship. It was fastened to the hull of the Grey Dolphin. A sailor with a rifle kept the sharks away. The carcass was hoisted on deck. Men with knives cut off slabs of blubber and these went into cauldrons. The oil was poured into barrels.

When each barrel was full the cooper fitted the top and sealed it with wax. The barrel went down into the hold. This went on until all forty barrels were full and sealed.

The Captain said, "Well done me buckaroos. We shall stay in these waters for two more days."

As in the story of "Moby Dick", Captain Melroe had a hatred for a large blue whale with four harpoons in it's back. The Captain called the whale, "The Blue Devil". In a previous voyage the Blue Devil had smashed one of the boats and four men were lost.

The Captain, sober these days had a score to settle. Besides harpoons, men were given rifles.

They scoured the sea in four directions, but there was no sign of the Blue Devil. "Maybe the next time."

"Raise anchor and we're off to the Pacific." It was a rough passage through the Straits of Magellan- Gales and high seas. Men swore and prayed. Would they ever see home again? Then the ship entered calmer waters of the Pacific and they headed north.

The voyage north was uneventful. They stopped at several ports to replenish supplies: Valparaiso, Bogota, San Diego, and San Francisco their destination. San Francisco at that time was a wild port town. There were ships from all over the world. There were men from many countries. There were girls who took their money.

Captain Melroe announced he had forty barrels of whale oil. "Give me your best bid."

Colin like the other men went ashore. There were saloons everywhere. There were cable cars and China town. As yet there was no bridge to Oakland. There was a train to the east coast, but if he went he would lose his share of the whale oil profits, so he stayed. He wrote a letter to Barbara. He was careful as San Francisco was famous for shanghai operations.

After a week the Grey Dolphin sailed again, retracing its' previous route. Once again in the Straits the sea was violent and the Grey Dolphin was tossed around. When they were through, the seas became calmer. They were glad to hear, "There she blows!"

The men worked faster and their mood was better, because they were going home. Once again Captain Melroe set aside two days to hunt for his nemesis, but it was no where to be seen.

"Raise anchors, we're bound for home!" Even the Mad Russian had a smile on his bearded face.

Before we leave the high seas, here is a brief note about Debra Marsh. Having a woman on many sailing ships, but particularly whalers, was considered bad luck. Men would not sign on as crew. Debra's parents died when she was a small child. Her Uncle and Aunt who had no children adopted her.

She was their daughter.

Her Uncle Ned taught her seamanship and navigation. On board when Captain Melroe was drunk, it was Debra March who was Acting Captain. On board ship she had a personal protector. If any man dared to make unwanted advances, the Mad Russian was ready to tear him apart and throw him to the sharks. She was exceeding beautiful, yet she presented a modest image. She wore pantaloons and a turban. On wet days she wore a souwester. When they stopped at some port she was one of the boys. Pleasant, fun, but not flirty. Colin met and talked to her several times. If he hadn't his Barbara he could certainly fall for Debra.

The Grey Dolphin stopped in Boston to sell its cargo. Then it headed to Lunenburg the home port. Captain Melroe, Debra, and Igor gave account of their voyage. There was a good share for each crew member. Captain Melroe announced, the Grey Dolphin would be going to the south seas the following year.

Isabelle Melroe gave Colin a hug and a kiss and wished his marriage to Barbara would be happy. She also wished they might have many children. Colin stopped at the Jolly Roger. One eyed Jack was there, but Colin had one drink and left. He walked along the wharf and asked, is anyone going north east. Yes, there was one fishing boat loaded with fish, that was heading for Port Hawkesbury.

After four years Colin was back. Did Barbara wait for him? Did she marry someone else? Colin went straight to see Jack McNeil at his boat building shop. Jack recognized him. Was he seeing a ghost? Colin smiled at Jack's discomfort.

"Jack, I'm back. I have a bit of green. Will you let me marry Barbara as you had promised?"

Finally Jack answered. "Many a time I told Barbara, that Colin would not return. Don't waste your best years. Marry Angus or someone else. That stubborn Red Head would not listen. She said, "I am betrothed to Colin. If he does not return then it shall be my fate to live alone for the rest of my years."

Jack held out his gnarled hand and took Colin's in both of his.

"Colin, me lad, I never believed I would be doing this. Forgive an old man for being so possessive. I give you my permission and my blessing. Go to your Barbara. She is waiting for thee. May the Lord bless thee with many bairns. I would ask a favour of thee. If it be that one of the bairns is a boy, name him after me, James not Jack".

Colin and Barbara were married and they had twelve children, six boys and six girls. Before the marriage Barbara put her foot down. "Colin, no more sea voyages for you. I waited four years to make this come true."

They moved to the Annapolis Valley where they had a mixed farm and grew apples.

In the year 2000, Barbara and Colin celebrated their 70th wedding anniversary. There were friends, neighbours, children, grandchildren, and great grandchildren. Their happy marriage kept them youthful and ever prosperous.

Through out Annapolis Valley and the Port Hawkesbury countryside people often discussed the latest news and movies. Inevitably someone would mention, "We do not have to see a Hollywood movie. We have our own Love Story right here. It is the story of Colin and Barbara."

22.
THE MYSTERY LADY

I SAW HER FOR THE FIRST TIME AT THE CARSTAIRS Farmers Market. Neither she nor I had come to buy vegetables or fruits. She had a booth and with a bit of deception she was selling magic, hope, and curiosity. I had no booth. I was talking to strangers. My goal was to gather material for a book about interesting people of Alberta. I would go to farmers markets, auction sales, garage sales, and anywhere that people gathered. If an interesting person was mentioned, I would follow that up with an interview.

For twenty five years I was a journalist. I wrote articles for Alberta dailies. Now I was on a part-time schedule, so that I could pursue my book. I was also doing free lance writing.

At this time I was fourty five and living alone with a structureless routine. Five years earlier my marriage to Debbie had ended. We had one daughter Edith, who was now married and they were expecting their first child. I had dated a few times, but I could not get serious and they did not seem to measure up to Debbie.

As I walked past the booths of vendors, this particular booth caused me to pause. A sign read, Let Madame Tamara Predict Your Future. The booth itself was interesting. The back panel was an electric screen with planets, stars, and space ships. These were blinking and moving. On the left side panel was jewellery. The panel on the right had imported articles and curios- there was a mosquito zapper, a Newfie cup with the handle inside, and some jumping beans. She sat at an ornate table. The table legs had carved snakes. On the table was the fortune teller's globe and a stack of charts. The lady, Madame Tamara was of mature years, but I could not guess whether she was thirty or fifty. On her head she had a band with astrological signs. I am sure she saw that I was staring at the objects and at her.

I said, "How much?"

"For two dollars I will read what the Taro cards say. For five dollars we will do an astrological profile. For ten you can get a complete prediction — Taro, and astrology. You can ask two specific questions."

I said, "I want to see what two dollars can produce."

She shuffled the Taro cards and arranged them on the table face up.

She said, "Your future is positive and there is a mystery that does not reveal itself."

I thanked her and walked away. I wasn't going to spend ten dollars on some hocus pocus stuff. I didn't believe that astrological prediction had any merit. They were to be taken as an interesting fantasy.

In the weeks that followed I couldn't dismiss her from my thoughts. I wanted to know more. She must have an interesting story to tell. The following week I was at the Sundre Farmers Market and there she was!

I approached her and said, "Give me the ten dollars prediction please."

She did the Taro card exercise. From my birthday she constructed a profile. She said, "The cards and the stars predict that your future is bright. I note that there is a temporary obstacle, but in time it will disappear. I also see a mysterious lady in your future. I cannot predict who she might be."

I said, "This is certainly interesting. I wish I knew who this lady could be. I am writing a series about interesting people. I am no astrologer, but I am guessing you have an interesting story, past and present. I would like to do an interview with you. Here is my card. If you are willing, I would be glad to talk to you."

Several weeks passed and then there was a call.

"You left your card and after much thought I am willing to share my secrets with you. Stop at the Sundre Dairy Queen and ask how to get to Tammy Miller's place."

At the Dairy Queen I asked the lady if she would tell me how to get to Tammy Miller's place. She broke into a slight smile, "So you are going to see the "Witch of the West". Be careful, she might cast a spell on you."

She then gave me the directions and said, "Good luck and keep your pants on!"

On the way to the unknown rendez-vous, would I be at the mercy of a sorceress and a temptress? Would I probably see a black figure emerging from a hovel? Was there a black cauldron cooking magical potions? Maybe I should turn around and go back?

When I drove into the yard, I was not sure this was the right place. The place was neat and the house was modern a two bedroom home. The woman that came to meet me couldn't be a witch. She had everything! Her dark hair fell gently on her shoulders. Her face in contrast was fair. She had a beautiful smile. She wore a white blouse, jeans, and athletic shoes.

"Hi Dan! I'm glad you came. I wasn't sure my story was appropriate for your book. It's such a beautiful day, let's go to the veranda." The veranda was on the other side of the house. From the edge of the veranda the ground was covered with shrubs and flowers sloping to the Little Red Deer River. A path led to a dock and a tethered boat. Down stream a heron was hunting for minnows in the shallow water. My gaze at the river was broken by a loud squawk. I turned around and there was a crow perched on one of the chairs.

"Jimmy, you're such a moocher. Jimmy is my boyfriend, but he never takes me out. Anytime I'm on the veranda he is sure to come and see what I have for him."

Was Jimmy a human boyfriend that she had turned into a crow? Maybe I better go before she turns me into a bat or a rat.

Tammy gave Jimmy a cookie. "OK, you can go."

The crow flew off with a cookie in his beak.

"Sorry for the interruption. Let's start with a drink. Would you like water, tea, coffee, wine, or juice?"

"Coffee will be fine."

"I will go and make some coffee. If you get bored, you may browse in this book." The book was a photo album. There were pictures of Tammy and an older man. The background of each photo suggested the pictures were taken in some foreign place. Tammy and this man had traveled a lot.

The coffee and the scones were delicious. I remarked, "By the pictures I would guess you have been to many places in this world."

"Yes Dan, for twenty years my husband and I travelled extensively and saw much of the world."

"How and why did you choose this place for a home?"

"My permanent home is in Las Vegas. This is my summer home. I'm here from May to October."

"Where is your husband?"

"Jacob passed away five years ago. Now I'm a lonely old girl." She laughed.

"Let's hear your story from the beginning. I'll turn on the tape recorder. You can start whenever you're ready."

"I know very little of my grandparents. My father's name was Tiko Tasker. My mother was Zara. In 1956 there was a revolution in Hungary. The protesters succeeded briefly. Then the army put down the revolt. Thousands of refugees headed for the Austrian border. My parents were not Hungarian, nor were they revolutionaries. They were Roma. They joined the escapees. They thought life would be better elsewhere. In the Austrian camps they learned some English. Then they immigrated to the USA. In America they found jobs with a circus. That suited them. They were Roma. They liked to be constantly moving. My father was a general helper, but he soon became boss of the electrical generator and cables. My mother was a fortune teller under the name of Madame Zara. I was born in 1960. Life in the circus is not like any other . This was a mid size circus. They would set up in a town for three days. The fourth day was dismantling and moving. The fifth day was setting up in a new town. The circus workers lived in trailers and moved with the caravan. In my early years my schedule was books in the forenoon and in the afternoon I would wander and watch the midway-dare devils, freaks, musicians, games persons, con artists, pick pockets, etc. The circus would travel from May to October. In October we headed back to Sarasota, Florida. This was our winter quarters. Winter was a time to repair equipment, practice new acts, etc. In the winter I attended a regular school. In 1978 my mother passed away. I took over the fortune telling tent as Madame Tamara. The summer when I was twenty, we were set up for two weeks at Tampa Bay. A middle aged man in expensive clothes asked for a ten dollar reading. From his birthday I calculated he was forty seven. Out of the blue he said, "How would you like to go for dinner with me?"

I replied, "That depends."

"It will be dinner, talk, and if there is a band, some dancing. There will be nothing more."

"Let me consult my cards." I knew I was going, but I shuffled the Taro Cards.

I said, Taro says, "You're OK. What shall I wear?"

"Let's make it casual."

"The dinner went very well. He was interesting, polite, and considerate. I enjoyed his company. I didn't think this would become serious. After all he was much older, even if he was handsome. The Taro Cards did not tell me there would be more dates. I got to like Jacob Miller. In fact I was falling for him. My father advised me to end the relationship."

"You're not his kind and you are a Roma."

"It was too late. I learned that Jacob was very wealthy. He had inherited a sizeable fortune. It was in the form of part ownership of three casinos — Las Vegas, Atlantic City, and French Riviera. Twice a year he met with managers and other owners of each casino. His income from the casinos was substantial, so he had time to pursue other interests.

A year later I married Jacob. The wedding was in Las Vegas. From my side was my father and two girlfriends, who were my bridesmaids. On his side were friends from the business world. I could have brought some interesting people from the circus — The bearded lady, the sword swallower, fish man, Siamese twins, the fat lady, etc. I thought such friends would shock the party. My father still had a concern about the marriage."

"He will use you and then dump you for another skirt." "It did not turn out that way. Jacob was my lover, partner, and more. Maybe he considered me his exhibit, but he never did reveal it. He was always proud to introduce me as his wife and partner. I was happy with Jacob. For twenty years we looked after business, travelled a lot, and had good times together. Our home was in Las Vegas, but on one of the Canada trips, he and I were captivated by the peace and natural beauty of this Sundre place. We bought the land and built the house. This was our home in summer when we wanted to escape from the city. After Jacob's passing I continued the same schedule. There were suitors, but they were after money, etc. I didn't find any one that interested me. That is my story. It is a story of a gypsy girl. I rose up the ladder, not by my beauty, but just by who I was and am. I was fortunate."

"Did you consider having children?"

"I did many times. I miss having a son or daughter. Jacob did not want children and I don't know why. Once he said. "I don't want to be a sixty year old daddy."

"You have plenty of money. Why do you bother with your fortune telling project?"

"Yes, I have plenty of money. Doing the fortune telling thing connects me to my mother and to my past. I enjoy people who are searching for a glimpse of their future. I give them a bit of magic and a bit of hope. It makes people look forward."

"I see that you are alone at this house. Are you not worried about security?"

"I have alarms and I have guns. I know how to use them."

"What do your neighbours think of a lady in the remote woods?"

"My closest neighbour is a mile away. They look after my house and they help whenever I need help. The towns people do not really know who I am. Some call me the Wicked Witch of the West. I laugh and keep them guessing."

The conversation carried on, but I knew it was time to leave.

I said, "Thank you for your story and for the delightful time you have provided."

As I drove back to Sundre, I thought that there are some people with a magnetic personality who draw you in so that you feel joy and satisfaction. You want to see them again. I believe Tammy was one of those people. The rest of the year I completed my work on interesting people. From time to time I thought of Tammy. I missed her.

The book was moderately successful. I received positive reviews. Someone in the Sundre area saw and bought the book. Gossip and interest spread. So the lady in the backwoods wasn't really a witch, but a wealthy heiress.

After the book's publishing I wondered if Tammy Miller still came in the summer to her remote Sundre home. I picked up the phone and called.

"Hello, this is Tammy Miller."

"Hi, this is Dan Melroe."

"Dan Melroe? Oh I recall. You were the one who pried out all my secrets."

"Yes, I am the one. I have thought about you. I would like to come and visit with you again."

"Oh that will be fine. Just come on down."

When I arrived at Tammy's home, she came out to meet me. She looked as elegant as she was the year ago.

I said, "I have a week to spend in the area."

She responded, "Why not spend it with me?"

That was music to my ears. That week we went on trail rides, nature walks, fishing, light dinners, and travelling around the area. I asked about Jimmy the crow. She wasn't sure if her two visitors were Jimmy and his girlfriend or just two other scrounging crows. I had brought a copy of the book for her. She wanted to see what I had written about her. The chapter was titled, <u>The Gypsy Girl</u> with a subtitle- <u>From Circus Tent to Mansion.</u> By the end of the week we had drawn much closer. Tammy and I wanted the relationship to continue.

I took Tammy in my arms. "Tammy, I love you and I want to marry you."

"Dan, I love you too and if the stars are beneficially aligned I will marry you!"

Tammy suggested we have a week to examine our relationship. If all went well we could confirm our union. I didn't know about Tammy, but I was nervous and apprehensive. What if she changed her mind? It turned out the stars said, "Get Married."

Tammy's neighbour organized a party in honour of our marriage. In Edmonton my friends and relatives gave us a larger party. My daughter was my escort to the altar. In Las

Vegas the wedding party was quite large since Tammy knew many in the business world. We decided that we would spend the first part of our marriage in the Sundre house.

In Alberta or anywhere in the world if you see a middle aged man holding hands with a beautiful gypsy lady, you will know that the couple is us.

I do not know whether it is the stars, the gods, good luck, or just our desire that brings two unlikely persons together. Whatever it is, let's celebrate its happening.

23.
SPECTACLE ON RUE 50 — A PARODY

LAST WEEK ON A SHOPPING TRIP I DECIDED TO TAKE 63RD Avenue on my way home. A few blocks along the way off 57 Avenue and on 50th Street was a scene that caught my attention. I slowed down and looked carefully. There in front of a house was a pile of furniture and boxes. This could hardly be a garage sale. I stopped to check. Among the boxes, sitting in an armchair, was a middle aged woman with earphones, listening to music. She was sipping Pina Colada from a tall glass. Beside her was a cigarette smouldering in an ash tray. At her feet was a dog, oblivious to everything. I did not stop to talk to her, but went on my way.

Two days later I chanced to talk to a friend Alex Middleton, who lives on 50 Street. I asked about the scene that happened a few days earlier. Alex usually tells the truth, but sometimes he exaggerates. This is the story as I reconstructed it with my own exaggerations about what went on at this house on 50th Street.

Mirabelle Woodland was a divorced lady in her mid 50's. She lived on a fixed disability pension, which she claimed was pitiful and inadequate. So from time to time landlords would tell her, "Pay up or be gone." Each time someone came to rescue her. Right now she was looking down the street for a white knight. To her surprise there was a knight errant. He wasn't on a white horse, but on a motorized scooter.

He stopped his scooter before Mirabelle's collection of boxes and chairs.

He said, "I say, art thou basking in the rays of the sun god or art thou waiting for a mover?"

"I'm not waiting for a mover."

"Then fair lady, it must be that you are waiting for your husband to come with a U-Haul?"

"I do not have a husband."

"Why what a shame. A beautiful lady and no admirers at her feet. What is your name may I ask?"

"My name is Mirabelle Woodland."

"Such a name could only have come down from heaven."

"And what is your name?"

"Dear lady, in the circles where I dwell, I am Captain Wilford Buckingham-recently retired from the Queens Own Horse Dragoons."

"With a rank and a title shouldn't you be living in London among royalty?"

"Alas my fair cuckoo, three women are pursing me for alimony. I have found it expedient to exit London. But I have found the City of Olds the most beautiful place in the world. I have not asked what are thy troubles this fine day."

"I am unable to pay my rent, so the Landlord has literally thrown me, my dog, and all my treasures out on the street. I have been promised help, but none has so far appeared."

"Do not fret my dear chickadee. Captain Wilford is here to rescue thee!"

"How are you going to rescue me?"

"My dear Chickadee I shall rescue thee by offering my hand."

"I need money not a hand."

"You misunderstand. I am offering you holy matrimony."

"You want to marry me and we haven't even had a date?"

"My precious chickadee, a lady such as yourself does not need to fret away precious moments on preliminaries."

"When would this marriage take place?"

"I say, haste is the call of the day! If you would mount this stead in front of me, we would speed away to St. John's Anglican Church where Rev. Lee Kim will unite us in holy matrimony. If he is not available, we shall repair to yon Baptist Church."

"Now, where will you take me after the marriage?"

"I am somewhat embarrassed. My lawyer is negotiating for a small mansion in the Vista's. So temporarily and in the interim we shall make do with my humble abode in yon The Lodge."

"What about my stuff?"

"Don't call it stuff my dear chickadee. Those are treasures and my man Bellingham will move those treasures to our new abode."

"You know this is kind of sudden for me. Will there be a honeymoon?"

"Better than a honeymoon. You will bask in the joys and pleasures of a nuptial paradise."

"What kind of pleasures are you talking about?"

"There will be many, but one you will enjoy is romping under the covers."

"That sounds sinful."

"Oh no, it is great fun. We can play find the button. You hide the button and I search for it. If I find it, I win the prize."

"I don't know if I should rush into this marriage. Maybe I will call my friend for advice."

"Who may I ask is your friend?"

"It is Gretchen McCain."

"Oh, do not mention that name! That pernicious dastardly ex-wife has thwarted three of my previous romances. I beg thee not to call her. Oh, Oh! I see those dastardly blood hounds approaching I must evade them. Farewell my chickadee."

A police cruiser stopped in front of the yard and Constable Penhold stepped out.

"Has there been a man on a scooter?"

"Yes."

"Has he offered to marry you?"

"Yes, in fact he did."

"That errant knight is Wilford Bratland. He is a resident of The Lodge. He is harmless, but from time to time he escapes the premises. I see you are moving."

"No, I have been evicted."

"Have you called Social Services?"

"Yes I called, but they have labelled me as a repeat problem?"

"What about a job to supplement your resources?"

"That would be so humiliating. If my friends found out I sweep floors and scrub toilets they would desert me. Such a scandal would be so disastrous!"

"Those are good jobs."

"Let the immigrants do them. My family has never stooped that low."

"You might think it over. I have to leave. I've got to catch up to Captain Wilford."

Mirabelle looked both ways but she could not see any white knight. She could not see anyone and it was getting chilly. Then as if from nowhere two vehicles, one from each end of the street approached and stopped before her collection and herself. Each vehicle had a sign in the side window. One read LDS Samaritan Team. The other read Baptist Miracle Team.

"It seems we are here on the same mission- to help Mirabelle."

"Yes, but only one team should get involved. Let's decide in a Christian way by flipping a coin. Heads you win, tails we lose. It's heads. So the Samaritan Team will go forth."

Four men in dark suits, white shirts, blue ties walked to where Mirabelle was reclining.

"I am James Foster of the LDS Samartian Team. This is Brother Thompson, Brother Jackson and Brother Michaels. I have already talked to Social Services and your Landlord. We have received your request for financial help. Our mission is to help and we are ready to do so. We try to have as few intrusions as possible, however we want you to succeed in solving the problem. We ask that you consider our suggestions. If you choose to have no intrusions tell us, and we will be on our way."

"I need the help and I will try to follow your suggestions."

"Very good. We can proceed. Brothers Jackson and Michaels will move your belongings inside.

Brother Thompson will review your budget. We will then make some suggestions. Brother Jackson will lead us in prayer asking for divine assistance."

"Dear Heavenly Father. We are thankful to be here to be able to help Sister Mirabelle Woodland. We ask thee that you grant us wisdom and humility, so that we may give her the assistance she needs. In the name of Jesus Christ Amen."

"For our records we have to fill out a form. Your full name please?"

"Mirabelle Georgina Woodland."

"Your marital status?"

"I've been married once and I hope to get married again."

"No, we mean– are you married, single, divorced, or widowed?"

"I've been all those. So chose your pick."

"Your age?"

"Do we need to write that down? OK. I'm fifty six, but everyone says I look thirty."

"Sex?"

"You are getting personal. I haven't had sex for sometime, but I'm hoping."

"No, we mean are you male, female or transgender?"

"Obviously, you can see I'm a female?"

"Your income after taxes?"

"Never enough."

"We mean in dollars and cents."

"I really don't know. I just write cheques. But I never have enough. You can see I'm close to poverty and starvation."

"OK sign here."

Brother Thompson was the first to speak.

"I've looked at her bills. She is spending far more than her income allows. I think she has to get a job to make ends meet."

"Let's come back in a weeks time and talk to her."

Two weeks later Mirabelle talked to her friend, Sandra Johnson.

"You know what those sanctimonious penguins told me to do? They said I should get a job. The gall to suggest such a humiliating solution. My family comes from patrician stock. We don't scrub floors and clean toilets. They would have me walk to the store. And they suggested some groceries I do without."

"What are you going to do?"

"I'll do what I've always done. Someone will always come along to donate money. First I'll talk to the Baptist Team."

"What if no one comes to assist you? Then what?"

"That has never happened. I'll write to Justin. I know he will send me a bigger cheque. For now, I will cross that bridge when I come to it."

"Que Sera Sera"

24.
FATAL EXCHANGE

A SOCIETY AT ITS FORMATION TRIES TO HAVE A HOMOGenous membership. Inevitably it breaks into layers of significance. In the top layer are the aristocrats defined by title, wealth, or pedigree. Below them are the "nouveau riche" who have wealth and are reaching for the top. Below them are several layers, each trying to be in a higher layer.

Thomas and Miriam Taylor of Boston maintained that they belonged to the aristocrat (upper) class, because an ancestor came on the Mayflower. Grandpa Caleb Taylor accumulated some wealth by buying a ship and trading in the Caribbean. His son Foster did not add to the family wealth. Grandpa's ship could not compete with the newer ships. Now Thomas presided over the family resources that had shrunk. He could barely cover expenses with his meagre salary as custodian and manager of the Standish Men's Club. Miriam was a member of the Ladies Pilgrim Sewing Club. She was a poor cousin since the other ladies had money to support charities and projects. Miriam pretended that she belonged to this exclusive Club. Thomas and Miriam had two daughters. As long as money lasted they were sent to an exclusive girls boarding school. They graduated from Auburn Academy, ready to meet prospective suitors with wealth. Besides being attractive, they were educated and sophisticated. They also claimed they were liberated women. Although they were identical, each had a personality and purpose that was unique. Marlene was the gregarious type with a persuasive manner. She found her niche with the Republican Party. She spent most of her time in Washington, but there were trips to many parts of the USA. Her job was to promote the Republican Party and to find people who could further its program.

Marlene's sister Darlene was identical in appearance, but had a character and personality that was almost an opposite to her sister's. She was an introvert, but her calmness and wisdom made her influential and powerful. She loved nature and would spend hours tramping through bush and meadow. In College she majored in English Literature. After College she was hired as a lecturer by Colleges and Universities.

At a lower level of society's strata was the family of Albert Prentis. He was one of the "nouveau riche". As a lawyer, his firm catered to wealthy corporations, so his income was above average even for a lawyer. He was able to send his two children Darin and Margaret to the best schools. Darin was completing his law degree. His father wanted him to join another prestigious Law Firm, get experience, and then return to his father's Firm.

Darin's best friend was his cousin Donald Prentis. In appearance Donald could be mistaken as Darin's brother. The two spent weekends and holidays doing activities that both enjoyed. Donald's parents were not wealthy so he did not attend prestigious colleges. After high school he took a community college program in accounting and went to work in Wells Fargo Bank.

While at Cornell, Darin was a member of the Republican Party Youth Group. This group made trips to Washington to the Republican Head Office.

It was on one of these trips that Darin met Marlene Taylor. She was attractive, vivacious, and brimming with confidence. She was the type that Darin would choose as a wife. They kept in contact. Darin got a position in a law firm- McLeod Smith and Roger. This was in Chicago. After graduation he would take a two month leave and then move to Chicago. His father was pleased with Darin's progress and accomplishment. He rewarded Darin with a paid holiday trip for two to Europe for one month. Darin planned the trip and booked the stops. The plan was to spend two weeks touring in France and then two weeks in Italy.

In June 1990 Darin Prentis's fortunes were at a peak. He had graduated at the top of his class. In October he would take the position in that prestigious Law Firm in Chicago. He had received a graduation gift that would be an envy for many. The suggested start for the trip was July 15th. Who should he choose as a companion? He asked his sister, but she could not get away at that time. He could ask his cousin Donald, but he thought of a better choice.

"Hello, this is Marlene Taylor."

"Hi Marlene, this is Darin Prentis. Do you remember me?"

"I do Darin. I'm trying to think why you called, but the answer escapes me."

"Marlene, I am inviting you to accompany me on a tour of France and Italy, starting July 15th."

"Oh my goodness! Your offer floored me. It sounds like an exciting time. But Darin, I do not have money for such an outing."

"Not to worry. All expenses are already paid."

"Would I be expected to sleep with you?"

"No, at each night stop there will be two bedrooms."

"With such an offer I can't say no. My sister and I are going to England the week before. On the 15th, unless I tell you otherwise, I will take a bus and meet you at the Paris Transit Centre."

"That's great, I'll be there."

In July, a phone call came in. "Hello this is Darin Prentis."

"Hello this is Amy Bowerman, calling you on behalf of McLeod Smith and Rogers. The plan was that you would join the Firm on October 1st. We have an emergency at the Firm. One of the partners has passed away. Another has left the Firm. We have a backlog of work. We are asking you to come now." There was a long pause.

"Hello Darin, are you still there?"

"Yes, I'm here. Your request is a mild unexpected shock. You see I have a once in a lifetime all paid tour of Europe."

"I can imagine your dilemma. I am merely voicing the wish of the Firm."

"I know. That position is very important to me. I will pack my bags and be in Chicago tomorrow."

"Very good Darin! The Boss will be pleased. Good bye for now. I will see you tomorrow."

Darin immediately called his cousin Donald Prentis.

"Donald, I have an offer for you that you will find hard to refuse. How would you like an all paid holiday in Europe for one month? Are you interested?"

"Of course I'm interested! I have a two week vacation. I'm sure I can get an extra two weeks. When will this holiday start?"

"July 15th."

"That's five days from now. Will I travel alone, with a companion or a group?"

"You'll have a female companion."

"Wow! Is she attractive?"

"Very attractive and has a very extrovert personality. She is a prize!"

"What if I fall in love with her?"

"It will be my loss."

"Wouldn't she notice that I am not you?"

"I don't think so. I have met her several times, but between long intervals."

"Am I expected to sleep with her?"

"No, you will have separate rooms."

"OK, I'm in."

"Come here immediately and I will give you all the documentation and the plan."

"OK, I'm on my way."

In Room 346 of the Balmoral Hotel in London, Marlene and Darlene were slipping off their shoes. Marlene said, "This hiking and looking at old buildings is for the birds. I prefer to hob nob with the powerful and rich."

Darlene replied, "I really liked our tour today. I can't wait to start on the walking tour to the Lake District. I want to see what Wordsworth and his Sister saw." After showering and changing clothes the two sisters went down to the Dining Room. They chose to have a light dinner and then they went back to their room.

Marlene spoke, "I have told you about my month long tour with Darin Prentis."

"Yes it sounds exciting!"

"Not for me. Do I really want to tramp over half of France and Italy? I'm asking a favour of you, my dear Sister."

"What can it be?"

"I want you to take my place."

"That's a big order! Wouldn't Darin see that I am a substitute?"

"I don't think so. We are almost identical in appearance. The tour will keep him busy and he won't see other differences."

"Call me foolish, but seeing the countryside of France and Italy is going to be a dream fulfilled. I'll do it. If I get into trouble, I will never forgive you. Oh, by the way am I expected to sleep with Darin?"

"No, you can't be that lucky. You are to have separate rooms. On the 15th you will take the bus to Paris Central Station and Darin will met you."

On July 15th at 3:00 pm the bus from London arrived. It wasn't difficult to spot "Marlene".

"Hi "Marlene", it is nice to see you after several months."

"Hi "Darin", I'm eager for the great adventure!"

"Let me carry your luggage." Donald took the two suitcases and they went to the taxi stand.

"Take us to the George Hotel, Monsieur."

At the Hotel they were shown to their rooms.

"At six, I will call you and we will have dinner in the Dining Room on the first floor."

"That will be fine."

The dinner was typical French. It started with a glass of wine, then salad, veal cutlets, garlic bread, etc. They passed up on the escargots for this occasion. Donald was a bit perplexed. He was told that "Marlene" was talkative, but at the table she seemed reserved. She spoke only when asked a question. Maybe it was the strangeness of this meeting. "Tomorrow I will pick up a rented Audi, and we will be off for Versailles."

At Versailles both were interested and quite comfortable with each other. There was so much to see. This was where the Sun King, Louis X1V kept his nobles in check. From here he ruled France, a strong Kingdom at the time. After all day on the tour, they had dinner. This time they tried the escargots.

The following day they drove through the Loire Valley. The scenery was very green and there were mansions along the route. The next day there was more of the Loire Valley. "Marlene" became talkative and to her the sights were breath taking.

At the end of the first week they were in Bordeaux Country. This was wine country, so there were vineyards in every direction. They didn't do much touring as it was drizzling all day.

The day and the evening were chilly. About midnight there was a knock on "Darin's" door. There was ""Marlene".

"Darin, I'm so cold. May I come and cuddle with you?"

"Sure." In the days that followed "Darin" was wishing for more chilly nights.

From Bordeaux they went south to the foothills of the Pyrennes. This was where the Knights Templar had their stronghold. It was where the people of the area followed a different version of Christianity. The R.C. Church could not or would not allow any departure from Rome. Many were killed. Many were burned at the stake. The Knights Templar were almost wiped out. The R.C. Church would not tolerate any heretics.

During their travels they took turns driving. "Marlene" was a good driver. As they turned east most of the roads were mountain roads, so "Darin" worried a bit about "Marlene" and himself driving on these roads. Through the Jura and Alps Mountains the roads were narrow and winding, and required utmost attention. "Marlene" was driving. At one of the curves, an oncoming vehicle was approaching at high speed. It might have been a police chase. The driver was well into their lane. "Marlene" cramped the wheel to the right to avoid a crash. It wasn't enough. He hit their car and both vehicles went over and tumbled to the rocks hundreds of feet below.

"Darin" was semi-conscious because he could hear sirens. Someone lifted him on a stretcher.

"What about "Marlene?" The attendant pointed to a covered body. He did not recall the trip in the ambulance. He became fully conscious on a hospital bed in the city of Grenoble. The Hospital and the Gendarmes were puzzled by the identity of the injured man and the deceased lady. Was the man Darin Prentis or Donald Prentis? Was the deceased woman Marlene Taylor or Darlene Taylor?

After two days in Grenoble, Donald on a stretcher and Darlene in a casket were sent back to Boston. Donald spent another week in the Boston Memorial Hospital and then was discharged. For the next two weeks he was recuperating at his parent's home. Fellow employees from the Bank sent flowers, cards, fruit, etc. Donald could not wait to get back to his job. His holiday in France seemed like a nightmare. In the two weeks Donald was recuperating he relived the two weeks in France. It wasn't the sights of the tour, but the images of Darlene that were etched in his mind. He realized he had fallen in love with "Marlene". She emerged first as a companion, next as a lady of beauty and exemplary character and in the final days as a lady with whom he was in love. In those final days he had not told her of his love. In those times, when tears blinded his sight, he asked as thousands before- "W*hy are the good ones taken so soon?*"

Donald felt a sense of guilt. If someone had to die, why was it not me? In his despair what would Darlene have him do? He thought she would have quoted poet Henley in "Invictus".

"I am master of my fate I am Captain of my soul."

Though there are obstacles and disasters that we face, it is we who decide how to live our lives.

After he was discharged from the Hospital, Donald was seeking closure. He went to the grave of Darlene Taylor. He knew it was futile to tell her that he loved her, but he hoped her spirit might hear his words. They both had lost so much. Tears watered the grave of his beloved. He muttered, "Good bye my sweet love, *and may flights of angels sing thee to thy resting place.*"

25.
RITA AND I

IN A FARM HOUSE ON THE SASKATCHEWAN BORDER Wesley Graham, "The Preacher" was going over the plan. His cohorts, Butch the Jackal and Jimmy the Weasel were fidgeting nervously. The Preacher began his career as a popular pastor of a church. He used his popularity to relieve some of the younger women of their virginity. For the older widows he relieved them of their life savings. Bruce (Butch) was a violent killer. He was a drug dealer and an enforcer. Even the Hells Angels would not accept him. Jimmy the Weasel was a small time crook. His crimes were shoplifting, bad cheques, and theft.

The Preacher said, "We have cased the place and that woman is a nuisance, but I think we can squeeze her family for some dough. Tomorrow we will take the boat to Kilarney Lake and drop off the supplies. The operation will be Friday. That will give us several days before they know what has happened. The first contact will be with those Missionaries. My guess is that they may go to someone for advice. I also learned that a dentist will be the second contact. He has a family so he will cooperate. Now I am going to tell you again, so it sinks into your skulls. You are not to be drinking or talking to anyone about the plan. We do not want to kill anyone. Understand!"

The two nodded their heads, "Yeah, we understand. When do we eat?"

"Right away! I'll cook those cutlets and potatoes. You can have one beer and no more. Remember tomorrow morning before daylight we take that boat to Kilarney Lake."

The Preacher, who was the mastermind had spent two years in prison. There he studied every book on computers. The last six months he had a real computer to practice. He had selected Olds as a likely place to fit into his plan. There were a number of elderly people who had large savings. He had cased the cemetery to check where one of a couple had died. There was a good chance the other was sitting on some dough. That is how he came upon that funny name-Shymkiw. It took several days, but the computer yielded the information. This old man had a Caregiver who was there everyday. "We can't extract money, but this old codger has stocks. His family could sell those and send us the money. The locks on the garage door are so poor even a kid could get in without any trouble."

"For a prelude this is what I would say, Rita is the anchor that keeps this home on an even keel. She has been my Caregiver for more than seven years. During those years she has performed many duties. A brief profile of her life shown on a graph appears as a upward sloping line. The slope is interrupted by a zig zag pattern before it resumes its trend. The zig zag interval represents the eleven years of positive and negative unsettling events. The most serious event is the vehicle crash that killed daughter Rita. This was followed by another car crash that injured a daughter April. How did Rita cope with these unsettling events? Not by despondency and withdrawal, but by determination and a faith in her God."

Tracey Viau knows Rita very well. "Rita, I've known you for years. In the last few years quite often you say Bill this, Bill that. Is there anything between you?"

"Oh no. Bill is my employer. He treats me fairly- small pay, but a variety of work. I spend a lot of time with him. No! There is no romance between us. I think we like each other."

"Rita, have you ever thought of getting married again?"

"Sure, I've thought about it."

"If marriage is like a baseball game, you get to have three strikes. Rita, you never know, but the third time might be a home run."

"But you never know what may happen."

"Rita you are a positive person. You keep being hopeful. I know you like your life as it is, but another love would be no sin."

"OK Tracey, if Mr. Right comes along, you will be the first to know."

"Confidentially, Rita what qualities are you looking for?"

"First, he can't be married already. I would want him to be a person who is kind, considerate, and has integrity. I would want him to be emotionally stable and responsible. I know everyone should be aware of the package of differences. They could be a Trojan Horse. I believe two people working on their relationship and helping each other to grow is very important. Respect of each others feelings and beliefs will make a harmonious union."

"Rita, you have quite a list. I don't think five star prospects exist. You may get a winner in a three star guy."

"Tracey, I'm not looking for anyone. Five star, three star, or one star."

"OK, we're just talking."

"Sure, I know this is just talk, but it is fun to dream."

"As a prelude of my profile to my life would indicate that I was born under a lucky star. The graph would show a gentle upward slope in most aspects of my career. My marriage of fifty nine years was happy with very few bumps along the way. My family is just fine. Each charting his own course. Since about eight years the line began a downward slope as health began to deteriorate. Since Rita's coming it has levelled out. As a compliment to Rita I would say, *Rita you are the wind beneath my wings.*"

On one of the garden tours a lady asked, "Have you considered marriage again?"

"Sure, it has to be Lady Right. A lady that compliments my life style."

" Have you been searching for such a lady?"

"I have to admit I have not."

"Did you expect her to drop out of the sky?"

"No, but that would be nice."

"What qualities are you looking for in the perfect lady?"

"Beautiful, emotionally stable, healthy, and fidelity is important. Financial matters are important. Its nice to have similar interests. Something both can do together. Like in Rita's list, the differences are quite important to consider."

"Oh boy, I don't think there are many ladies with all those qualities."

"Maybe not. But I can dream and maybe a four or a three star gal will come along."

"Just a minute. Don't you have an attractive lady coming to see you each day? She's right there under your nose and you don't see her."

"That's a loaded question. I'm not going to say more, except to say she's nice and I like her."

It was Friday July 5th 2019 and a gentle rain was falling. The TV screen flickered with each clap of thunder. One more hour of TV and I would turn in. I thought I heard a noise coming from the garage. I turned down the TV. Yes, there was something or someone making the noise. I opened the door to the garage and everything happened at once. One arm was around my neck. Another was holding a cloth over my mouth and nose. Still other hands were putting shackles on my hands.

Then all became black. I was slipping into a sleep . I can only guess what happened next.

When I became conscious, I was strapped to a seat in a vehicle, and I was blind folded. I could hear someone in the van.

The Preacher's plan was to include Rita in the kidnapping. As soon as Bill was unconscious, a call was placed to Rita.

A voice said, "I need your help can you come?"

Rita dressed and drove to Bill's house. The garage door was locked. There was no one in the kitchen or living room. So she proceeded to the bedroom. Before she touched the light switch an arm went around her neck. Another hand covered her mouth and nose with a cloth and she was shackled. She was then taken to their van.

I don't know how long we had been travelling. I did not know where we were going.

The Preacher said, "We will soon be there. The Weasel will drop off Rita's van and then join us. Jackal you will sit beside me in the front and Weasel will sit at the back."

Later I would learn that Jimmy The Weasel would drop off Rita's van inside Mistawasis (Hobbema) Reserve, northeast of Ponoka. After Jimmy The Weasel got in, we kept driving. It seemed several hours. Finally the vehicle came to a stop. One of the men-The Weasel or The Jackal led us to a boat. We were off again. It wasn't long and we were escorted off the boat to some kind of building. We heard the Jackal say, "Are we going to shoot them now or later?"

"You crazy coot. We are not going to shoot them unless we have to. We want the money. Shooting them won't get us the money. Remember, you are also wanted State side. If they get you, you will fry."

Then we were pushed unto something like a bed and a cloth was placed over our noses and mouths. I do not know how much later I became conscious. The blind fold had been removed and we were unshackled. It was daylight but there was no sign of our abductors. We were inside a one room cabin on an island. Far off we could see a distant shore. Rita did not panic. She just said, "What has happened to us and why?"

"I don't know why, but I'm guessing this is kidnapping for money."

"But I don't have much money."

"You just happened to have a connection to me."

"What are we going to do?"

"Can you swim?"

"Yeah, but the shore could be ten miles away. Can you swim?"

"No."

"Then we stay and hope someone rescues us."

Back in Olds, Elder Black and Elder Davidson looked out.

"Rita's van is gone. She usually leaves just before eight."

"Maybe she wanted to surprise that man she works for-what's his name?"

"Oh some funny name-Slovak or Russian or whatever."

Evening came and still there was no van. Elder Black phoned her number. It rang but no answer. They text her but no response. Sunday morning and still no van. I'm going to mention this to Bishop Taylor. As soon as they spotted the Bishop, Elder Davidson said, "Bishop, we are missing Sister MacPherson. It is not like her to go and not tell anyone."

"I don't think it is serious, but just in case I'll ask in our Ward Council this morning. If no one knows, then later I will announce it to everyone in the Sacrament meeting. Then you Elders can drive over to where she works and check the place. She has sons and daughters in Edmonton and Grande Prairie. Maybe she has misplaced her phone while there. She does that you know! Tomorrow morning if she is still missing we'll search. I can't imagine anyone kidnapping her, but then she is overly friendly. I pray nothing bad comes to her."

"Brothers and Sisters, I have an unusual announcement. As of now, I do not think it is serious, but we have not been able to contact Sister MacPherson. If anyone has any information let us know and say a little prayer that we reach her safely and soon."

On Monday, the phone rang in the Missionaries apartment at 6:00 am.

"Hello this is Elder Black." "Go to your Church. There is a message on the door." Whoever it was hung up.

Elder Black said, "There is a message for us on the Church door. This is like in the movies."

At the Church door they opened the envelope.

The message read- *Contact the families! Do not call the police!*

We want $500,000 for Bill and $300,000 for Rita.

We will call you in several days. HAVE THE MONEY!

Elder Davidson turned white.

"This is not a game. What shall we do?"

"Let's talk to the Bishop."

They called the Bishop. His house phone rang. His wife Lindsay answered.

"Hello."

"We have to see Bishop Taylor immediately!"

"He has just left for the Clinic. Go there and I'll call and tell him that you have an urgent matter."

At the Clinic, "We have to see Dr. Taylor."

"I know. I'll get him."

"Hi, I can't imagine what the urgency is about?"

Elder Black showed him the message. His face also went white. This was trouble with a capital T.

To the Missionaries he said, "Do not tell anyone about this. Go about your work and pray." To the receptionist he said, "Cancel all my appointments for the day. Reschedule them. If there is an emergency send them to Dr. Fisher. I'm going home. If there are calls, tell them I'm not available today."

Before the doctor left the phone rang. "Dr. Taylor's office, how can I help?"

"Get the dentist on the phone now!"

"What do you want to talk to him about? I'm his receptionist."

"I don't give a shit who you are, just get the doctor or I'll shove a stick of dynamite up your ass."

Pamela did not hesitate. "Dr. Taylor, there is a crazy man who wants to talk to you."

"Dr. Taylor here. How can I help?"

"Look here Smart Ass. We know the Missionaries are with you. You're in this up to your eyeballs. Just make sure the money is there. We'll contact you. Do not talk to the police. We know you have a family." Whoever it was hung up.

When Dr. Taylor came home, his wife Lindsay wondered why.

"We may be in trouble."

"What kind of trouble?"

"Rita and the man she works for, have been kidnapped and I have their ransom note."

"Spencer, we can't handle this ourselves. We should notify the police."

Dr. Taylor phoned the police station.

Sergeant Sherman told him to go to the far corner inside of the No Frills. An officer would meet him there.

Dr. Taylor followed instructions, went to the store and waited. He had a chance to price eggs, dairy products, etc.

After about half an hour a woman with a shopping basket slowly came his way. She said, "I see sour cream is on sale and eggs are getting so expensive. What do you think."

" I really don't know, my wife does the shopping. I'm waiting to meet someone."

"Isn't that a coincidence. I was also supposed to meet a Dr. Taylor. Do you know him?"

"I'm Dr. Taylor."

Out of her hand bag she pulled out her badge. "I'm Corporal Theresa McKay. You have a message for me?"

The Corporal read the ransom note and kept it.

"Dr. Taylor, I want you to go home. Take precautions. I will contact my Superiors. Don't worry. Everything will turn out OK."

That evening Dr. Taylor's phone rang. "Dr. Taylor, this is the Team. Come to Rita's apartment."

"It may be locked."

"That's not a problem."

When Dr. Taylor arrived at Rita's apartment, two men in suits met him and showed their badges.

"When the kidnappers call you, call us immediately at this number. Tomorrow you go to your practice as if nothing happened."

The following morning the two families were contacted and asked to come to Olds immediately.

When they arrived the officers advised that compliance was the best course. An officer could accompany each group to their bank, where an emergency sum would be packaged and ready to go.

There was no call for several days. That was strange. Everyone involved waited. Family members worried. Had the kidnappers panicked and killed the victims?

A week after the kidnapping Constable Elliot of the Ponoka Detachment paid his monthly visit to Chief Fiddler of the Mistawasis (Hobbema) Reserve. They talked in generalities. Because car theft was rampant in this area, the Constable asked if there were any unfamiliar vehicles on the Reserve.

"As a matter of fact, I heard some teens were ripping around in an older van. I think they drove it until the gas ran out." "Let's go and find that vehicle."

When they found it, the van was a sight to behold. The windows were broken. The tires were flat and it was resting in a muddy ditch.

"Who is doing all this?"

"You know who."

Constable Elliot took down the license number and radioed it into headquarters. That triggered an immediate alert. That van was involved in the kidnapping. The next morning ten Mounties were on the Reserve. They questioned everyone and even some in the Wetaskiwin area. Known criminals were taken in and grilled.

"Where did you hide the bodies?"

"We didn't steal the van. It was just sitting beside the road."

"You better come clean. Sooner or later we'll find the bodies. You won't be seeing daylight for a very long time."

After days of questioning and searching, nothing substantial came to light. The usual crooks were shaking in their boots.

That same weekend Jimmy Ratner the Weasel, was nervously pacing in his dingy room in Wetaskiwin. He was waiting for a call. He already had plans for his share of the ransom money. If those two scum bags had double crossed him, he would hunt them down. That's what you get when you deal with crooks he thought. He would wait a few days and if they did not contact him, he would go to the farm headquarters. He would have a word or two for the Preacher and the Jackal.

In the morning of July 6th, Rita and I woke from the drugged induced sleep. We were in a one room cabin. We had slept on the one bed with some stinky blankets. There was no sign of the kidnappers anywhere. I took an axe and smashed the lock on the cupboard. There were food supplies- canned meat, fish, stews, and vegetables. There were boxes of rice, oatmeal, raisins, flour, etc. I estimated the food would keep us alive for a month. However, we thought it would be a few days and we would learn whether we would live or die.

Rita said, "This place is a mess. We'll soak these stinky blankets in the lake and then hang them to dry. We have no choice but to sleep together. Can I trust you?"

"Rita, I will try my best."

After a few days we realized we might be here longer than we expected. With charcoal we made a calendar on the wall. We crossed each day as it ended. The first X was on the sixth. Now we were on day thirteen. A routine began to set in. We cleaned, washed, cooked, and set up a pole with hooks to catch fish. During the time we spent there we caught eight fish. This was a nice treat.

The days passed, our concern was that not only when our kidnappers returned, but also what would we do when the food ran out? We began to ration food and our plan was that towards the end we would take the cabin apart and make a raft.

Back in Olds there was now a new Missionary. He was alerted to a possible call. Dr. Taylor waited and his family kept up their precautions. The Police were puzzled. This was not the usual pattern of kidnappers. At the Church Wednesday was set aside for prayers for Sister MacPherson. Secretly, most believed Rita and Bill had been killed and their bodies hidden. Bishop Taylor urged members to pray and keep up the faith. He said it was quite alright to include Bill in their prayers.

On about the seventh, the Weasel wasn't going to wait any longer. He got in his battered Honda and drove to the farm headquarters. When he arrived he was wary. There could be cops waiting for him. He walked to the back of the house. The van and boat were still there. That was strange. He opened the door and a horrific smell came at him. He speculated. Did the guys shoot each other? Did the police shoot them? He took a rag soaked in beer and tied it around his face. He entered again. On the table was an empty whisky bottle, some glasses, and a pill bottle. The label read OXYCODONE. In the bedroom he saw two bodies on the bed. They were bloated. The skin was open and maggots were feasting. He rushed outside. At this point he didn't want the ransom. He wanted no connection to the kidnapping and those dead bodies. Just in case the cops found out he wanted to present a reply that he did the right thing. He re-entered. The phone was alive. He didn't know the number to call, so he dialled 911.

"This is 911. Do you want ambulance, fire or police?"

"Police."

"RCMP, Lloydminister detachment."

"Ten miles south of Lloydminister are two bodies in a farm house." He hung up and drove away.

The Police with a Forensic Unit found the bodies. There were photos, examinations, and finger prints taken for identification. The bodies were identified as Wesley Graham the Preacher, and Bruce (Butch) Cassidy, also known as the Jackal. Then the search was on for any other partners. Yes, the name of James (Jimmy) Ratner came on the screen. He was also know as The Weasel.

They found The Weasel he was charged and taken to the Wetaskiwin detachment. Then came the questioning.

"James Ratner, you are charged with the kidnapping of Rita MacPherson and Bill Shymkiw and the murders of your partners, Wesley Graham and Bruce Cassidy. You have a right to remain silent and you have a right to Counsel."

"I didn't have anything to do with that."

"We have your fingerprints at the crime scene."

"Can I see a lawyer?"

"Sure, here is the phone." Edward Bayda arrived.

"Fine day Gentlemen, I see you have been harassing my client."

The Constable led the lawyer and the Weasel to an empty room.

After talking to the Weasel Bayda said, "Gentlemen, you know and I know that my client is innocent. Charges should be dropped and he should go free."

"Mr. Bayda, you have been successful in the past. This time we have your client Dead To Rights."

Lawyer Bayda whispered to the Weasel, who nodded his head.

"Gentlemen there is no doubt I will win this case, but we are willing to Plea Bargain."

"What do you propose?"

"Drop all charges and my client will tell you where the kidnapped hostages are."

"We will accept if the hostages are alive. If they are dead then murder charges will be laid."

"I guess we have no choice."

As the days passed and we put more X's on the wall calendar we experienced a closeness. Sometimes we would sit on the bed and just hold hands. A tenderness would pass between us. We were experiencing a mood that few have-wondering if we would ever see our families again. I shall always remember July 27th. It was a misty day with a gentle rain. We stayed inside and I made a fire in the stove to take the chill out of the air. I think that day Rita was in a pensive mood. Usually she talks a lot, but this day she was quiet as if she had some heavy thoughts on her mind.

"Bill, do you think we'll come out of this alive?"

"Rita, I don't know, but I hope."

"Bill, each day I pray silently that all will turn out well."

" I hope someone is listening. We could use some divine assistance."

"Bill, I never thought I would say this but here goes, from the beginning I have got to love you. I didn't dare tell you because a closer relationship was not practical and I never could be sure how you felt about me."

"Rita, I have fallen in love with you a dozen times, but like you a closer relationship would be complicated and not with the expectations of society."

I held out my arms and she came in and our lips met. She whispered, "Why is love so painful?"

"I too felt the agony. Maybe because it has become so deep."

On July 31th we had one can in the cupboard. We heard a motorboat. Were we going to be rescued or were the kidnappers returning? We were ecstatic to be rescued!

When we returned to Olds our families were relieved and overjoyed to see us alive and well. Some commented on my beard. There was no razor where we were. At the Church, members had smiles and some had tears of joy. Their beloved Rita was back! Bishop Taylor had the last word, "God has answered our prayers."

26.
GETHSEMANE

THE JESUS STORY HAS TWISTS AND TURNS GALORE. THE first three centuries of the Christian era were a period of confusion. Let us start at the beginning.

In the beginning were the Jews. Our Gregorian calendar says the year is 2019. The Jewish calendar says the year is 5778. You can see that the Jews had almost 4000 years of history before Christ. In that long period they began as a wandering tribe of herders in the Tigris — Euphrates Valley. They progressed to be a settled people. During the empires of Alexander and the Romans there were Jewish groups from India to the British Isles and around the Mediterranean Sea. They had a Hebrew language. They had developed a sophisticated religion of one invisible God. Most of that period they had no nation, so it was their religion that defined them and their culture. For a brief period of about 100 years in the year 900 BC, when their neighbours were weak and preoccupied they had a nation and kings– Saul, David, Solomon. Most of that period and into the Christian Era they were under someone's rule. Quite often they were persecuted and in bondage. Through their Prophets and writings they longed for a golden age when they could be free and have their own king or ruler.

We should start the Jesus story with a man called Joseph. He was a craftsman in Nazareth in Galilee. He was married to Anna. For fifteen years they tried to have children, but no success. Joseph wanted an heir so he divorced Anna and looked for a new wife. In his area there was no one suitable. The only female that might do was a thirteen year old girl. We will know her as Mary. Joseph agreed to a betrothal pact with Mary's parents. From that day forward she was destined to be Joseph's wife. She would remain with her parents until she was sixteen. Then she would be formally wed, move into Joseph's home and be his wife.

Before her sixteenth birthday, a complication arose. Mary was pregnant, who the father was only Mary would know. Joseph was faced with a dilemma. He could cancel the agreement and ask for compensation. He could disown her and let the community deal with her. She would be stoned for adultery. His third option was to shield her and marry her as she was. This was his choice.

Mary bore a son that they would call Joshua (Jesus). After Joshua there were four more boys and two girls. (Gospels will say they were not Mary's children).

As a boy Joshua was precocious, obedient, and helpful. Joshua grew and learned his father's trade. After his bar mitzvah Joshua joined the men where they discussed Jewish history and scripture. At the age of twenty he married Deborah. A year later she died in childbirth. Joshua was despondent and devastated. He went to Joseph.

"Father, I have to leave for a while. This place and Deborah's death tears at my heart. When the family needs me, I shall return."

Joshua joined a caravan of traders whose owner was Joseph of Arimathea. On his trading forays he went as far as Egypt in the west, Asia Minor to the North, and Persia to the east. During these years he was exposed to different cultures, languages, and religions. He also began to analyze his own religion — Judaism. He felt his own religion should eliminate corruption and revise some of its laws and rules. In a way he in his mind he was constructing a more humane religion.

When he was twenty nine he heard that his father had passed away. He went back to Galilee to head the family as was the custom. With his intellect, knowledge, and experience he was head and shoulders above the people of Galilee. He was charismatic. In the synagogues they would gather around him and he would tell stories and his views regarding Jewish laws and rules. That is how he became a Rabbi in communities on the shores of the Sea of Galilee. He also gathered a loyal group of followers and believers that we will know as his apostles/disciples. They would call him Rabbi Joshua.

On a visit to the community of Magda, he was attracted to a young widow. Her name was Mirium. The scriptures would demonize her and call her Mary Magdalene, a reformed prostitute. She was not that at all. She came from the village of Cana. She married a man from Magda who was an owner of many boats. Before they had any children he died. She was a young widow with some wealth.

Ordinarily she would have gone back to her family in Cana. She chose to stay in Magda and manage the boat business. Because she remained single people assumed she must be a prostitute. That was not the case at all.

Joshua liked Mirium and he liked her wisdom and independent spirit. Of course she was a beauty. He proposed and she accepted. The two families were pleased and a wedding was held in Mirium's family home in Cana. In the scriptures you can read about the wedding. The story will tell of a miracle. It was not that at all. He had brought extra goatskins of wine. So when the regular wine ran out he brought out his extra supply. After the wedding as was the custom she joined her husband in the household at Nazareth.

The weather was fine that spring, so fields and gardens were planted. The grass was lush so that the lambs and goat kids were fat. Hens had their broods and even the bees were raising their broods. Trees and flowers were budding. Joshua and his younger brother had more work than they could handle. All was right with the world.

That evening after the meal Joshua said, "I have a matter weighing on my heart." His brothers and sisters knew what was to unfold. We have already described Joshua as a man who was charismatic, intelligent, perceptive, etc. In spite of his exemplary character, he hid a serious flaw. If he was faced with a serious problem, he would become determined to arrive at a solution. Most times the result was acceptable, but there were times his actions brought negative consequences.

Mary asked, "What could be causing you anxiety? Everything I see seems as though God's blessing is upon us. Our cup overfloweth."

"For three nights I have had a dream or vision, where a man in robes is standing before the Temple and he says, "Joshua you must come to God's house." I have decided to go to Jerusalem for the Passover which will be in two weeks from now, in the month of Nissan."

Mary spoke, "We can celebrate the Passover here with our family and friends."

"Yes, but I believe the Spirit of God is calling."

Mirium spoke, "Joshua I plead with you! Do not go to Jerusalem. Here in Nazareth you have family, friends, and people who are eager to hear your message. In Judea they have heard of you. The Sanhedrin and some of the Judges want to destroy you. They want to put you to death."

"I'm not afraid, the Lord will protect me. Mirium, will you come with me?"

"Of course."

"I too," said Mary.

"I'll go too," said James.

"Then we must prepare for a two week stay."

Mary said, "We will bake more bread. We have dried figs, cheese, and honey."

"There are still four wine skins of three year vintage."

Joshua said, "I know we have no money, but I trust God will provide. Tomorrow after prayers in the synagogue we'll be going to Tabor. I believe the walk will be two or three leagues. I will talk to the disciples, maybe some will come with us? Mirium, will you come with me to Tabor?"

"Yes, I will. A woman beside her Rabbi will make the women in the gathering more comfortable."

On the first day of the walk to Jerusalem everyone was in a jubilant mood. In the evening the women slept on the roof of a residence. On the second day the pace was slower.

Joshua said, "John, go ahead of us and tell the poor that the Rabbi from Galilee is coming."

On the third day they stopped about a league outside the city walls.

On the fourth day they entered the city and it is written people greeted the Galilee pilgrims with palm branches. In the city there were so many people-crowds everywhere. The Galilee pilgrims scattered in small groups and announced that in the morrow Rabbi Joshua would speak to them in the square before the Temple.

When the next day arrived, Joshua wanted to go to the Temple to pray before he spoke to the crowd. He walked past the money changers and salesmen selling all sorts of trinkets and mementos. A guard stopped him.

"Where are you going?"

"I am going to the sanctum to pray."

"Oh no you won't. You must buy an offering before you enter. The Money Changers will change your money to Temple money. With the Temple money you buy a sacrificial offering.

It can be an actual lamb or dove or just a money donation to the Temple."

"But I have no money."

"Then you don't get in."

"But the Torah says God does not ask for money."

"But we do!"

Joshua was upset and he complained loudly to everyone that the House of God had become a tax collector. Arguments followed. The line up was not moving.

"You are becoming a nuisance. Leave now!"

"All right, I'll leave."

He went to the end of the row, and as he walked out he tipped each money changers' table over. Coins were scattered in every direction.

Joshua in a loud voice said, "This is a House of God and Prayer, and you have made it into a Den of Thieves!"

Andrew, who had accompanied Joshua said, "Rabbi let's get out of here."

Judas said, "There's going to be trouble."

The guards reported the incident to the High Priest Caiaphas.

"I want you to find this Rabbi and bring him before the Sanhedrin. Here is money if you need to bribe someone. This man can cause us trouble with the Romans. Find him!"

That afternoon the guards searched the crowds and asked. They spotted a man who a guard had seen with Joshua.

"You are with that Galilee group."

"No, I'm from Hebron."

"I'm sure I saw you with the Rabbi. There is money. The Priests mean no harm. They want to talk to him about his ideas. Do you know anything?"

"Maybe I saw him. How much are you offering?"

"Ten silver pieces?"

"Maybe I was mistaken."

"How about twenty pieces of silver?"

"I'm not sure. It will be difficult to find him in the crowds."

"Thirty pieces of silver and that is the final offer!"

"All right. I will find him and tell you where he is. You will come and the man I kiss is the one."

That afternoon Joshua passed the word that his disciples should meet in a rented room for a supper. The scriptures have a full description of that last supper. The disciples were puzzled. Joshua was talking as though he was leaving them. He also asked them to meet in Gethsemane for a vigil. He spoke of betrayal. Could that be possible? No disciple would dream of betraying their Rabbi.

The evening and night in Gethsemane is a critical part of the Jesus story. Joshua experienced an agony like no other. He was torn by two choices. The rational choice was to leave Jerusalem as quickly as possible. The second for which he sweated blood was to let events untold and let God demonstrate to these people his overwhelming power.

By morning he was apprehended. They took him to the Sanhedrin where the Judges questioned and condemned him. They said he had broken the laws of God and death was the proper consequence. They took him to Pontius Pilate.

"We have a man here that should be crucified."

"Crucified? What has he done?"

"He has broken the laws and blasphemed."

"What do you mean by blasphemed?"

"He claims to be the Son of God."

" Are you the Son of God?"

"If you say so."

"Take this man to Herod. He should deal with this Jewish nonsense."

Herod said, "Oh No! I don't want Jewish blood on my head. Take him to Pilate."

"Are you here again?"

"He must be crucified before the Sabbath begins."

"But he has not done anything deserving a crucifixion."

"If you let this man go, he will stir up the crowds. You will have a riot and rebellion on your hands. Caesar Augustus will hear that his Governor can't keep peace and order."

"Let me suggest a solution. We have two men to crucify. Barabas is a blood thirsty terrorist and this Rabbi is accused of an imaginary crime. We can release one and crucify the other. What should we do to Barabas?"

"Release him?"

"What should we do to this innocent, but foolish Rabbi?"

"Crucify him!"

"I wash my hands of this injustice. Centurion, take this man, flog him and let him carry his cross to Golgotha."

So it was done and Joshua would hang on the cross for days and eventually his bones would be thrown into a pit.

Here is the part you will not find in the scriptures, but it is in the Book of Truth. Merchant Joseph summoned his most trusted servants. "We will try our best to rescue this man. When Joshua is on the cross and pleading for water, raise this sponge to his lips. The herbal essence will speed up his body to slip into unconsciousness. I will do the rest."

Joseph went to Pontius Pilate.

"My dear Governor, I have a favour to ask of you."

"A man of your wealth should not need any favour, but ask."

"As soon as that man called Joshua shows he is dead, release his body to me."

"That would be against Roman law."

"Would this bag of gold and silver have the law set aside?"

"Who am I to refuse such a sensible solution. Centurion, when that man Joshua appears to have died, take him down and hand his body to this man."

Joshua's body was taken down and Joseph's men wrapped a shroud around it and placed it in a tomb belonging to Joseph. They closed the tomb. The scriptures will say that the Romans placed guards. That is nonsense. Romans weren't stupid. Why guard a closed tomb of a dead man?

After midnight Joseph's men rolled away the stone. Waved another substance in Joshua's face.

He stirred, and although groggy and in pain he was conscious. They left the shroud and Joshua was on his way to Jaffa.

Mirium was the first to find the empty tomb. She spread the news to any disciples she could find. Some now believed that there was a resurrection and Joshua had ascended to heaven. A few were not sure.

Mirium returned to Nazareth. She was agonizing. Should she stay with Mary like Ruth of old or should she go back to Cana and Magda? Meanwhile another servant of Joseph was on a mission to Nazareth. Mirium saw a stranger coming her way.

"Are you Mirium, the wife of Joshua?"

"I am, but Joshua has died."

"I have a message for you from my Master, Joseph of Arimathea."

" A message?"

"Joseph wants you to accompany me to Jaffa, where he has someone for you to see."

"How can I know you are really from Joseph?"

" I have a letter written in Greek."

"Anyone could write this letter."

"I also have Joseph's seal."

When he pressed it on the back of the letter, it left an imprint- a six sided star with a circled JA in the middle.

"I will go, but what shall I tell the family?"

"Tell them you are going for a brief visit to your family in Cana."

After two days of travel, they arrived in Jaffa at the door of Joseph's house.

"Come Mirium, open the door and see!"

She opened the door and stood in shock. Was this a trick? There stood Joshua. It could not be! He died on the cross. Joshua came forward and held her. She was crying. It could be no other than her husband. There were scars on his head from the crown of thorns. Both wept with joy.

"Tomorrow, we can go back to our home in Nazareth."

Joseph spoke, "I do not like to disappoint you, but you will never go back."

"Why?"

"Joshua, your teachings are the seeds of a new religion. This religion needs time to grow and establish a firm foundation. If you return, it will be said that the crucifixion and resurrection were a hoax. You will go to a new home. Mirium, this money is for your boats. Tomorrow morning you will sail to France where your new home awaits."

The ship took them to Cyprus, then Malta, and to southern France. Next was a day's journey to sunny Provence. The new home was comfortable and hectares of grapes and olives covered the fields. There were bright flowers everywhere.

After the crucifixion, the disciples gathered. Except for Thomas, they believed that an Angel had taken Joshua up to heaven. They also believed it was their calling to spread Joshua's teachings. How should the new religion take shape? James, the brother of Joshua, said the new religion should be strictly Jewish. Paul, a new convert said, they should water down the Judaism and make the new religion acceptable to Gentiles. For the next three hundred years the new religion struggled to define itself.

The year 325 is significant in the Christian story. Emperor Constantine summoned leaders of various Christian factions to come to Nicae and establish one religion. There were two large factions — Nicaeans and Arians. The Nicaean faction prevailed. They defined the character of God. Other religions had one God. Christianity would have three — Father, Son and Holy Ghost. Each had equal Godly powers. They could act individually and in combinations.

The Church, after 325 resembled a men's club. So in 431 at the Council of Ephesus Mary was elevated as the Mother of God. She was viewed as a semi goddess. It is through Mary that you reach Jesus. Catholics regard Mary as the portal to Jesus.

On a hot summer day and four years in their new home, Joshua thought he saw a caravan or was it a mirage?

"Mirium, come! What do you see?"

"It's a caravan and an old man with a staff is walking towards us."

They could not believe their eyes! It was Joseph of Arimathea. There were tears of joy. The caravan set up a camp, but Joseph was escorted to the house. Mirium, heavy with child scurried like a young girl preparing a feast for their guest. Little Joseph went from Mom to Dad seeking safety from the man with the stick.

After the meal there was talk. Joshua brought out a flask of the best wine.

Joseph asked, "Do you miss Galilee?"

"We do. We have abundance and beauty here, but often I will take Little Joseph on my lap and sing the Psalms of David. Like the Prophet in Babylon, we weep and yearn for Zion."

"What is with you and God?"

"I have had time to think. I had this expectation. I believed what I wanted to believe. But if not for you, I would be dead. I thought God would come down in a blaze of glory and show his omnipotence.

Today I believe God will act according to His will and not mine. I have come to realize great happiness here on this place. I love Mirium and Little Joseph dearly and maybe soon we may see more blessings. If the baby is a girl, we will call her Mary Ruth."

In the morning the caravan was ready to move. Joseph bade farewell to Joshua and his family. "I am getting old and I do not know if I will see you again. I bestow blessings on you, and the generations that will follow."

As the caravan disappeared in the distance, Joshua, Mirium, and Little Joseph held each other with a mixture of sadness and joy. Little did they know that the future would bring big changes unimagined!

27.
A MANSION ON THE PRAIRIES

IAN MACLEOD AND ERIC FORTIN WATCHED THE DANCING flames in the fireplace. The two old men were comfortable. While outside wind and sleet were assaulting the walls of the mansion known as Stirling Manor. It really wasn't a mansion but a large three storey brick house. It was built on the edge of the town of Capillano. It was sixty years ago when Ian and his bride Jasmin had decided to make this place their home.

"Eric, it has been sixty years since you and I became partners."

"Yes, that was a long time ago. The incident that brought us together, I wish that it had not ever happened."

"How do you remember that incident?"

"I was living in Edmonton. My father was foreman of a construction company. He taught me how to operate the big machines — Cats, Scrapers, Graders, etc. He was encouraging me to follow in his footsteps. My ambition was elsewhere. I wanted to be a light weight boxing champion. I was short, barely five feet four inches in height and only 130lbs. I had taken martial arts training and now was preparing for my first boxing bout. There were hours of practice involved and my hands were becoming lethal weapons. Before I had a chance to enter the ring, I received a call from an old friend, Sidney Anderson."

"Come to Capillano. The County is building ten miles of road. There are good wages for anyone that can operate a machine."

"I was broke and as yet my promoter had not scheduled any bouts, so I went to Capillano. As in every town of the Prairies the beer parlour was the oasis. Sid suggested we have a couple of beers and plan for my possible job. There were several tables at which men talked, swore, and laughed. One table away from where Sid and I sat was the table of Thor Jolson and his three companions. They may have been there for sometime. The waiter bought us our drinks and Sid suggested we go and see the foreman, Mat Staples about a job." Meanwhile Thor summoned the waiter.

"Tommy, that kid who came in should not be in this place. He isn't old enough."

"I checked. He is old enough."

"I don't believe it. Hey kid how old are you?"

"I'm old enough."

"I asked you how old are you."

"That is none of your business."

"I'll make it my business. How old are you?" I realized this could be ugly. He walked up to our table and poured beer over my head.

"How old are you?"

"If you go back to your table and sit down, I'll tell you my age."

"Look here midget, I don't take orders, I give orders." He poured another glass of beer on my head. I stood up and my fists were clenched.

"So the little pip squeak wants a fight. I'll give you such a beating that your own mother won't recognize you."

"I'm ready for you, but we don't have to break furniture. Let's go outside." The parlour emptied. This was going to be a show.

"OK midget. You have the first swing. Ha! Ha!"

" No I'm better then you, so go to it if you can."

"Oh! I can." He swung and I ducked. My fist plunged into his fat beer belly. He kept swinging and I kept ducking. My hands were doing damage. Soon his arms were dropping and I went for his head. Blow after blow and his face was a bloody mess.

"You're not going to make a fool of me."

He reached into his boot and brought out a knife. "OK midget, I'll cut you to pieces and feed the parts to the dogs." I realized this was going to be him or me. Adrenaline rushed into all parts of my body. When he thrust the blade at me, one of my hands struck his wrist and the other took the knife. In one motion I plunged it into his midriff. I pulled out the knife and threw it as far as I could. Thor slumped. His pals took him to a vehicle. He was taken to the Camrose Hospital. Four days later Thor was dead. I was charged with second degree homicide. That's when I asked you to take my case."

"I remember. That was my first homicide case. I needed to summon all my skill to defend you. I was nervous. It did not look good. Thor was a bully, but he was still a Capillano man. At the trial I kept reminding the jury that this was a case of self defence, plain and simple. I got the acquittal verdict, as I was hoping. I remember you came to my office to thank me, but you said you had no money. That was when I put you in charge of a farm that I had just bought."

"Eric, what are your plans for the week?"

"I'm going to the north farm and check with the boys to see if they have two John Deere 9600's ready for harvest. Tomorrow I'll check with the guys on the south farm." At this point a lady in her early sixties entered. She brought some tea and scones for the two old timers.

"If you were women I could understand, but two old men in their eighties repeating the same old lies?"

"My dear daughter, we never tell lies. Ask Eric."

"Eric, you repeat the same old lies that my father spins."

"Violet, your father is as straight as an eight foot two by four."

"I've seen some two by fours in my time. I'll be back after a while to pick up the tray. Father, remember you have an appointment with Dr. Adams tomorrow about your heart."

"That old pill pusher can't cure a horse."

"Then why do you go to him?"

"I don't want to hurt his feelings and us mature men have to stick together."

"Ian, tell me again how you came to be a lawyer in Capillano? How did you choose Capillano to begin your law practice?"

"Eric, I've told you this story many times before. I fear your memory is failing. Here it goes: I was twenty two when I had obtained my degree from Dalhousie. I looked around in Nova Scotia but nothing caught my attention. In a law magazine the Alberta Law Society advertised towns that were looking for a lawyer to set up a practice. That is how I chose Capillano. I arrived here with twenty dollars in my pocket and a trunk full of law books. I rented a shack that had been a shoemaker's shop. The rent was five dollars a month. I went to the Bank and borrowed $150 to buy some furniture and keep myself alive for a couple of months. After I won that case where you were charged, I had a lot of business. Every criminal and crook wanted me to defend them. I won some and lost some. Either way I got paid. The most memorable incident besides your trial was when Jasmin Dufour and her parents came to my office. I was immediately struck by Jasmin's regal bearing. The Dufours were not from this area. Their town was Lamont. There must have been some reason that they came to Capillano. They wanted me to prepare some legal documents. The gist of their intention was that the Estate should go to Jasmin after their demise. In turn she would care for them until that time came. Some would say that I was smitten. I will admit that I was. Besides her physical attractiveness, we in the words of Shakespeare had a "Marriage of Minds". There followed a courtship. When she was thirty four and I was thirty one, we married. I showed her the place where I wanted to build. She liked it. We pooled our resources and built this big brick house and we named it Stirling Manor. Jasmin was ecstatic and I let her plan the interior. Then Violet and James came along. She wanted more children but her doctor advised her to stop at two.

Those were beautiful times as the children grew. In the evenings when the days' work was done she would sit and play the piano. Music filled the house. Violet became a R.N. and began working at the hospital. James had a brilliant mind and at the University he majored in Economics. He fell into a trap. He became an alcoholic. He would work for one or two months and either boredom or stress would get to him and he would go back to the bottle. After a wasted life he has joined the AA. Each day I hope that he might conquer his demons." At this point Violet came to pick up the tray.

"Small children and eighty year olds need their sleep. Dad, it's time for bed."

"Violet, someday I will sell you to a vacuum salesman."

"I've already had one salesman so no thanks. Remember you're going to see Dr. Adams."

The following day Violet took her father to see the Doctor. Dr. Adams said, "Ian, I see you're still with us. Are you taking that laudanum I prescribed the last time?"

"Doc, the Pharmacy does not carry laudanum anymore. It was discontinued fifty years ago."

"Well that's a pity. Take off your shirt." Doc Adams took a horn and began listening to Ian's heart and breathing.

"Doc, when are you going to get a stethoscope, instead of that horn from a century ago?"

"My horn is all I need and your heart is beating on two cylinders instead of four. I will send you to a specialist in Edmonton. I will also give you a prescription for laudanum."

“Doc, the pharmacy does not have any laudanum.”

“Tell the pharmacist to order some and in the meantime he might give you a substitute.”

Ian went to his office to check the mail. Violet came in.

“What did the Doc say?”

“He said, I should get some laudanum and he said I should go see some quack in Edmonton.”

“Father, I think you should close this hole of an office and retire full time.”

“Retire? Balderdash! What would I do?”

“What all retired people do. You know father, people in town keep saying your office is an eye sore.”

“Yes, and a lot say it is a tourist attraction. I’ve heard by the grapevine that when I close the door permanently, they will take my dear office and put it on the museum grounds. I wonder if they will let me practice law on the museum grounds?”

“Come on Father let’s go home. It’s time for your noon lunch.”

That evening after supper when Ian and Eric were in their chairs before the fire, Eric asked, “What did Doc Adams say?”

“He said, I have sometime before I’m called up yonder provided I take his prescribed laudanum.”

“You know Ian, we are fortunate to have Violet run the show here at Stirling Manor.”

“Yes I realize that, although I don’t want to make it public yet. Life has not been too kind for Violet. When she began her nursing career she was charmed by an encyclopedia salesman. I wasn’t sure about that match but neither I nor Jasmin said anything. Harry Trudeau, the salesman brought in very little income so Violet had to work. When the children, Grace and Thomas came, Harry went off with another woman. Violet didn’t lose any sleep over that. She returned to Stirling Manor and went back to the hospital job. Jasmin looked after the children. Today Grace has a Beauty Salon in Edmonton.

Thomas went to India to find the purpose of life. The last we heard he was a Buddhist monk in an Ashram in northern India. What about your story?"

"As you know, I married Helen Simpson. We had a good marriage. We had two boys. Today, Derek is Captain of Queen of the Isles, a Ferry out of Tsawassen. Matthew has a logging operation in the interior of BC. I have six grandchildren."

"Eric, have you ever thought about doing something meaningful before we are called?"

"I have."

"Your children and my children do not need any financial help, so I am ready to listen to any plan or legacy you might suggest. Eric, we have worked together for sixty years so a joint venture might be an appropriate initiative. After we are gone this house or mansion will be too big for Violet. She will have all the money she will ever need. I'm going to talk to her and run some plans by her."

Violet took Ian to Dr. MacGill in Edmonton. He suggested a slower pace.

Ian closed the office and the town did move it to the Museum grounds. If you are ever in Capillano go to their Museum and step into the tiny lawyer's office. There are the well worn chairs and a desk. In the inner room is an old typewriter and shelves of old law books. On the wall is a picture of a young man. The printing below reads:

> Ian Alexander MacLeod BA; LLB. suma cum laude.
>
> Dalhousie University.

Violet agreed to her father's and Eric's legacy project. After they were gone to their rest she would move to a condo in Edmonton. Stirling Manor would be converted. Ian would donate the building and Eric would contribute money to redesign and refurnish the Manor. It would be a home for mothers seeking escape from abusive partners. The Stirling Manor sign would come down and instead a new sign would read: JASMIN — HELEN HALL

28.
THE LONG WAY HOME

IN THE SUMMER OF 1955 I WAS TAKING A UNIVERSITY class in Saskatoon. At the residence where I stayed I struck up a friendship with Arthur Kratzman, who was also taking a University course. The following is his story.

Arthur's home was Melbourne Australia. In 1943 he had completed the first year of a teacher's course. Circumstances were dire. The Japanese were getting close to invading Australia. Every male over seventeen was required to enlist in the Armed Forces. Arthur chose the Australian Air Force. He thought that up in the air was more exciting than being on the ground or on the water.

He took the basic training in Melborne. Then he was off to the other side of the world. He was in Canada, where he would train under the BCAT Plan. His first stop was an airbase in Dafoe, Saskatchewan. Dafoe was in the middle of nowhere. The closest town was Watson, a small village. Regina was more than 100 miles south and Saskatoon was 150 miles west. Dafoe trained crew for Bomber Command. Arthur was excellent in mathematics so he was placed in the Navigation School.

Besides young men at the base there were about 100 young women in the WAAF. Arthur began to court a brunette named

Sheila Armstrong. Before the budding romance became serious, Arthur was transferred to Nanton, Alberta.

Nanton was also a small place but the community staged dances and socials for the airmen. At a dance he met another brunette, Jane Stratford. On leave Arthur and Jane went to Calgary and Lethbridge. His training was almost completed and he would be going to Britain. Arthur told Jane that the war was about to end. He would come back to Nanton and take up his teaching career. They married in a short ceremony. A week later he was flown to Britain. He was part of the Squadron 166. Because he was Australian, they named their Lancaster — Flying Kangaroo.

His airbase was Kingsley Crofton in Lincolnshire. Their squadron was now on active duty. They would assemble over the North Sea. There would be about a 1,000 planes escorted by fighters. Then they would fly over Germany and drop bombs on industrial centres. Flying on a Lancaster was no picnic- anti aircraft guns and German fighter planes were waiting. The casualty rate of Bomber Command was fifty percent. After each sortie when the squadron returned, there was sure to be missing planes and crew. Each time they went out they were never sure if they would return. As in Canada, there were leaves when men went to nearby towns and cities.

On these leaves he joined his buddies at pubs, dances, and socials. He wrote letters every few days to his wife in Nanton. The letters from his wife became shorter and shorter. She said she was just too busy. About six months after he left Nanton, she wrote that she was pregnant. Arthur wondered? When she stopped writing he concluded that the marriage had ended. He felt that he could pursue a new female romantically. He was especially attracted to Betty White. She made it plain that she would not become serious until the war ended.

The Flying Kangaroo had made twenty three sorties and had survived. On one sortie it was badly shot up, but the crew were safe. On another sortie the tail gunner was wounded. In 1945 the War was in its final stages. Allied forces in the west were closing in on Hitler's Nazi Germany. Air Command was still pounding German Cities. Air Marshal Sir Arthur Norman, head of Bomber Command was probably in a vengeful mood! He ordered a massive strike on the city of Dresden. The whole city went up in flames and explosions. It was on this sortie that the Flying Kangaroo was hit as it turned for home. The crew bailed out. Arthur landed in an area of trees and brush.

Arthur knew that if the Gestapo found him it might mean death. He hid his parachute as best he could and started going south. He walked at night and hid during the day. After three days he reached the Carpathians. He was so hungry that he didn't care whether he was caught of not. He stopped at a farm yard. He was lucky. The farmer was Slovak rather than German. The farmer fed Arthur, but did not want to harbour a fugitive. He gave Arthur some food and directed him to a road that would take him to Yugoslavia territory.

His first encounter was with Serbians. Because of his uniform they sent him to a Partisan Unit in the hills. The Partisans interrogated him and invited him to join their Unit. He said he wanted to get back to Britain. The reply was that would not be possible. In the Partisan Unit were a few women. He found Anna Tito especially attractive but this was war so there was no romantic involvement. The Unit was to engage a retreating Ukrainian SS Division. Their tactic was to strike and then get away.

The War ended in June 1945 and Arthur made his way to the British zone. From there he was back to Britain and to his airbase. He learned that the Flying Kangaroo had three killed and two taken prisoner. The Squadron no longer existed, so Flying Officer Arthur Kratsman could return to Australia. He chose to go back to Canada. He wanted to know if Jane Stratford was still his wife. He found her but the meeting was awkward. She told him that when she was informed that he was missing in action, she presumed that he was dead. She married a local man, Dwight Morrow. He asked about the baby, but she said it was not his. He went back to Australia, but did not feel at home. People and places had changed. His high school girl friend had married. He decided to take up his teaching career, but it would be in Canada.

He got a job in a rural school called Viking. He wondered if the WAAF brunette, Sheila Armstrong had married. He located her. She was working as a secretary in a Real Estate office in Melfort. Both were willing to resume their courtship. Before a year had passed they were married.

When I first met Arthur in 1955 he was married and had two children. Each summer he was taking courses towards an Education Degree. After that summer we never met again. I went back to teaching in a High School. Arthur continued his studies towards a Masters Degree then a PhD. Some years later I learned that he was Dean of Education in Edmonton. I regret I never made contact with Arthur. Today, I know that he is not in Edmonton. Has he passed away? Did he eventually return to Australia? It would be nice to know.

29. THE DANCING PEROGIES OF VEGREVILLE

FOR THE PAST TWENTY YEARS I HAVE BEEN A REPORTER for the Edmonton Journal. My beat has been to follow up human interest stories in the northern half of Alberta. Zachary Zuk has been an old friend for many years and he makes his home in Vegreville. Zak told me this story. It sounded so preposterous that I thought he was pulling my leg. However, through all the years I have never known Zak to tell a lie or fabricate a tale. So I'll just accept the story as Zak told it.

This is a story about a piece of dough with a filling. In many cultures it has different names. In western Canada the perfectionists call it varynyky. Most people call it a perogy and that's the name we'll use. Shakespeare said that a rose by any other name would smell just as sweet. So we can say that a perogy by any other name would be just as delicious. The perogy has a long history.

Thousands of years before the Christian era it probably originated in China. As people moved the perogy went along. Today machines can make a perogy at factory speed. It becomes special when it is made by a woman for her family. Her family knows it's made by a person who has love in her effort. Her hands bless this common food and make it special. It is a food enjoyed by peasants and kings.

To appreciate the story you should know the legends attached. Just as Christians have a myth or legend that on Christmas Eve at midnight animals will talk. There is a similar legend about the perogy. When people are not around, perogies will talk to each other. Another legend states that a perogy has some connection to eastern religions. It is part of the greater whole and yet it is a separate part. Each perogy will go through many incarnations. Its aim is to become reconciled and join the Big Perogy. Now we proceed with the story.

It was Friday June 15, 2019 that some two dozen ladies arrived at the community centre in Vegreville. Their destination was the kitchen area. They would be preparing food for a wedding that was to be held the following day. The coordinator of this group was Stella Greba. She was an impressive woman, attractive, six feet tall, and 185 lbs all muscle. When she gave an order, it was followed. She divided the ladies into groups. Some would make cabbage rolls, others would make perogies and still others would be making nalysnyky. Other ladies cooked sausage, ham dishes, beet relish, creamed onions, etc. Stella went from group to group checking the progress. At each group the ladies exchanged all the important news. At group four the talk was about the bridal couple.

"I don't see what Amy saw in that Clint bum?"

"Maybe she had to get married."

"Not Amy."

"Maybe Clint has lots of money."

"No way, that bum hasn't two nickels to rub together."

"I heard his parents are looking for a franchise, maybe Tim Hortons or Subway."

"If that happens, Amy will be doing all the work while Clint will be in the pub."

"You are too hard on the boy. I think he'll turn out alright."

"I'll believe it when I see it. Did you see those shifty eyes?"

By three o'clock in the afternoon the work was completed. Stella named six ladies in the group.

"I want you here nine o'clock sharp. We'll have to roast cabbage rolls and sausages. We'll have to boil those perogies. There will be the fruit salad to make." After everyone left Stella closed and locked the doors.

In the evening Patrick Perogy spoke, "That Lynda Dansky dropped me on the floor. Now I feel dirty and itchy."

"Don't worry Patrick, you'll get clean when they drop you in the hot water."

"Is that what they do?"

"Of course."

"I'm not going into that hot water, no sir not me."

Patrick looked around and saw his cousin Peter, a big fat perogy.

"Peter we need your help. You have been a good old Liberal Perogy for many years. Pull some strings and get us out of this hot water." Peter Perogy got out his special cell phone and called the PM's number. The PM's butler picked up the phone.

"PM's residence, Cedric Hamilton speaking."

"I want to speak to the PM."

"The PM is getting ready for bed. Are you a Liberal?"

"You bet your bottom dollar I am."

"What is your concern?"

"I have it on good authority that there is a plot to kill a lot of Perogies. I want to speak to the PM."

"Mr. PM, there is an urgent call for you and from a Liberal supporter."

"Well I was just getting ready for bed. Sophie is waiting. Put him on."

"Hello PM, I hope I didn't get you out of bed? There is an important security matter here in Vegreville."

"Where's that?"

"In Alberta."

"Don't I have enough trouble in Quebec, but those Alberta Red Necks are after me. What exactly is the crisis?"

"There is a plot to kill a lot of Perogies and then boil them in water."

"Are you serious?"

"Very serious."

"I'll get on it at once, tell the Perogies to hide wherever they can."

"Thank you Prime Minister."

"Just when Sophie is waiting, I have to deal with nut cases in Alberta and BC. Cedric get me the Attorney General and Minister of Justice."

"What is her name?"

"I think it is, Jody Wilson Rabbit."

"I'll get her on the line."

"Good evening Mr. Prime Minister, what do you want to speak to me about?"

"There is a plot to kill hundreds of Perogies in Alberta, we have to stop this crime."

"Where in Alberta?"

"Some place called Vegetableville."

"I've never heard of that place."

"Just a minute, I'll ask Cedric.... The place is called Vegreville."

"I'll consult my Deputy and we'll proceed carefully in any legal actions."

"I'll expect results or there will be a Minister in hot water. Oh by the way, when you return to Ottawa drop in. I want some advice about the Veterans Affairs Portfolio."

"Why are you asking me?"

"I'm not asking, I just want a minister from BC. Good night Jody."

"Good night Prime Minister."

"Well what did the PM say?"

“He said, he’ll get on it at once. See it pays to be a Liberal. He also said we should hide.” “Where can we hide?”

Some suggested the flour bin, under the cabbage rolls, behind the paper towels, etc. It was Abigail Perogy that had the answer.

“The Government Building is empty from Friday to Tuesday. No one will look for us there.”

“OK it’s off to the Government Building.”

On Saturday morning at nine o’clock the selected ladies were at the Hall kitchen. Stella got everyone moving. Cabbage rolls and sausages went into the ovens. Fruit was cut up for salads. Water was boiling for the perogies.

Gladys Sanduk came to Stella. “Stella the perogies are not there!”

“What do you mean?”

“They are not there on the trays.” Stella looked and yes there were no perogies.

“I’ve never heard of such a problem. In Mundare at one of the wedding someone stole a kishka, but Perogies”

“What is a kishka?”

“It’s sausage. I’m going to call the cops.”

“Sergeant Maxwell speaking.”

“This is Stella Greba at the Community Centre. We have a serious crime here.”

“What kind of crime?”

“Someone stole the perogies.”

“Stella are you joking? This isn’t April Fool’s Day.”

“I’m very serious.”

“How many were stolen?”

“Maybe four to five hundred.”

“Holy Smoke, I’ll get some men there in a hurry.” The Sergeant turned to his Secretary.

“Get every person in the building here and ask for the Canine Unit.”

Two squad cars came careening around the corner with sirens blasting. People, dogs, and cats scrambled to get out of the way.

Someone asked, “Where’s the fire engine?”

At the Centre men spilled out of the squad cars and took positions inside and outside the building. A Corporal was looking for finger prints. The Sergeant and the two men were searching under the cabbage rolls, in the flour bin, in the wash-rooms, and under the stage.

“Well I never! There is no sign or clue where the culprits went.” The Sergeant’s phone beeped.

“Sergeant Maxwell speaking.”

“This is Jody Wilson, Attorney General. The PM wants the riot and massacre stopped immediately. Do you hear that?”

“I hear, but we have no leads. Rest assured we will get those criminals one way or another.”

“OK but remember if this crime is not stopped both of us will be looking for jobs.”

“Yes Minister, we’ll go all out to do our job.”

At two o’clock in the afternoon on Saturday, Sylvia Kupka and her Band were dragging their instruments and amplifiers to the stage of the hall. After all the equipment was set up and tested, Sylvia said, “Let’s play a few bars of tunes we will be playing — Alberta Wedding March, Vegreville Polka, Presentation Two Step, and Anniversary Waltz.” The Band members were satisfied, put away their instruments and left to return at six.

At six guests began to arrive. Sylvia on the fiddle and her Grandson on the guitar greeted each with a snappy tune. The parents of the newlyweds greeted each guest or guests warmly. There was a container for money donations. One of Amy’s bridesmaids took the wrapped presents and put them in a safe place. One of Clint’s best men offered anyone who wanted a drink of Seagram Special. Each guest could take a sample of the wedding cake. The guests would proceed to greet and congratulate the newlyweds. After handshakes and kisses the guests would go to the buffet lineup. Two teen girls handed out plates and drinks. Everyone piled their plates high with all that delicious food. When they came to the end of the line there was sour cream, but where were the perogies? Stella replied, "Some SOB has stolen all the perogies!" There were various and angry responses. "What is this country coming to? It's those damned politicians. We've got thieves around every corner and blockades on the railway."

Some of the responses were too vulgar to mention. Anyone who would steal our perogies is as low as the belly of a snake. The anger did not subside. Some went back to get another Seagrams drink.

At the Government Building the Perogies found everything they would want. There was food, drinks, and blankets. Colin Perogy and his pal Vinny Perogy were manipulating the tech controls. They were able to access the audio in the kitchen, and the dance area at the Community Centre. When the Perogies heard Sylvia's dance music, all the Perogies started dancing. The four dance tunes were repeated over and over. How do you know they were dancing?

Nick Chomsky and Doris were the caretakers of the building. On Sunday afternoon they went to do some cleaning and they found the door unlocked. "Doris did you lock the door on Friday?"

"Yes I did."

"Doris, I think you are getting more senile by the day."

" Nick, one more word from you and you'll be doing all the work yourself." Before they opened the second door they heard music. They peeked in and saw all the Perogies dancing! "Let's get out of here. This must be the Devil's party."

"We have to talk to Rev. Fr. Domka about this." The Rev. Father said, "It's a Satanic ritual. I'll phone the Bishop and see what he says. In the meantime don't mention this to anyone. If the media gets hold of this everyone will say we are a bunch of crazies in Vegreville."

Doris could not hang on to the secret. She just had to tell her daughter. The news or gossip spread like wild fire. Everyone had an opinion. Some said that Nick and Doris must have been drunk or on drugs. One man said he saw the Perogies rise in the sky turn into horse flies and fly north to Wood Buffalo Park. One woman said that she believed that the Virgin Mary took the Perogies up to heaven so that the Saints could see the Dancing Perogies. Another person said all this was a hoax and that Stella and her group never made any perogies. My friend Zak was certain that the six army trucks took the Dancing Perogies to Ottawa and to the PM's summer residence at Meech Lake.

The Police kept searching for the stolen perogies, but with no success. Their search was not futile. On Gust Nelson's farm they found a still and ten gallons of home brew. On the Reserve they found eleven cars that had been stolen. Near Leduc they found a three acre field of marijuana. In Camrose they apprehended four wanted criminals. In Two Hills they found a shed full of stolen property. Sergeant Maxwell was sure he would get fired so he put in an application with the Calgary Police Force.

In Ottawa there was the usual chaotic scene. The Leader of the Opposition rose and said, "Mr. Speaker when will the PM tell us about his connection to the Perogies?"

"Mr. Speaker, the Perogies are hard working and of course they are Liberals. Furthermore I can inform this House that my Government will introduce a new program for the working people. Each person whose income is middle class or lower, will receive twelve perogies free per month. Those whose income is above middle class will have to pay for their perogies. Mr. Speaker, it is all about fairness, diversity, human rights, and saving the planet. Our party unlike the Conservative believes in dialogue. Two years from today all perogy makers will be using solar power to boil the perogies."

"Ha! Ha! Ha!"

At Vegreville the Mayor called a special meeting. He said, "The Media has spread a lot of half truths. We are the laughing stock of the country. They refer to us as wing nuts. What should we do?"

The youngest Council member, Marilyn Trach said, "If we are dealt lemons, let's make lemonade."

"This is not about lemons. This is about our Town's profile and it is not good."

"I meant, use it to our advantage."

They did. On their website and on their billboards the message read, "Come to Vegreville and see the World's Largest Easter Egg and hear The Story of Dancing Perogies."

Tourists and Albertans made a detour to see the wonders of Vegreville. They took photos of the Easter Egg and asked, "Where are The Dancing Perogies?" The residents replied, "They were in the Government Building but now they are gone. But go to the Museum and see the video of The Dancing Perogies. Here's a coupon courtesy of the Town." The coupon read: Go to any cafe or restaurant and for one dollar you will get a dozen perogies with sour cream.

The Council and the Chamber of Commerce decided they needed another monument, maybe a huge perogy on a fork? Someone informed them that such a statue already existed in the Town of Glendon. The Council decided to erect a smaller statue at the entrance of the Government Building.

In Ottawa there was a change of Government. The new PM was asked about The Dancing Perogies at Meech Lake. His reply was, "I will not be using that residence so they can stay there indefinitely."

Zak said, "There is a prophecy, whenever there would be a woman PM, then The Dancing Perogies would return to Vegreville. We Are Awaiting That Special Event."

It is possible they will return sooner. If the residents of Vegreville block the railway or if the PM sent the Perogies at Meech Lake back to Vegreville.

30.
TIME MARCHES ON FOR JOHNNY MCLEOD

IN A PREVIOUS STORY WE LEFT JOHNNY IN 1979 WHEN HE had completed grade six. The year when he was in grade seven (1980), was a busy one. He had his paper route. He could ride his bike without holding the handle bars. His customers became friends and they liked Johnny's courteous ways. He never had enough eggs to satisfy his customers. In school, he found learning easy. He liked the sports. On Feb.14th he gave Peggy a Valentine. In class sometimes their eyes met and Peggy would give Johnny a beautiful smile. At the end of June Johnny, Stevie, and Peggy were promoted to grade eight.

In July Stevie rode to Johnny's place. "Johnny I have some important stuff to tell you. We don't want the whole town to know, so let's go to the goat pasture." They sat on their favourite log and Stevie said, "Two years ago we made a pact. We promised never to marry. Now, I think we should break the pact and get ready to marry."

"Why?"

"You always ask why. We should make plans to marry because that's what people do. In our garage Jack King and Nick Sanders were putting a motor in Jack's car. I heard Jack say that Doris, his girlfriend was a hot number. Nick said that he had asked his girlfriend Nancy to marry him, but she was dragging her feet.

"What did Jack mean, the girl was a hot number?"

"I will ask Stan Boyd. He knows all about motors and women. The way I figure, if we don't get married, we'll be two old bachelors living in a shack and eating crackers and sardines for the rest of our lives."

"Do you think we should get married now?"

"Johnny, you're such a dunce. If you get married now to Peggy you would have babies popping out. How would it look if you and Peggy came to school with a baby carriage? No, we get married after we finish this stupid school nonsense. We should plan ahead."

"What kind of plan do you have?"

"First we have to get the girls interested and then we offer them the cheese and they'll say yes."

"How do you plan to get the girls interested?"

"Girls like three things: Guys who smoke cigarettes, guys who drink beer, and guys who wear white shoes."

"Why white shoes?"

"That's what I saw in a magazine."

"What's the cheese?"

"Girls will marry guys who have cars and money."

"I have some money from paper route, sales, and jobs that I do now."

"Johnny, you have to have a pile of money. I'm planning to work in the garage or I might go to the potash mines. What about you?"

"I haven't thought about it. Grandpa and I have our farm. We could raise more laying hens."

"That's chicken feed. Maybe we could both go to the potash mines. For now we get the girls interested. I brought some cigarettes." The boys lit the cigarettes.

Stevie said, "Just suck the smoke and blow it out through your nose." There was coughing, gasping, and choking. Johnny thought this marriage business might not be worth all the trouble and where was he going to find white shoes.

Stevie said, "The next time I come we will practice drinking beer."

That evening while Grandpa was dosing and pretending to be reading the paper Johnny said, "Grandpa, is it true that if a guy smokes cigarettes, all the girls will come to him like flies to honey?"

Grandpa came to full attention. "Johnny, who tell you dat crazy ting? Dat Stevie Boyko no good."

Johnny wanted to know more, but he saw Grandpa was not going to tell him. If Stevie was right and since Grandpa smoked, then there should be flocks of ladies coming to see him.

Two weeks later Stevie came to the farm and they went to the log in the pasture. Stevie brought out a bottle of beer. They took turns drinking.

"What do you think?"

"It doesn't taste very good. I think a Coke would be better."

"You have to follow the plan."

"Where did you get the beer?"

"Stan Boyd our mechanic, has a box behind the tires."

"You stole it?"

"No, I borrowed it. Someday I'll put one back. Stan Boyd won't miss the beer, because most of the time he doesn't know where he left the spark plug wrench."

Johnny did not feel good about the plan. He said, "Stevie, I don't want all those parts of the plan. I don't like smoking, stealing beer, and I will not wear white shoes."

"Suit yourself, but if you end up in a shack eating crackers and sardines all your life then don't blame me."

"What did Stan say about the girl who would be called a hot number?"

He said, "Put your nose in your school work. You are still wet behind the ears. Hot numbers are not for you." The marriage plan was dropped and even Stevie forgot about it. Johnny never asked Stevie why he didn't get a pair of white shoes.

When the boys were in grade eleven, they still were friends. Stevie did not quit school and go to the potash mines. One day as they were walking home after school Peggy said, "I just don't get that Algebra."

Johnny replied, "I could help you."

"Would you?"

"Sure."

"Come whenever you can."

Johnny did go to the Sutherland home and the two worked and Peggy made progress. It was slow work but Johnny was patient and he did not mind being close to Peggy. At Christmas, Peggy gave Johnny a watch. Johnny gave her a card, but he wished he had chosen something more. Mrs. Sutherland was very hospitable and after each session there was hot chocolate and cookies. Johnny wondered if he dared to tell Peggy he loved her. He fantasied about the two getting married.

In grade eleven the two high school teachers held career sessions with each student. Stevie said he would take a mechanic's course. Peggy said she wanted to be a kindergarten teacher. Johnny couldn't think of anything except doing what he was already doing. One of the teachers said, "Johnny, with your high marks and your interest in animals, you should think of being a vet."

Johnny talked to Grandpa about taking a veterinarian course. Grandpa was delighted. He said, "You know we saved money for your Mom to became a nurse or teacher and that money is still there and it has grown. This little farm will always be here for you, but now is the time for you to reach higher."

Johnny spoke to the teacher, "Can you help me to really see what veterinary practice is all about?"

The teacher said, "I have a friend in Wadena who is a vet, and I'll ask for a favour."

Dr. McIntyre told Johnny to come whenever he could.

Johnny went on several weekends and accompanied the vet, as he visited farms to treat cattle and do surgeries. This was what he wanted to do. He told Peggy his plan and she was pleased. She said, "It would be nice if we landed in the same town." For Johnny, Peggy seemed more beautiful each time he saw her.

In grade twelve Johnny gave up his paper route. He devoted all his time to his studies. He needed perfect marks and a recommendation from Dr. McIntyre to get admitted to the newly established Veterinary College at the U of S.

There was disappointment for Johnny, because Mr. Sutherland the post master, was transferred to Wadena. He would see Peggy only on weekends. In mid June a letter came and it stated that Johnny was admitted to the Veterinary College. He shared the news with Grandpa. Grandpa invited his friends and the bottle was brought out for celebration.

"My Johnny be wet doctor. What you tink bout dat?" His friends said that was great and it deserved another "more rich" drink.

The graduation was the event of the year. Johnny received a scholarship for $3000. All this was exciting, but his thoughts were about Saskatoon, Grandpa, and Peggy.

In the fall of 1985, Johnny left for College. Grandpa was slowing down so he used his OAS cheque to hire Mrs. Host and her teen son to help on the farm. Peggy went to Teachers College in Regina. At the Veterinary College the pace was hectic with lectures, assignments, and endless labs. His twenty classmates were brilliant students and competition was intense. There was little time for social events. He came home whenever he could, and he connected with Peggy when she was home.

After three years at College, that summer presented two momentous events. One evening as he and Grandpa sat at the kitchen table, Grandpa said, "Johnny, I wait for you be wet. Maybe I not make it. I want tell you we be some years together and you make me happy. When I go do not be sad for me. Do a good job. Help people. Get married and have kids."

"Grandpa, you will be around many more years. I want you at my graduation and my wedding. You will get to see my children."

Johnny knew that his wish was possible but not probable. He saw his beloved Grandpa failing in health that year.

The second event brought joy and concern. Peggy had completed three years of her Course.

She took a teaching job at the small town of Quill Lake which was ten miles from her Wadena home. In late November she was driving home on No.5 when a mild blizzard made driving treacherous. A vehicle was coming straight at her. She froze and there was a crash. Police and ambulance came and Peggy was taken to the Wadena Hospital and then to Saskatoon. She had bruises and her leg was broken. The break turned out to be serious, it was a compound fracture. She spent time in the hospital and therapy followed. While she was in Saskatoon, Johnny visited her every day.

"Peggy, everything will turn out alright. We'll have a wedding dance soon."

"Johnny, I hope you're right but I worry that I may not dance too well with one leg."

After the New Year, Peggy returned to her job but in spite of all the medical skill, she still had a noticeable limp. During the Christmas break Peggy expressed her concern.

"Johnny I think I will always have this limp. Do you want me as I am?"

"Peggy, you have been the only one since grade five. I will always love you and will marry you."

Peggy came into his arms. "Johnny I love you, now and forever."

During the fourth year Johnny felt that his studies were nearing an end. Although there was one more year to go.

In April a young lady came to the lab. "The Dean wants to see Mr. John McLeod."

Johnny could not guess what the Dean wanted, maybe an offer to be a lecturer for the first year students?

"John, I regret to be the one to present you with sad news. We have received a message from Margo. Your Grandfather Mike Starchuk has had a stroke and has passed away at the Wadena Hospital."

Johnny bit his lip but tears welled in his eyes. He was shocked. He could not imagine that Grandpa would go so soon. Dean Winters said, "I sympathize with your grief. Take what time you need and don't worry. We will make adjustments so that you may graduate next year."

"Thank you."

Johnny went to Margo but although the ride was not far, it was a sad trip and Johnny wept unashamedly. Grandpa had become more to him then he had ever realized. The funeral was a simple affair. Father Andrew Panchuk of the Orthodox Church conducted an abbreviated ceremony and the body of Mike Starchuk was laid to rest beside the grave of his wife Ann.

After the funeral, Johnny went to see his friend Steve Boyko (Stevie). "Steve, you and I have been friends for many years through good times, bad times, and crazy times. I'm asking a favour. Take charge of my Grandpa's Estate. Sell whatever has to be sold. Save some items, especially my bike, and do whatever has to be done."

"John, it will be an honour that you chose an old friend. I'll do the best I can. Go back to your studies and make all of us proud that you are one of us."

After high school, Steve married Greta Duncan and they had two children. Steve took over his father's garage and enlarged it. His mechanics were so skillful that business came from every community around Margo.

The fourth and final year of his studies was filled with satisfaction and anticipation. He would get his degree and he would get married. The Dean offered to take him on as Assistant Professor, but he said, "I want to go among the farmers and practice my skills." For Christmas he planned to see Steve and then spend four days with Peggy. He wanted to get her something special as a gift but he did not have the money. He scraped together $200 and bought her a locket. His stop in Margo was brief. Steve said he was in the midst of settling the Estate.

When he arrived at the Sutherland home, he knew something was not right. Peggy seemed so tired and joyless. Had she found a new boyfriend and was finding it awkward to tell me?

"Peggy, you are hiding something. Tell me." Peggy went into his embrace. She put her head on his shoulder and began to cry.

"Peggy tell me what's wrong."

"Johnny, I love you, but I'm fearful. I didn't want to tell you earlier, but in the last month I've been dealing with cancer. The doctors guess that it developed from my broken leg and it has now metastasized. Tomorrow I'm going to Saskatoon for treatment for chemo and radiation. Johnny, I don't know if I'll make it for our wedding."

"Peggy, you're a fighter. You'll make it. If you are worried we can get married today."

"No Johnny, that would be our reaction to fear and desperation. I have loved you since grade five. You have been the only one in my dreams and in my real world."

"Peggy, you'll make it and we will have many years. I'll come and visit you at the hospital as often as I can."

"Johnny, please don't come. I will be very sick. If things don't turn out well, I want you to remember me as your love during better days."

As they embraced, tears and kisses mingled in the mountain of sadness. Johnny gave her the gift but it was a bitter sweet moment.

Johnny went back to his room in Saskatoon. He had not prayed since those early years when his Mom had died. Now he pleaded with God for Peggy's recovery.

Two months later he received a message that Peggy did not make it. He went to the funeral. She looked beautiful and peaceful. There weren't any words to describe the loss he felt. She was his future wife. She was more. Her beauty, kindness, sincerity, compassion, and a host of good qualities were a testimony that the world had lost a good person.

In May at the spring convocation, John Michael McLeod was granted the degree-Doctor of Veterinary Medicine (DVM). suma cum laude. This should have been a celebratory event, but for Johnny it was a sober reminder that life is precious and fleeting. Two of the most important people in his life were not there.

Because of his standing, colleges at Olds and Guelph offered him positions as a professor. He was offered a fellowship from Harvard to pursue research. There were congratulatory wishes. One letter from Dr. Scott Duncan at Wynyard caught his attention. It read: Dr. McIntrye at Wadena knows you and recommends that I contact you. I am retiring and I want to pass on my practice to a vet that will carry on my work. Please come and see me.

On the way to Margo, he stopped in Wynyard. Dr. Duncan's Vet Clinic was old but with a few charges it would be first class.

"Dr. Duncan how much are you asking for this practice and facilities?"

"Dr. John, I don't need the money. Offer me what you can afford and all this will be yours."

"Give me a few days to make a decision."

At Margo Steve handed John a cheque for $30,000.

"This is payment for your property."

"Steve, this is more than double of what I expected. Who was the buyer?"

"Dr. John, Greta and I are the buyers. That little farm has so many precious memories. I want my children to sit on the log in the goat pasture and try their first cigarette. We may build a bigger house because we are planning on many more children. I will keep your bicycle until you are ready to take it. Dr. John I know you have lost your beloved Peggy, but I think she would want you to find another "Peggy". Good luck and come and see us as often as you can."

Dr. John did buy the clinic at Wynyard for $10,000. He bought a Jeep to take him to all the farms in that district. After about a month Dr. John realized he could use some help. There were trips and surgeries where he needed an extra pair of hands. He advertized and hired Vicki Thompson a Vet Tech. who had just completed her course at the Olds College. She was not Peggy but she was just as attractive and charming. She fit in superbly. Sometimes when a long day had ended he invited her for lunch at one of the cafes.

It was a rainy day and he had three farms to go to. It was such a day. It was dark when he returned to the clinic. Vicki was waiting. *A light* came on for Dr. John. He cleaned up and came back to the office. She was still there. He said, "Vicki will you marry me?"

Vicki replied, "Dr. John, or should I call you Johnny? I thought you would never ask. Yes, I will marry you!" They were in each other's arms and the lights went out. Dr. John said, "Someday I'll fix those lights but not today."

CPSIA information can be obtained
at www.ICGtesting.com
Printed in the USA
BVHW040012101220
594973BV00006B/104